CROSS BLADES

MM HOCKEY ROMANCE

J.M. JACKIE

A playful hand slithered over my shoulder, and I recognized Zara's younger brother, Harpreet.

"Come on, white boy, let's see what you can do!" he called out, shimmying his shoulders and twisting his wrists in invitation. I laughed and shrugged before following him onto the dancefloor and busting out my white boy moves, amusing everyone around me. *Damn, this was fun.* The atmosphere was infectious, and I found myself swept up in the moment. Zara's mother, Jasmeet, pulled me into a dance beside her, and we started really tearing it up, unleashing a whirlwind of moves, a fusion of traditional steps and modern grooves.

Sweat clung to my skin as I lost myself in the music, the pulsating beats guiding my footsteps. The room was a blur of flashing lights, the rhythm of the music syncing with my heartbeat. I had so much to drink that, by the end, I didn't even know whose wedding it was anymore.

"Having fun?" Zara bounced into my arms; her tiny frame dwarfed by my sheer size. "You should have called me over!"

I laughed, encircling her narrow waist and kissing her on the lips. Zara shied away because her parents were nearby, but her eyes sparked, instantly making my cock harden in my slacks. "Yeah, you're here now," I replied, trying not to fist the fabric of Zara's bright green sari. It flowed like a cascade of emerald water, rippling with every step she took, as if it were a vibrant river winding its way through a lush forest.

"Tease." She shoved at my chest. Then she was off with her cousins again, disappearing like a flash of color amidst a sea of flowers.

"Another drink?" Harpreet spoke, already pouring what was left of a bottle of champagne into a flute. "Last call."

"You said that five hours ago!" I laughed, shaking my head, when he offered it to me. "I'm so drunk, I think I'm going to puke."

1

FACEOFF IN THE CITY

EVANS MULRONEY

Detroit Michigan 2013

*D*o or do not, there is no try. Yoda's voice rang in my ear, and I forced another smile as a horde of people came flying at me. *Meet my parents,* she said. *It'll be fun,* she said. *Yeah, right.*

Now, I was drenched in sweat at an extravagant Indian wedding, desperately trying not to forget the names of the endless stream of people she kept introducing me to. The air pulsed with the electrifying beats of Bollywood music, wrapping around the room in a vibrant, intoxicating melody.

I found myself engulfed in a sea of colorful saris, caught in the whirlwind of streamers hanging from the ceiling. On the dancefloor, bodies moved in sync with the rhythm, a kaleidoscope of twirling colors and infectious energy. Amidst the crowd, I even spotted Zara's grandmother, hips gyrating with wild abandon.

For an outsider, the experience was overwhelming. But the sight of Zara, her face illuminated with sheer joy, her hazel eyes glistening with laughter as she danced with her cousins, made it all worthwhile.

CONTENTS

"Puke over there then. This carpet is worth more than your life," Harpreet said, draining the flute in one go. "Damn, that's the good stuff!"

I raised an eyebrow, feigning offense. "Wow, Harpreet, I thought we were friends. Threatening my life over a carpet? That's just cold."

"Oh, I'm your friend, alright. Your friend who appreciates the value of a good carpet," he replied, pointing to the luxurious floor covering beneath our feet.

"Fine. No puking on the carpet," I said, trying to sound serious but failing as another fit of laughter escaped me. "But seriously, I think I've had enough to drink. My legs feel like jelly, and I'm pretty sure I forgot my own name a few minutes ago."

Harpreet clapped me on the back, nearly causing me to stumble. "Nonsense! The night is young, my friend! Besides, you haven't truly experienced an Indian wedding until you've danced until your legs turn to jelly and you can't remember your own name. It's a rite of passage."

"Nah, I think I need some fresh air," I said, feeling like the floor was unsteady beneath my feet.

"I'll come with you," Harpreet replied, and together we walked outside into the crisp, wintry air. As we stepped out of the sprawling wedding hall, the wintry breeze slapped against my face, awakening my senses. Away from the chaos, the night was wrapped in a quiet, serene ambiance, the darkness broken only by the warm glow of scattered lamps.

It felt like stepping into a snow globe. The air was crisp and pure, carrying a faint scent of alluring spices that hung tantalizingly around us. Harpreet took out a package of cigarettes, his cropped black hair swaying in the wind, and his green kurta pajama bright against the night.

"I'll quit tomorrow, I promise," he said, almost defensively, knowing damn well that the promise was as fragile as smoke dissipating in the wind.

I laughed at his feigned optimism, though I declined his offer of a cigarette.

"So, have you decided yet? Word on the streets is you're ready to go pro," his voice carrying a hint of curiosity beneath the winter night's quiet. The question hung in the air, as loaded as the scent of spices. Clearing my throat, I thought back to what had happened earlier with Zara's father. We've only been dating for a few months, things weren't serious at all, but it seemed to Zara and her family that they were, and by the end of dinner, I felt like they were all waiting for me to decide what would happen to our relationship if I went pro for the NHL.

A decision I had no fucking clue how to make. "Ah, well—I'm not sure. Zara's great. Everything is great. I'm not sure what else there is to say. Once I'm done with school, we'll see where it goes."

"But you'll be graduating next year," Harpreet pressed on with an annoying smirk. "My friend, one thing you should know is that Zara isn't someone who will wait around. Trust me. If you aren't serious, she'll be gone with the wind."

"Thanks for the vote of confidence," I laughed, but it felt hollow. Zara and I hadn't even really talked about what was going to happen next...

"Alright," Harpreet said, flicking his cigarette away. "Your funeral. I'll see you inside."

Watching him disappear into the building, I sagged against the brick wall, silently wishing the night would end. I was dead tired, and I still had to drop Zara off at her dorm room before heading back to my own. Taking out my phone, I scrolled through the text messages before pausing on Alex's name.

The last message I sent was left on read, as were several others I sent during the week. Sighing through my nose, I tapped out another text to my best friend, hoping he'd have the decency to respond this time.

What are you up to? I texted and pressed send, the pang in my chest spreading.

Ever since Zara and I started dating four months ago, I've noticed his entire attitude has changed. He withdrew and kept to himself most days, which wouldn't be unusual except I kept getting the feeling he was trying to shut me out. Scrolling through my emails, I landed on the last one I received from a scout at the game a few nights ago.

Fuck, that shit was crazy. Jayden had played his fucking heart out, Grayson too, and it literally put our team on the fucking map. I heard Jayden and Grayson had been scooped up and soon they'd have their pick of going directly pro.

It was unreal to think back to where we started, to where we were now. Skimming over the email, my heart raced with anticipation. Several scouts had expressed interest in me, not too surprising considering I was in the NCAA Division I at the University of Michigan. Coach was highly optimistic about my potential to go pro and join one of the AHL (American Hockey League) teams, with the Grand Rapids Griffins being the closest option. However, I understood that this was all speculative. My future depended on the choices I made and the opportunities I would receive. It was possible that I might even get drafted directly into the NHL like Jayden and Grayson, but that decision was still to be made.

I went back to my message to Alex and saw that it was read. Bastard. I thought, slipping my phone back into my pocket. *If he doesn't want to talk, why not just say so? What is with all the silent treatment?* It was fucking with me, but I was a pretty easy-going guy and I've known

Alex since I was three. He could be a surly bastard when he wanted to, but he always came back.

But why do I feel like things are different this time?

"Hey!" Zara's voice startled me out of my thoughts. "I was looking for you," she said, walking over to me. The bright green sari Zara wore seemed to have a life of its own, twirling and twining like a vibrant emerald serpent, accentuating her every movement. *Shit, I must be drunker than I thought.* Black eyeliner made her hazel eyes look smoky as she wrapped her arms around my neck. "Come back inside. They're about to cut the cake."

"Babe, I've got to go. I have practice at five am tomorrow," I responded and kissed her pout. "I'll make it up to you later, I promise."

"No," she whined, pressing up against me. I felt her perky breasts beneath the fine fabric of her dress, and my cock thickened. Zara always knew how to get me going. Licking my dry lips, I leaned closer to her, hands braced against her waist.

"Yeah? What are you going to do to make me stay?" I said, my voice husky.

Her eyes flashed with wicked delight, and her mouth curled into a smile. Looking left and then right, Zara tugged my hand and led me to the back of the wedding convention center, where the lights were dim. She shoved me against the wall and then, descending upon me, captured my lips in a heated kiss that got me hard in seconds. I groaned. My large hand came up to her breasts, kneading the fabric as her mounds filled my palms. "Fuck," I hissed, and our lips met with a renewed urgency.

The scent of her perfume made me go dizzy with desire. I could taste our shared breath, and feel the thud of our combined desire as I pulled back to attack her beautiful, long neck. Zara's skin was bronze, washed into the golden light of the street lamps as I sucked on a spot along her collarbone. Groping blindly, I kissed the top swell of her breasts, nuzzling my face deeper, wishing like hell I could tear this off and take her brown pebbled nipple into my mouth.

"Shit—I want you to fuck me, baby," she whispered. "You looked so fucking hot tonight. Who knew white boys looked amazing in kurta pajamas?"

I laughed breathlessly and fisted her long hair. Zara's lips were flushed red, and her eyes were vibrant, pulsating hazel that made her heart stop. *God, she is breathtaking.* "I knew it. You are only with me to get into my pants."

She giggled. "You caught me. Now take them off Evans before I lose my patience."

I love it when she gets bossy. It's so fucking hot. Growling low in my throat, I kissed her again. Her lips were soft, almost silken, and pillowy against my own. I could feel the soft tickle of her breath beneath my nose, my fingers carding through her hair as we breathed each other in. Fuck, I was ready to go, and if Zara didn't find a secluded place for us, I'd take her right here and now.

"Aheem," a voice cleared their throat, and we jumped apart. Harpreet stood there with his arms crossed and his foot tapping.

"Shit!" Zara cursed, righting her sari. "What are you doing watching us, you creep?"

"Mom's looking for you," Harpreet said, his eyes narrowing into pinpricks. "You've got roughly ten seconds to get in there before Harleen pops a blood vessel in her head over one of her bridesmaids going MIA."

"Crap," Zara sighed and turned to me. "Call me when you get home. And don't drive drunk. I called your sister to come get you, and she should be here soon."

Disappointment panged through me. "You don't want me to stop by your dorm?"

Zara's mouth kinked. "Not tonight, baby. This won't be ending until the wee hours and you've got practice tomorrow. Text me when you get in. We'll talk soon, I promise." She sealed it with a kiss and then flounced off with Harpreet in tow.

Damn. My cock was pulsating in my slacks and I sighed, knowing it was probably going to be another night with just my hand. Checking the time on my phone, I realized I had one missed call from my sister and a text saying she was waiting in the parking lot. *That was quick.*

Zara was always thinking ahead, and it was one reason why I liked her so much. She knew I had practice tomorrow, and that hockey was important to me, and she even made arrangements for me to get home safely. If that wasn't the perfect girlfriend, then I didn't know what was. Striding towards the front entrance, I saw Kateryna's sleek black BMW in the parking lot, her high beams flashing as if trying to tell me to hurry the fuck up. Rolling my eyes, I walked over to the car, my long legs eating up the distance between us. I unlocked the door and got in, my nose wrinkling at the obnoxious floral spray of perfume Kateryna seemed to bathe her car in.

"What's up, loser?" Kateryna said by way of greeting, her bright blue eyes turning to me. "So, just how drunk are you that you had your girlfriend texting me to pick you up instead of an Uber driver?"

"Not drunk enough," I muttered and then leaned back in the seat. "Just drop me off at the frat house. I've got practice tomorrow, pumpkinhead."

"This is the thanks I get for driving your drunk ass home," Kateryna muttered, using one hand to tug on her messy blond updo. "You're lucky I had practice in the area or else you'd be walking home."

Ah, siblings. Can't live with them and can't live without them. "Shut up. Your voice is making my head hurt."

Kateryna scowled at me but kept her eyes on the road. "I have no idea what she sees in you, anyway. Zara is way out of your league."

I yawned, ignoring her. Kateryna could be grumpy when it was past her bedtime. I knew she was doing me a solid favor by not forcing me to take an Uber. "So, how was practice?"

Her face lit up immediately. Kateryna also played for Michigan University but on the women's junior hockey team. "Well," she began, stretching the word out for effect, "practice was pretty good. I finally nailed that slapshot I've been working on. Top right corner, no goalie in the world could've stopped it!"

"Impressive. But let's not forget who taught you that move."

Kateryna scowled, hating the reminder that she used to follow me everywhere and beg me to teach her how to play hockey. "Yeah, yeah, whatever. But can you dangle through defensemen like I can?"

I snorted a laugh. "Dangle through defensemen? You might need a GPS to find your way around them. Remember that time you got stuck behind the net for five minutes?"

Kateryna rolled her eyes. "Oh, shut up. That was just a strategic pause to let you catch your breath. I didn't want to embarrass you."

I chuckled, raising an eyebrow. "Strategic pause? More like a scenic route to nowhere. And speaking of embarrassing, you still owe me for that last shootout. My five-hole goal had you seeing stars."

"Beginner's luck, dear brother. Let's see if you can repeat it when it counts."

"Remember that time you mistook the referee for a teammate and passed him the puck?" I teased. "That shit was fucking gold."

"Why don't you stick your head up your ass and see how far you get?" Kateryna shot back.

"Ouch," I said, feigning hurt. "Touchy."

"At least I don't mix up my teammates during line changes. You practically handed the opponent the puck on a silver platter."

I laughed and pinched her chubby cheek. Kateryna slapped my hand away and before I could blink, she was pulling up to my house on campus. Stretching my limbs, I yawned again and cracked my neck. "See you later, pumpkinhead. I won't tip you because your Uber services were horrible. One star rating for sure."

"Shut up and get out," Kateryna laughed, pushing my arm. I kissed her cheek. "Night, bro."

"Thanks. Drive safe," I said as I climbed out of the vehicle.

Watching her pull away from the curb, I shivered against the cold. I'd forgotten my coat at the wedding, far too drunk to remember to bring it. Instead, I hugged my arms to my chest as I turned and walked back to the frat house. The night deepened, and a profound silence blanketed everything as I walked up the stone steps into the house. Everyone was asleep and the world outside hushed to a whisper, with only occasional rustlings breaking the stillness. Opening my bedroom door, I tugged off my shirt and tossed it aside, then my slacks and loafer shoes. I'd have the clothes dry-cleaned tomorrow. I flopped on the bed face first, a wave of dizziness coming over me before sleep yanked me under.

2

PUCK DROP AND CHEMISTRY SPARKS

EVANS MULRONEY

The blaring noise of my alarm clock jolted me awake. I groaned, rolling over I checked the time to see that it was after 4 a.m. *Crap.* I had practice in an hour. Getting out of bed, I felt like a zombie. A headache throbbed in the back of my eyelids, and the room kept spinning. *Fuck, I'm never drinking that much ever again.* Yeah, right, who was I kidding? I got out of bed, ready to start my day with a hot shower and some black coffee. I checked my phone and sighed. Still no response from Alex.

Whatever. It was his ass coach was going to fry.

Turning on the shower, I moaned, stepping into the hot steam as it unlocked my stiff muscles and lathered my body in soap. After that, I grabbed my gear and headed straight to the hockey rink.

An icy mist blanketed the area as I breathed in the crisp air. This place was my sanctuary. Skating gracefully across the ice, I began my warm-up drills as the guys trickled in. Grayson and Jayden were the first to arrive, followed by Chris and a few others. My heart raced as I anxiously awaited Alex's arrival; if he didn't hurry, Coach would have our heads.

More teammates joined us on the ice. We exchanged fist bumps and nods, our camaraderie evident. Finally, Coach Cornell called us together, his bald head and piercing eyes shining in the fluorescent lights. "All right, you potato sacks," he barked, "we're running drills for our upcoming game against the Ice Panthers. Grayson, lead the way. I want you all looking like figure skaters out here!"

We responded with a resounding "Yes, Coach!" and lined up for practice. My heart pounded as I scanned the group. Still no sign of Alex. It was unusual; he never missed practice.

"Evans!" Coach's voice boomed, and I jumped. "Where's your better half? He's forty-five minutes late!"

"Ah ... I'm not sure, Coach. Should I call him?"

"Forget it!" Coach snarled. "He'd better be here next time, or you'll both be running suicides for a week!"

I gulped at the prospect. *Where on earth is Alex?* I zipped down the rink, weaving through cones, and executing rapid stops. My heart thundered in my chest as we aimed precision shots at the net. It wasn't just Grayson and Jayden I was up against. I was battling against my limits, striving to prove myself. I understood I had to pour my soul into the game, pushing myself to the brink if I desired a direct route to the NHL.

"I haven't seen this much confusion since the last time someone tried to explain the plot of 'Inception' to me! Get your heads in the game!"

Coach's voice cut through my thoughts, and I hurried to get my head back in the game. We played for several more hours until it was close to 8 a.m. and I had a few hours to relax before getting to class. Heading back to the locker rooms, everyone was buzzing with excitement about the upcoming games. "Hey," Grayson said, nudging my shoulder, his brown hair flopping over his brow. "Where's Alex? We were short today, and this is the second time he hasn't shown up."

I knew it was Grayson's job as team captain to check in on everyone, but these questions were grating on my nerves. I honestly had no fucking clue what was up with Alex, and we were all adults. I wasn't his babysitter. "Not sure, man. I'll call him later to see what's up."

Grayson nodded but looked skeptical. He tore off his shirt, and my gaze snagged on the hickies littering his chest and neck. Jayden and Grayson weren't exactly quiet about their relationship, and I had nothing against them being gay, but seeing it was jarring to me sometimes. I grabbed my stuff and headed to the sauna since I'd already showered earlier, but I felt a lot of tension in my body and I needed to relax before the next game.

Grayson waved goodbye with Jayden and Ian hot on his heels, while I left the locker rooms and headed to the sauna near the back. A flash of reddish-bronze caught my attention, and my breath caught.

Alex stood with his back to me in Coach Cornell's office, his head hanging low. Blood roared in my ears when I took in his muscular form, his long taut thighs, and the way his black shirt stretched across his strong back. *What are they talking about?* I didn't want to pry, so I continued my journey toward the sauna, hoping I'd catch him later to talk. It was still pretty early in the morning, so nobody was around. I slipped inside the sauna and sighed as the rolling press of heat seemed to penetrate my very being, drawing out the stress and fatigue. I found a spot near the entrance and closed my eyes, letting the soothing warmth transport me to a place of serenity.

Fuck, this was the life. The world outside melted away, leaving only a deep and restorative calm. I could finally have some time to think without the pressures of life weighing me down. A white towel hung snugly around my hips, and I spread my legs out and leaned my arms back, groaning as the heat infiltrated my brain. The sound of the door opening and closing snapped me out of my relaxation. I was startled, my eyes flying open, only to see a flash of auburn before my vision.

"Fuck, you scared me," I laughed, but a knot formed in my throat.

Alex possessed a striking appearance, with reddish bronze hair that cascaded like molten copper over his brow, catching the light in a mesmerizing dance of warmth and depth.

"Did I? Sorry," his voice gruff said as he sidled up beside me, his frame lithe compared to mine, but just as powerful.

"Where the fuck have you been?" I demanded, cutting right to the chase.

Alex's jaw tightened, but then his expression smoothed out into something secretive and cunning. Thick lashes framed his rich dark eyes as he blinked up at me. "What do you mean?"

"Cut the shit," I snarled. "Coach will have your fucking head if you miss another practice like that. Grayson is being patient, but everyone here is serious about making it pro. Coach doesn't want any slackers, so you better get your act together."

Alex laughed like I was telling a joke, and something seemed off about him. "Sure, Evans. Whatever you say."

"I'm fucking serious, man, and what the hell is wrong with you? You've been ignoring me for two weeks straight and I—where are you going?"

Alex stood. The white towel hugged the swell of his perky ass, making it stand out starkly in the low lights. My throat went dry as I watched him pour more water on the sauna rocks, intensifying the heat. "It's already hotter than the devil's ass in here," I grumbled, not sure why he wanted to do that right now.

"It's not nearly enough. What's wrong? Afraid you can't take it?" Alex said over his shoulder, his lips pulling into a mocking smirk.

What the hell is he talking about? We have a class in a few hours. I wasn't sure what the hell was going on with my best friend, and to be honest, I didn't really like it.

"So..." I probed when Alex sat back down beside me. "What's going on? Is it your mom? Did something happen?"

There it is again. Alex's jaw ticked.

The veins in his neck throbbed as if he were holding himself back from something. I stared at him. Not sure what thoughts were running through his head. Very few people knew Alex's mom was a cocaine addict and that he'd spent most of his life trying to get her into rehab. "She's fine. Another hit and it's like nothing ever happened," Alex muttered, knowing that there was no point hiding it from me. "I'm sorry, Evans, shit's been ... well, shit."

"Did you tell Coach?"

He nodded, but his expression was tight. "This is my last chance, or he says I'm out."

"Fuck," I breathed, and we both knew Coach Cornell wasn't the type to play around. "Come stay with me—we can share a room like we used to—"

"I doubt Zara would be okay with that," Alex laughed, but it sounded too high. Fake. Alex was never this fake with me. *Something horrible must have happened.* My heart thudded in my ears as I stared at my best friend, watching his side profile. Alex blinked but kept his eyes forward.

His eyes were like peach blossoms, curved and hooded, adorned with rich hues of dark brown, like the enchanting colours of autumn leaves. "She won't care. I promise," I spoke, tearing my gaze away.

"She will. You guys have been inseparable since—well, what can I say? She's perfect for you in every way..." Alex trailed off, almost as if implying that he wasn't perfect for me, which was odd.

I nudged his arm. "What are you talking about? You're still my best friend. What does she have to do with anything?"

Alex's body glistened with sweat, the soft rise and fall of his chest brought out every curve of muscle on his creamy skin. My gaze dipped to that happy trail that plunged into the white towel and the swell of his cock where it lay flat against his thigh.

Shit. I cursed and dragged my eyes away. *What the hell am I doing staring at him?*

A flush spread across his cheeks. Alex reclined on the sauna bench and allowed his body language to take over the conversation. His toned legs spread slightly with his towel stretched between his thighs. His fingers knit behind his head as he leaned back and shrugged.

"Nothing, I guess." Then his eyes slipped closed as if he were going to sleep. I didn't want this conversation to end just yet, but I knew how prickly Alex could get when talking about his mother, so I let it rest for the moment, content to lie back and enjoy the stifling heat. I'd get out of here in a minute... Sleep tugged me under, and before I knew it, I was succumbing to darkness.

***

STRANGE RUFFLING NOISES made me twitch. My eyes felt like they were welded shut as I struggled to peel them open. *Fuck, what happened?* A wave of dizziness crashed over me and I realized I had fallen asleep in the fucking sauna. Shit, that was so fucking dangerous. Wiping the sweat pooling on my brow, I groaned and sat up straighter, only to stop dead when my eyes crashed into a swirling autumn haze.

Alex was on his fucking knees in front of me.

His palms were flat on either side of the bench, his shoulders wedged between my massive thighs while my cock hung fat and heavy, slapping against my stomach. My towel had been unwrapped, lying limp and wet on the bench.

What the fuck?

There was a hint of determination in Alex's gaze. Hard. Unyielding. And before I could think, his fingers wrapped around my shaft with a delicate caress. More heat throbbed my sensitive skin, and I cried out when Alex's thumb raced up the mushroom tip. "What are you doing—*fuck*—" I choked on my own spit when my cock stiffened further, filling out his palm. I grunted, and grabbed his shoulder for purchase, trying not to blow my load right there and then. My breath came out heavy with steam and the scent of lust, my vision swimming as he stroked hard and fast, his pink tongue darting out to lick his lips.

"*Shit—Alex—*" I was overcome by emotions. Panting hard and fast, straining into his touch, trying not to fuck into his tight fist. A moan caught in my throat. Teasing strokes massaged pleasure into me bit by bit, like being struck by lightning each time. "*Ah—Ngh—*" I gasped.

Alex's hair was a captivating blend of red and bronze, akin to a fiery sunrise captured in each strand. His eyes held mine, like those of a sly fox, as he dipped down and opened his mouth.

Stardust burst before my vision as he took me in from root to tip. His eyes never left mine, like he was daring me to do something. To push him away. To tell him this was wrong. It was wrong. So fucking wrong, but it felt so right. Alex's tongue flicked along the slit, swirling and slipping along my shaft until his lips touched the base. Slow, careful, inquisitive motions were met with eager and needy moans.

Less caution yielded more sounds.

"Fuck—" A curse wrenched from my lips. Alex's tongue drew sharp patterns and moved with practiced ease up and down the length of my cock, paying attention to the bulbous tip, circling the thick, pulsating vein. *It is the hottest thing I've ever fucking seen in my life.*

Muscular thighs tensed just inches from his head. Beneath Alex's towel, he was getting hard as well. The bobbing of his head kept steady. No need to get overenthusiastic. He kept my cock rubbing against the inside of his cheek while lapping his tongue against me. *Fuck yes.* God, my cock grew until it stiffened between his lips and pushed towards the back of his throat. What the hell was happening, and why wasn't I stopping it?

"You taste exactly like I thought you would," Alex said as he pulled off, his palm clung to my thighs. "Always like I dreamed."

"Alex—what—" I barely got the words out before he plunged again, taking me deeper than ever before, hollowing out his cheeks as he sucked. Hard. Pleasure sparked behind my eyelids. My cock pulsed and twitched, come erupting in searing waves down his throat.

Sweat beaded on his brow but his concentration was unbroken. It was as if he had all the time in the world and would spend it doing just this, sucking my cock. Fisting his hair, I arched my hips. I whined as I came. My orgasm ripped through me like a silver bullet and I fucked into his mouth, chasing my release as waves of pleasure rolled over me.

"*Fuck—fuck—*" I groaned, going limp, and Alex drank it all down like he was a fucking expert.

Alex wiped his lips and stood. Hooking his fingers under the folds of the towel, he stared down at me. His eyes flashed with fire. Our gaze locked, and then I was moving before I could even register it, unravelling the towel and letting it flop to the ground in a cold wet slap. My hands settled on his narrow hips, his rock-hard abs and jutted hip bones dug into my fingertips as I sucked in a breath of his clean scent. Tears burned my eyes. It was so fucking wrong. For years, Alex has been everything to me. My best friend and confidant. I didn't want to ruin things between us, but I wasn't going to fool myself either. *I wanted him. I always have.*

Pressing a trembling kiss to his stomach, Alex ran a hand through my thick blond hair, gathering it in his fist. "Do it."

Alex propped his leg beside me, almost hooking it over my shoulder, bringing his swollen cock right up to my face. A large part of me wanted to explore every inch of him, but my heart was racing too hard to do anything more than nuzzle against his skin. Breathing in, my tongue flitted out, tasting the salt of his precum before swallowing the head whole. Alex groaned, his hand tightening in my hair. I've never done this before. He knows that yet he held me firm, almost as if he were punishing me.

"Touch me," Alex barked, and my hands came up to grab two handfuls of his tight ass, spreading his cheeks apart as I hooked his knee over my shoulder and wrenched him forward with enough force to send him stumbling. Alex laughed, but it bit off into a cry as I took him deeper, making his cock hit the back of my throat. Breathing through my nose, I tempered my breath. More sweat streaked down my chest, damping my back as I sucked him in with a force I had never known.

Alex made the most delicious noises. Squeaks and hisses that sounded like a kitten. The wooden bench creaked and moaned beneath us and then Alex was thrusting his hips in wild abandon.

"*Fuck—Evans—I'm gonna come—*" he whined, blunt nails digging into my scalp. I growled, and Alex doubled over, breath hitching as warm, hot liquid flooded my mouth, making me choke.

I almost gagged, but swallowed it down, relishing the taste of him inside my mouth. Sweat stung my eyes, and I was dripping wet, before Alex sagged and finally pulled away, collapsing on the bench next to me. Our chests rose and fell, as we stared deep into each other's eyes.

I heard a steady stream of voices outside the sauna, and panic set in like a searing hot coal burning its way down my throat. We scrambled to get dressed, throwing on the towels and righting ourselves just as the sauna door opened and a few guys walked in.

Alex stood first, his eyes latching onto mine, blazing like the fiery red glow of dawn. A smile curled his lips, and he walked out like nothing had happened. My heart jammed into my throat. *What the fuck just happened? I am straight.* I had a girlfriend, and Alex just obliterated all of that. My hands curled into a fist, the moments from earlier now curdling in my gut like sour milk.

What the fuck have I done?

3

THE RIVALRY BEGINS

EVANS MULRONEY

P anic gripped me, a relentless force that clenched my chest, rendering each breath a struggle as the world around me blurred into chaos. *Did that really just happen? No.* I raced to the showers, lathering myself in soap, wanting to rid myself of the feelings coiling inside my gut.

It was a mistake. Nothing more. *A mistake? Sucking your best friend's cock was a mistake?* My frantic thoughts spiraled. Bile rose hot and thick in my throat as I hurried to get out of the locker room.

I'm not gay, and neither is Alex. A large part of me wanted to chase after Alex and demand what the fuck just happened, but I couldn't stop my hands from shaking. Going about my daily routine, I went to my law class, plastering on a fake smile, when I saw Zara sitting at the front of the lecture hall waiting for me. *Fuck*. Several guys from my team and frat house sat around her, along with a few of her other friends I'd come to know.

"Hey," I said, snagging a seat right between her and Chris. Leaning in, I kissed her gently on the lips and took her hand in mine, loving the way our skin contrasted.

"What happened to you last night?" Zara's enchanting hazel eyes held a hint of mischief, and her waist-length, pitch-black hair framed her face like a curtain of ebony silk. The cardigan she wore was a sensual white cashmere that seemed soft to the touch.

"What do you mean?" I asked, taking out my textbooks.

"I called you three times to make sure you got home properly," Zara replied, tucking a strand of hair behind her ears. "Kateryna picked you up?"

"Yeah," I laughed and realized I forgot to thank her for doing that. "Shit. I must have been so drunk that I passed out. Sorry, baby. Thanks for doing that, by the way."

Zara beamed and then took her hand back to get out her own notes.

"Take out your textbooks to section 5:9 and we'll be going over what you need to know when going for the bar…"

Shit. Another fucking headache that I needed to deal with. Zara was smiling at me expectantly, and I had to look away. Hockey was really the only thing I wanted to do for the rest of my life, and she knew that. Studying law had just been to make my parents happy. I didn't actually think I'd be good at it or that I'd make it into a career or anything, but now that I had met Zara's family, I could tell their expectations were high. Zara knew I wanted to go pro, and I was confident she would support my decision, no matter what. The question was, would her parents? Most of their concerns probably stemmed from the thought of me getting injured during a game and never playing again.

Like Cricket.

Shit, what happened to him is like what horror stories are made of. I still remember the sickening crunch on the ice when his knee snapped. We'd lost one of our own that day. It killed me to think about it. Cricket was one of us—the light in a dark tunnel. I knew it still ate Grayson up to his core every day, blaming himself for what happened.

Sighing through my nose, I kept my eyes on my teacher, trying to dispel the tightness in my chest.

Anxiety wrapped around me like a suffocating blanket, squeezing the air from my lungs and making my heart race like a wild stallion. Zara touched my hand, and I jumped, not realizing I'd been staring at the teacher for the past five minutes. "Are you okay?" she mouthed at me, and I nodded.

Of course. Fine. Dandy.

Swallowing around the knot in my throat, I tried not to think. Not to feel. If I did, I felt like I'd go crazy. Best to ignore it. Everything. Nothing happened in the locker room today. *I'm not gay. Alex will come to class and we'll laugh it off like we used to.* He'd continue to be my best friend and this entire thing would blow over.

Images of me running my hands through reddish bronze hair made my heart lurch. The way he looked up at me, cheek resting on my thigh like it was the most natural thing in the whole fucking world. And maybe it was. If I allowed it to be.

Pink lips parted, taking me in inch by inch. His tongue swirled the head and his nose buried deep in my blond pubic hair. Apprehension descended upon me like a sudden thunderstorm, with lightning strikes of worry flashing through my thoughts, and the deafening roar of fear drowning out reason. *It wasn't real. It didn't happen.*

Damn, Alex! My hand curled into a fist, and rage spread like molten lava through my core. *He did this to me! And he knew I'd hate him for it.* We weren't lovers. We were friends. Damn him for crossing the line between us and damn me for not stopping. We were both to blame. Taking out my phone, my thumb hovered over his contact information and the hordes of text messages I'd sent within the past two weeks that had gone unanswered. *Maybe something was wrong.*

Alex was acting out of character. Looking around the room, I turned to Chris, who sat beside me and hunched over his textbook, taking notes. "Hey," I whispered, and his green eyes turned to look at me. "Did you see Alex this morning after practice?"

Chris snorted. "Yeah, bastard walked right past me when I asked about what we were going to do for our assignment. I don't know what's up with your boy, but he better get his shit together. Coach isn't having it and neither is Rex."

"Rex? What's he got to do with anything?" I asked, frowning.

Chris' brow rose. "You don't know? Shit. Well, apparently Rex and Alex were working together on some big assignment for their degree in Engineering and Alex fucking bailed last minute, leaving Rex to finish the project on his own. Dude, I know shit happens, but at least be honest, besides, Mechanical Engineering is hard. If he's struggling, then he needs to speak up. I texted him this morning about it and if he doesn't respond, I'll ask for a new partner. You can let him know that."

Fuck. That wasn't at all like Alex. What the hell was he thinking, leaving Rex out to dry like that? Running a hand through my hair, I nodded, and Chris went back to listening to the lecture. The more the day went on, the more I was convinced something was wrong. Alex loved studying Mechanical Engineering. As a kid, it was all he wanted to do other than hockey. Why in hell would he treat Rex like that? Weren't they close friends? My chest tightened as the bitter taste of jealousy flooded my senses, casting a murky shadow over my rational thoughts. Rex was cool, but a part of me didn't like how close they'd become over the years. Thinking back to Alex's behavior, I really should have known something was off about him. However, the thought of confronting him again made my stomach knot.

What if he tried to kiss me? Would I let him? Warmth blossomed in my cheeks and I stamped it down hard. This was wrong. I had cheated on Zara with Alex and I was fucking fantasizing about doing it again. But I wasn't fucking gay.

Right? I pushed everything to the back of my mind and went back to studying. No. It was the heat of the sauna. A lapse in judgment. Things would return to normal. *I am straight. I have a girlfriend. Alex is my best friend. We'd study together. Then go pro together. That was the plan.*

Yet, my chest cracked open like a sledgehammer hitting a boulder. The feeling of his lips on mine sent a rush of liquid warmth through me. *I want him. Now and then.*

And the realization tore my world apart.

***

"HEY," ZARA CAUGHT MY ARM, linking it with hers. "Are you okay? You seemed so out of it during class today."

"Ah—yeah—just tired. I'm more hungover than I thought," I said, then cleared my throat.

"Sure," Zara said. "Listen, I have a bit of a break now. Can we talk? We can head to my dorm. You don't have another class until 3 p.m. right?"

The fact that she knew my schedule should've made me happy. Instead, my brain short-circuited on the words "can we talk?". *Fuck, nothing good ever came after hearing those words.* A part of me wanted to blow her off and head home, but whatever she wanted to talk about might be important, so I smiled and said, "Yeah. Sure." Taking her hand in mine, we walked down the halls. *I used to love this.* Walking the halls with a girl like Zara made everyone's heads turn with jealousy. She was the hottest girl in school and the fact that she chose me used to make my heart soar. Now all I could feel was dread coiled in my gut. *I didn't deserve Zara. Especially after this morning ... especially after... that.*

I bumped fists with a few guys I knew, and Zara stopped to talk to a few of her friends before we finally made our way back to her dorm room. The second she opened the door, I walked in and threw my stuff to the side, flopping on her bed. Spreading my long legs out, I sighed and was immediately immersed in a world of pink. It was as though an explosion of fluffy pink teddy bears had filled the space, creating a cocoon of comfort and warmth. The walls were adorned with soft pink posters, and the bedspread was a sea of delicate rosy hues.

"I can't believe you aren't sick of this color yet," I grumbled. A collection of pastel cushions adorned her bed, like a plush oasis. Even the curtains, desk accessories, and décor items followed the pink theme.

Zara laughed. "At home, my mom hated it. That's why I have to overcompensate when I'm away at school."

"How are your parents doing after the party?" I asked as she walked over to me and began peeling off her stockings. My gaze narrowed on her long hair falling over her shoulder, and her eyes trained on mine.

"Why? Do you want to know what they said about you after you left?"

"As long as it isn't mean, my fragile heart can't take the criticism," I replied and she shoved my shoulder.

"They liked you. Harpreet helped sing your praise while piss drunk."

"That's my boy, Harpreet," I chuckled.

Zara rolled her eyes. "I guess the fact that we're both studying Law helped too, but yeah, thanks for coming. I appreciate it." She leaned in and kissed me on the lips. Usually, by now, my cock would be straining against the zipper of my jeans, but something strange was coiled in my chest. *Could she smell Alex on me? Could she taste him?* I pulled away, my heart hammering against my ribcage. Should I tell her? What would she think? I'm not gay, so maybe she didn't need to know, right? Panic swept over me like a sudden storm, darkening the horizon and churning in my gut.

"So, what did you want to talk about?" I said, hoping a change of topic would ease my mind.

Zara's mouth kinked. "Guys are so dense. I just said that so we could be alone together."

I gaped at her. "Really? You made it sound so serious, I thought for sure something horrible had happened."

Zara stood. Stripping off the front part of her cashmere sweater dress, she exposed her perky breasts, the brown nipples erect and wanting. "Nah, you looked hot today, and I missed you last night."

My throat went dry. Sun-kissed skin filled my vision as she straddled my lap, the bronze ochre color, much like the mellow-brown light that bathed the forest. I groaned, taking her narrow hips in my large hands. I loved how small she was and how she fit perfectly on top of me. Nothing like Alex.

I almost choked on my own spit with that last thought. *What? Why the hell am I thinking about him?* Zara licked her lips, her cashmere dress riding up at the hips. Reaching down, I lifted her dress, my hands mapping out her firm ass, spreading those cheeks. Pressing her lips to mine, she moaned, and I kissed her back, licking into her mouth before slipping my tongue through. Her soft hands found my chest, thumbing the fabric of my shirt, and I rolled her hips against my clothed crotch. It was good.

Great even. Yet, images of Alex staring up at me on his knees made my cock thicken.

Those brown eyes were dewy wet, lips slick with my come as I fucked into his mouth. Blood roared in my veins and I thought about pushing her away, and telling her I was too tired from practice, but I knew it would just make things worse between us. My head was a mess.

All I could see was Alex. All I thought about was Alex. *I'm not gay.* I growled into the kiss, flipping her onto her back and grinding my hips into her crotch. Zara gasped and laughed, her gaze smoldering before her eyes slipped close and her knees parted. I got to work, stripping off the dress. My heart was pounding when I saw she wasn't wearing any underwear. "You minx," I chuckled, and she laughed, threading her fingers through my thick, blond hair. "How long have you been planning this?"

"Since last night," Zara replied, breathless.

Nestling between her thighs, I stared at the clean landing strip on her cunt. It was wet. Glistening with desire and I leaned down to take her into my mouth, swirling my tongue around her clit. Zara grunted, her nails digging into my scalp and the scent of her peach blossom perfume filling my nostrils. The taste of her was tangy and sharp, and I enjoyed every minute of it. Slipping my finger between the folds, I fucked into her gently, letting her drive her hips forward. Losing myself to the motions, I thought back to Alex.

Do it. He'd said it as if it were the easiest thing in the world. *Bold. Daring.* I remembered how his cock felt in my mouth. *Down my throat.* Fuck, my dick was harder than ever before at the memory. I pulled out of her pussy and she groaned, and I was far too impatient to take off the rest of my clothes. Opening the zipper of my jeans, my cock sprang free. Hard and aching. I reached into my bag and I realized with a start I was out of condoms. "Shit—do you have any condoms?"

Zara opened her eyes, startled. "No. Crap." Disappointment filled her face. "Just pull out."

"Okay," I replied. It wasn't ideal, but it wasn't like we hadn't fucked without condoms before. But with my hockey career about to take off, my parents had suggested I take extra precautions. Crawling over her, I leaned down to take her nipple into my mouth. She moaned, arching into me, while I flicked and sucked the delicious bud, then my finger slipped inside her folds while I fucked into her slow and sweet. *Damn, it's so fucking hot.*

And my cock was hard, yet inside I felt something was missing. I didn't feel the roiling heat I'd felt with Alex. *That suffocating need to take and taste.* Pulling my finger out of her, I grabbed hold of the base of my cock and lined it up with her entrance. Capturing her lips, I pressed inward, my breath stuttering as my cock was engulfed into insurmountable heat. Fuck. I gritted my teeth, trying not to blow my load right there and then. Zara clung to my shoulders, her tiny hands gripping hard.

"Yeah, that's it, baby, fill me up."

She is perfect. Hot. Tight. She loves to have sex. Smart. I knew she'd be a damn good defense attorney, and yet when I bottomed out, I felt nothing. No blistering white haze I'd felt with Alex. Or the flash of reddish bronze that nearly brought me to my knees to worship his body and his cock. My heart didn't feel raw, nor did liquid pleasure curl down my spine.

It felt good.

And empty.

I thrust into her, holding her body close to mine as tears burned my eyes. My hips were flush against her, my rhythm was hard and jerky.

Brutal and off-pace. I felt like such a fool. Too stupid to know what Alex probably had known for years. *I hate him for that.* For the way he always did that to me. Forcing me to see the things I never wanted to see. Zara's pussy was slippery and wet, easy to fuck. I shivered and panted against her mouth while my hips moved at a harsh pace. Zara's sighs and moans filled the air, and I wanted to drown myself in all of it, knowing it would be the last time.

She was perfect, but not for me.

Alex's flushed face danced before my eyes. Cunning eyes that curled at the edges like a foxtail. A tight ass that begged to be rammed. *Alex would take it all.* I didn't have to be gentle. *I could bend him over and fuck him as hard as I wanted.* Zara's cunt spasmed. She cried out as she came, clenching hard around my dick. Memories crowded in again, of Alex mouthing my cock, licking and suckling it as if he were drinking sweet white nectar. My orgasm slammed through me at the thought. *Alex bent in half, his ass bouncing on my cock.* I grunted, then hurried to pull out, but it was too late and I was already coming.

"*Fuck—*" I hissed and then pulled free. My cock twitched and emitted milky streams all over her firm stomach and thighs. "Shit," I breathed, placing my hands near her face. Zara laughed, her face wet with sweat, and my heart lurched as I stared at the come all over her. Lifting her hand to my forehead, she smoothed out the wrinkles there.

"Don't worry, I'm on the pill. It's fine."

"Yeah. Right." I swallowed, not wanting to be an ass and doubt her. I never liked having sex without protection, but we were so worked up that it just happened. Wiping the sweat from my brow, I collapsed next to her and sighed. Zara cuddled close to me, and her breath evened out. I stared up at the ceiling, my eyes stung as everything came crashing down around me. What the hell was I doing? Why had I slept with her? What would she do when she found out what I did? With Alex?

I'm not gay.

Never was.

Yet, what happened this morning made me realize how I'd been feeling the past few weeks. Alex never ignored me. Since we were kids, he's always been there for me. Desperation had clawed at my chest for even a fraction of his affection. I didn't want to be without him.

And I knew deep down, that if it came to it and I had to choose between him and Zara.

It would be him. *Always him.*

I had to break things off with her. Then have a serious discussion with Alex.

I was not gay, but what I'd done this morning was pretty fucking gay. And the worst thing about it was that it didn't scare me as much as I thought it would.

4

HAT TRICK OF SURPRISES

EVANS MULRONEY

Walking through the snow, my mind was a mess, burdened by thoughts of Alex and Zara. Two people I cared about the most, and now I was stuck at a crossroads. Zara was the perfect girlfriend. Yet, a part of me knew that wasn't enough. My body burned for Alex. My best friend.

The possibility that he might share my feelings shattered my world. Was I in love with him? The mere thought quickened my heart. The biting wind slapped against my cheeks, but I kept walking. What did it all mean?

Upon reaching my frat house, my shivering body longed for warmth. A few other guys lounged in the common area, but I was too exhausted to engage in conversation and headed straight to bed. Despite my early class, I needed rest before returning to campus. As I lay on my bed, I checked my phone, but there was nothing from Alex. Bitterness crept into my heart as I dialed his number, only for it to go straight to voicemail. "What the hell?" I whispered. Why did he sleep with me if he was just going to ignore me?

Anger roiled through me, and my hand curled around my phone. *What the hell was he doing?* Alex was never the type to play around with people's feelings. He knew I was in a relationship with Zara and still made a move on me. What did it mean? I thought back to his face, the way his eyes looked dimmed, almost defeated, and the sadness that seemed to permeate around him like perfume. What the hell was going on with him? Staring at my phone, I started typing out a message to him.

We need to talk. Call me. I pressed send and then fell back on my bed, exhausted.

Today had been a whirlwind, and it wasn't even fucking over yet. My eyes slipped closed and sleep dragged me under. I awoke to a frantic beeping of my alarm. Glancing at the time, I realized it was already around 2:45 p.m., and I had a class in fifteen minutes. Panic surged within me. Crap. I hastily rolled out of bed, grabbed my essentials, and wrenched open the door. I rushed out the door, sprinting to class, hoping I would not be late.

***

THE DAY CARRIED ON with little fanfare and there was still no word from Alex. I had left several messages and calls, but he hadn't responded. Something ugly coiled in my gut and by Thursday I was making my way toward the apartment he shared with his mother downtown. I revved up my sleek black Ford-F 150 that my father had given me as a graduation present and headed straight to Alex's neighborhood, making sure to park around the corner so nobody tried to steal my rims.

Garbage littered the snowy streets, and I kept my eyes sharp for any sudden movement. This area wasn't exactly safe, and I knew how much Alex hated it here, but I needed to talk to him. This couldn't continue. If anything, my parents could get us a place and we could live together for a while.

The apartment building itself was a stark contrast to the pristine surroundings of the university campus. It was marred by graphite scrawls on the walls and reeked of the acrid stench of urine in the stairwells. I ascended to the ninth floor, cautiously stepping around homeless individuals who had taken refuge there. Alex had earned a full scholarship to Michigan University for Mechanical Engineering, but his scholarships kept him going there. His mother could never afford it, and Alex resented it every time I offered to help him.

I walked down the long corridor, my footsteps echoing in the dimly lit space, until I came to a halt in front of a battered brown door. My heart raced as I noticed the bright orange-yellow tape plastered on the door, alongside a grim eviction notice. What the hell? I tore the notice from the door, my hands trembling. *Evicted? Last week?* The world seemed to spin around me. Panic surged, and everything rushed to my head, leaving me on the verge of collapsing.

No. No. Alex couldn't be gone.

I pounded on the door, desperation making me feel mad and crazed, with emotions threatening to tear me apart. "Alex! Open up! Alex!" I shouted, the echoes of my voice reflecting my inner turmoil. *Where the hell is he?* A door creaked open, and a disheveled woman with her clothes hanging off her body, pupils blown wide, greeted me with a drawl.

"Hey, sweetie? You looking for someone?"

"Alex. Do you know the guy who lives here? Where did he go?" I barked at her, my voice cracking with emotion.

"Oh, him? Left a few days ago. I don't know where. Shirley owed me fifty dollars and still she left. So uptight. Hey, why don't you come inside? I'll show you a good time—" Her suggestive words hung in the air, but I didn't wait to hear more.

A whirlwind of panic raced around me. This couldn't be happening. Blood rushed to my ears as I fled the building and burst out onto the wintry streets. The harsh wind slapped against my cheeks as I shivered in the cold. Tears welled up, blurred my vision, and spilled over. I fumbled for my phone and dialed Alex's number again, only for it to go straight to voicemail.

I wanted to scream.

If Alex was stuck with his mom, that meant he was in danger. Or worse. Shirley was an addict. They wouldn't get far without her addiction making things worse for them. I tried to think of where they'd go, but Alex kept most of his life private. I only knew his mom was an addict because we had stumbled upon her getting high one day when I dropped him off after school.

Alex had opened the door to Shirley bent over the table, the in straight lines laid out before her while she snorted. Humiliation had crawled up Alex's neck and he probably would have slammed the door shut if I hadn't been there watching. We were fourteen at the time, and by then, I knew Alex and I lived in different worlds.

Shirley May hadn't always been like this.

Once, she had a husband. A large house in the suburbs next to my parents, where Alex used to live. *Then life hit. Her husband left her.* She lost her job and unfortunately ended up getting hooked up with the wrong type of guys. Alex never told me what happened the night he came to my house and slipped into my room, his face bloodied and his boxers torn, but deep down, I knew.

Alex needed me, and I would do everything in my power to be there for him.

Over the years, things didn't get better. Shirley spiraled and if it wasn't for me keeping Alex tethered, he probably would have too. "Fuck! Fuck!" I hissed, searching through my phone, wondering who I could call. I dialed Rex's number, hoping he'd seen Alex.

"Hello?" a deep baritone voice responded.

"Rex," I breathed out. "Fuck man, have you seen Alex? I'm going crazy looking for him."

"Dude, I haven't seen that guy for weeks, and if I do, I might fucking kill him for leaving me hanging like that."

My jaw dropped. "What? Weeks?" No way. I saw Alex a few days ago. There's no way he hasn't been at school for weeks. Was he crazy? Did he want to get kicked out and lose his scholarships? What the hell was happening right now? The alarm surged through me like a lightning bolt, flashing with intensity and leaving me as disoriented as a compass spinning aimlessly in a magnetic storm. *First the eviction and now this? Where was he?*

"Yeah, dude. I'm not sure what's going on with him. I thought he was my boy and shit, but it turns out I was wrong—"

"No," I replied, my voice cracking. "Something is wrong."

Rex scoffed. "Nah, bro. He's just being a bastard. Look, save yourself the trouble and drop him, man, I'm tired of cleaning up after his ass—"

"Rex," I snapped, my patience running thin. "You don't understand. *I can't fucking find him*. He's missing."

Rex paused. "Really? No shit. I knew something was up with him, bro. He was acting fucking weird. Do you want me to get a few guys together to see if they can find him?"

"Anyone. Speak to anyone who saw him last."

"Okay. Shit. I'll call you back if I hear anything." Rex hung up, and I wondered if I should call the police. *And say what?* I tried to swallow around the blockage in my throat. What could I say? Alex's mom kidnapped him? That I need to speak to my best friend who's ignoring me? Alex was a fucking adult. If he didn't want to talk to me, then what could I do? Running a hand through my thick blond hair, panic rose in my chest. I should call the police. Just in case. Alex could hate me for it later.

And before I could think, I was rounding the corner to my truck and speeding off toward the police station.

***

IT WAS STUPID. I knew it was, but I had to try. Nobody tried for Alex except me. He needed me, and I couldn't let his mother take over his life. Approaching the front desk, I noticed a line of disheartened faces waiting for their turn to report or inquire about cases. The tension in the room was palpable, and an air of indifference seemed to permeate the place. Overworked officers shuffled in and out of view, their expressions etched with fatigue.

When it was finally my turn, I explained my predicament to the officer behind the desk. "I need to report a missing person," I stammered, anxiety coursing through me.

The officer, a middle-aged man with a weary demeanor, peered at me over the rims of his glasses. "Missing person? You'll have to wait 48 hours. The person has to be missing for at least that long before we can file a report."

Fuck, I already knew that, but I felt a rising sense of frustration. "But this is urgent! I can't wait 48 hours. Something's wrong. Alex left suddenly, and I need your help to find him."

He sighed, clearly unimpressed. "Is Alex an adult?"

I nodded. "Yes, he is, but—"

"If he's an adult, he can leave whenever he wants. We can't file a missing person report for that. You'll have to wait 48 hours."

"But it's not like him to just disappear," I pleaded, desperation quivering in my voice. "There's something wrong. I need your help now."

"I'm sorry, but there's nothing we can do until that time has passed."

Fuck, I wanted to slam my fist against the countertop, but I knew that wouldn't be helpful. The people waiting in line cast sidelong glances, their worries etched into weary faces. Whatever. I left knowing that it would be a waste of time to start. I ended up heading back home, my mood stormy as I walked into the frat house and straight to my room. My phone buzzed with a message from Zara, but I ignored it and sat on my head. Alex was gone.

But where? And how? I checked his social media and my heart lurched when I realized it had been deleted. What? My vision blurred, and it took everything to remain upright. Did he plan to leave? Did he know he was being evicted? What the hell was happening right now? I sat there for several moments, my eyes staring disbelievingly at the screen. Shirley did this.

She made him do this. Anger sparked hot and low in my gut.

I will find him. Even if I had to tear down the city to do it.

***

"WHAT'S WRONG?" ZARA SAID, by way of greeting. The wintry air hung heavy around us, with the cold air cutting through like icy daggers. Icicles clung to the eaves, glinting in the pale sunlight. I had been on my way to class when I literally ran into her, startled and frantic.

"Alex is missing."

Her face remained blank. "Oh."

"I'm on my way to talk to Coach about finding him—"

"Why don't we talk first? Maybe I can help?"

"I don't have time to sit down and talk—"

"Just for a minute," Zara said, already grabbing my hand and leading me to a nearby bench. "You know I have amazing deductive skills."

I warred with myself. A part of me didn't want to be delayed, and Rex still hadn't gotten back to me. Time was of the essence, but I knew Zara wasn't doing this to delay me. She would genuinely want to help.

We sat together on a bench beneath a willow, the branches swaying in the breeze. I told her everything from start to finish, but her face looked pinched as I shared the news about Alex's disappearance. "I don't think he's missing, baby," she said, her words sending a swooping sensation through my stomach. "I think he left, and he didn't want you to know."

"Impossible. I'm his best friend. He wouldn't leave without saying anything."

She gave me a sympathetic look. "Okay, if that's the case, then why is his cellphone still working?"

"What do you mean?"

Zara's lips pursed and she took my phone, showing me the messages. Read. They all said 'read'. "He's getting them ... maybe... he doesn't want to talk to you."

I stood. Not wanting to hear another word. "I need to talk to Coach. I'll see you later." I left, ignoring her calling after me. I couldn't accept that. She didn't know anything about Alex or our relationship. We'd been best friends since grade school. He would never just cut me out of his life like that. Striding toward the Coach's officer, my rage was burning hot by the time I wrenched open the door without knocking. Coach Cornell was hunching over his notes, his brow furrowed and he was startled when I walked into the room. "Evans? Something happened—"

"Coach, we need to find Alex! He's missing, and I don't know what happened."

"Missing?" Coach Cornell's brow climbed his forehead and then relaxed. "Evans—Ah—"

"He was here a few days ago, but other than that, I don't know what happened to him. Please. I need your help to find him—"

Coach Cornell gave me a puzzled look, his brow furrowing. "Calm down, son. Ah—" He rubbed the back of his neck. "I don't think Alex is missing. He—Ah. Quit. Last week," he revealed, his words hitting me like a sledgehammer. "I thought you knew. He came to my office and told me he was leaving."

"Quit? He quit the team without telling me? Without saying a word?"

Coach Cornell nodded gravely, his eyes reflecting his sense of confusion. "I'm sorry, son, but that's what he said. He seemed pretty determined, too. Lately, his performance hasn't been good, I think we both knew I wasn't going to keep him on ... I was planning to announce it to the team later today."

The room spun around me, and a sense of loss and betrayal washed over me, leaving me feeling like a ship adrift in a storm. The desperation I had felt since Alex's sudden disappearance deepened, and I struggled to comprehend the truth that my best friend had chosen to leave without giving me a chance to understand why. Coach walked over to me and patted my shoulder. "Things happen. Try not to think too hard about it. Alex will come around when things have cleared up with his family."

"He told you?" I asked, my throat constricting.

"Some, but I could guess most of it," Coach sighed. "Go home. Get some rest. You look like a bus hit you twice, Evans. Don't blame yourself. Alex is his own man, and he'll make his own choices."

Like his choice to cut me out.

Everything came to a screeching halt. Rex's indifference. Zara's pity. They all knew, and I was the last one to get it. For weeks, he'd been ignoring me. Withdrawing. But I had been the last to see it—the last person to notice my best friend. I bit back a scream and nodded to him once before I left his office.

After a few minutes of aimless wandering through campus, feeling the chill seeping through my jacket, I finally trudged back home. Tired and defeated, I tore off my jacket and slumped onto my bed. With my head buried in my hands, I tried to make sense of the whirlwind of emotions that had consumed me. Suddenly, my phone beeped in my pocket and I pulled it out to check who it was.

My breath caught. *Alex.*

My heart soared, and I opened the text message, tears stinging my eyes.

I'm fine. Don't look for me. We aren't friends anymore.

And the world fell from my feet.

5

PENALTY FOR LOVE

ALEX MAY

I didn't mean for this to happen. Shit. I cursed, hurrying out of the sauna, my face sleek with sweat and my orgasm still pulsating through my veins. It had been a huge fucking mistake. Striding toward the locker room, I got dressed, not caring that my body was still soaking wet and the taste of Evans was still hot on my tongue. *What have we done?* My heart jackhammered in my chest, but I kept moving. Throwing everything I could in my duffle bag, I left the lock nearby for Coach when he came to pick it up. *I am leaving.* Tears brimmed my eyes before spilling over, but I couldn't linger here. I slammed the locker shut before walking out of there for good. Taking out my phone, I texted Rex to let him know I'd be on my way to his place soon, right after I stopped by my apartment to pick up my mom. *Fuck, she'd throw another fit.* One that I wasn't sure I could handle with how emotional I felt.

Everything happened so fast. One minute I was staring at Evans, my heart expanding past the point of pain at having to explain that I was leaving. Those ocean eyes were like sunlit currents, yanking me under. Evans had fallen asleep, and I had watched him, my heart in my throat.

I just wanted to look. I told myself while I raced to my beat-up 2005 blue Mazda, the car was practically all rust now, and I wouldn't be surprised if it broke down in the parking lot. With trembling hands, I opened the door, threw my stuff in the truck, and then got in. Staring straight ahead, I finally let the bitter feelings sink in, like a jagged rock down my throat. I dropped out. Officially.

All the years I had worked to get here. Overcoming stereotypes about having a drug-addicted mother. Becoming the first person in my family to go to university, all of it was gone. Including losing my best friend, Evans.

I clenched my fists, a torrent of indignation coursing through me as I railed against the unrelenting unfairness that life often presented to me. I punched the steering wheel. Pain burst like a flare inside my knuckles, juddering up my arm, and I flinched back, hissing. "Fuck," I snarled and stared at my hand. The skin swelled with redness, and I gritted my teeth against the throb. My phone buzzed with a text message coming through.

Yeah, man, everything is set up. Come whenever. Rex responded.

I didn't bother with a reply. I'd see him soon, anyway. Starting the car, I drove out of the parking lot, my thoughts a whirlwind mess. What the fuck did I just do? My body shuddered. Images of Evans sitting on the sauna bench flashed before my eyes. The filmy white towel barely covered the swell of his cock or his powerful thighs. With sculpted muscles that ripple beneath his taut skin, Evans' sunny blond hair and bright blue eyes made everyone around him swoon. I always wanted to bask in his light.

He was the most popular guy in school and I was his dark shadow.

Everybody knew we were best friends, but nobody understood why. Evans was talented. Smart. I had no doubt he'd make it pro next year, and it was a damn shame I had to miss it.

But it was for the best. All I did was drag Evans down.

I just wanted a look. A taste. Licking my dry lips, I thought about how I had stared at him for several moments. I tracked each drop of sweat as it trailed down his sun-kissed skin. Then I moved, crouching in front of him. For years, I lusted after him. Wanted Evans so badly I thought I'd burst with it. Then my hands moved. Evans was a deep sleeper and had been ever since we were kids. I unwrapped the towel, peeling it off layer by layer until it exposed his flushed cock to the humid air.

My throat went dry. Dizziness and desire threatened to drag me under, but I would never hurt him. *I just wanted to look.* To bask in his everlasting warmth and be filled with so much of it that it bled through every orifice. Resting my head on his thigh, I took slow, deliberate breaths, eyes latched onto Evans' cockhead. I wondered what it would be like to take him in. Suckle him. Lap at the mushroom-tipped head until it grew and swelled to fullness.

Blue eyes flittered open. An ocean so vast and endless was suddenly peering down at me. He was startled, shocked to see me on my knees and naked. Then I acted. And shit went to hell from there.

"Damn," I cursed, wondering what had possessed me to behave like that.

Evans wasn't gay. I knew by now he'd be panicking, and shame crawled over my skin. I wasn't a home wrecker. I knew Zara, and she was a damn good person. *Why would I do this to her? Hurt her like this for my own selfish desire?* Pulling into my apartment complex, I killed the engine and got out. Walking up to my apartment, I couldn't help but notice the grim surroundings. The place was marred with filth, garbage strewn about, and homeless individuals occupying the premises. As I approached my brown door, my heart sank at the sight of the glaring orange eviction notice that seemed to taunt me.

A seething anger welled up within me, and I felt a burning desire to unleash my fury on the world and everyone in it. Losing my job last month was a heavy blow. Balancing the demands of hockey and school had become unbearable, and on top of that, my mother had relapsed. We were three months past due on rent, and the prospect of eviction loomed like a relentless storm.

With a heavy heart, I used my key to unlock the door, and a resigned sigh escaped my lips as the stench of vomit hit me, emanating from the living room. I forced myself to push the distressing thoughts aside and get to work. *Don't think,* I told myself, as I began picking up the trash scattered around the room.

Our bags were packed and ready to go, lined up by the door. However, I knew that leaving would be a daunting challenge, an ordeal that threatened to tear me apart from the place that had been our home. As I picked up a crumpled piece of paper, I caught a glimpse of my mother sprawled out on the floor, her skirt riding up and a pool of her own vomit beside her cheek. *Shit.* The room seemed to spin as I rushed to her side, hands trembling.

"Mom?" I demanded, panic welling up inside me. Horror and dread coursed through me like lightning bolts, my heart pounding in my chest. "Mom! Fuck!"

She stirred, shaking her head and trying to shove me away, and I wanted to grab her and shake her silly. We were getting evicted and all she could think about was getting high. I fought through the wave of disgust washing over me, hooked my arms under her knees, and lifted her. Placing her on the couch, I cleaned up the mess, not trying to think too much or else I'd go insane. By now I was used to it. "Alexei," she moaned, thrashing on the couch. "It burns. God, it burns."

Gritting my teeth, I ran a hand through my hair, trying to figure out what to do next. We had to get out of here before the landlord called the police. The eviction notice was sent weeks ago, but I had been so distraught that all I did was ignore it and try to find a job to pick up extra work, but everything fell to shit.

"Just—give me a second," I replied. I didn't want to yell at her. I never did, but this situation was far too stressful and if it wasn't for Rex, I would have lost my mind already. Grabbing our stuff, I ran downstairs to my car to pack what I could away, and then I went back for my mother. *Fuck the furniture, most of it was trash, anyway.* Then I cleaned up the vomit with a small washcloth and changed her clothes.

"Don't be mad Alexei," she laughed, trying to cup my face, but I shoved her hands away. Anger burning deep in my core. Shirley's hair was plastered to her forehead, her once bright brown eyes were wide and manic, and her mouth curled over yellow teeth.

"I'm not mad. Can you walk?" I asked, knowing the answer already.

She shook her head and stretched out her hands like a child. I bit back my frustration and lifted her, then closed the door and tossed the key on the ground. Let the old baster find it, I thought as I took the elevator back down to my car. A brusque wind nipped at my skin, and the threadbare coat I was wearing did nothing to keep out the bitter cold. I got my mother situated in the back seat.

As I slid into the driver's seat and turned the key, the engine sputtered weakly but refused to come to life. "You've got to be fucking kidding me," I spat, staring at the piece of shit that I'd had for the past five years. "No. No!" My heart raced as I tried again, pumping the gas pedal and imploring the aging vehicle to cooperate. But it remained stubbornly silent, mocking my efforts. "Shit!"

I wanted to fucking scream.

"Alexei…" my mother cried weakly in the back, and the strong smell of piss filled my nostrils. This cannot be happening. Snowflakes fell in a strange, slow-motion dance, transforming the world into a nightmarish tableau that left me feeling disconnected from my own body. In this desolate land, fear and desperation clung to me like a shroud. *At twenty-one, I was homeless.* My mom was a crack addict and there wasn't a way out of this hell. A light buzzing yanked me out of my trance and I grabbed my phone out of my pocket.

You still coming, bro? A text message from Rex came through.

Tears burned my eyes before spilling down my cheeks. I dialed his number, my throat working as he picked up on the first ring. "Hey man, I got everything ready for you guys. Are you on your way?" His deep voice made my body sag with relief.

"I—My car broke down," I admitted, not caring if he could hear the tears in my voice.

"I told you that piece of shit wouldn't last. Send me your location. I'm coming now."

"And—" I swallowed around the dagger in my throat. "Bring a blanket. My mom, she had an accident."

"Don't worry." Then Rex hung up, and I clutched my phone like it was my lifeline. I sent him my location and then sat back in my seat, hugging my jacket closer to my chest. A part of me thought about calling Evans. I knew he'd come. Pick us up and take us back to his frat house like it was nothing. He'd done it so many times before, but things were different now. Evans had a girlfriend; he was about to go pro with hockey. I couldn't be the weight that dragged him down.

I refused to be.

No, Evans is going to make it.

Snowflakes descended with an eerie silence as we sat by the side of the road, muffling the world around me and creating an unsettling disconnect from reality. My mom moaned in the back seat, but I was too lost in my illusions to care. In my mind, I was far from here. Evans and I were laughing, the ocean in his eyes while he kissed me on his bed, spreading me out before claiming my lips again.

We both made it to the NHL.

I was able to study Mechanical Engineering on the side. Our names were in flashing lights as we walked hand in hand down the red carpet. A blast of a horn jolted me from my fantasy, and I turned to see Rex pulled up in his silver GMC Sierra 3500 HD. The car was like a woolly mammoth as he parked it closer to mine.

Stepping out of the vehicle, Rex straightened his black winter jacket and nodded at me. I got out and sighed when he came over to me. "Are you okay?" he asked, concern flashing in his brown eyes. "Bro, you shouldn't have left my place. We should have just come here together."

"I know," I responded quietly, knowing how foolish it was to try and do everything alone. "I'll toss my shit in the back and my mom..." I clenched my teeth. "I'll try not to ruin your leather seats."

"Fuck the leather seats," Rex scoffed. "Just let's get you guys somewhere warm."

I stomped down another wave of tears and walked back to my car to hide my face. Rex followed me, and I handed him the garbage bags full of our clothing and some of the things I was able to get from the apartment. Shirley muttered to herself in the back seat, twisting and turning, her body shivering. Rex laid down a blanket for her and we were able to get her into the back seat safely.

"What are you going to do with your car?" Rex asked, slamming the back door.

Fuck, I don't know. It's not like I had the money to tow it or for the mechanic to fix it. "Leave it here," I replied, ignoring his incredulous look, and I climbed into the front seat.

The ride back to Rex's house was blissfully quiet, and I was glad he knew when to stop asking questions. As we approached the grand estate, I marveled at its pristine white facade that glistened under the soft, wintry sun, while the windows sparkled with frosty patterns. Snow-covered lawns stretched out before it, their serene whiteness punctuated by the occasional evergreen tree, creating a tranquil and magical scene. Rex pulled into the driveway, his chestnut brown hair falling over his eyes as he turned to stare at me. "Everything will be okay."

A bitterness swelled in my throat, threatening to strangle me alive. "Sure. Thanks."

I got out, not waiting to hear his reply, then got my mother onto her feet. The stench of urine was like a slap to the face, and I felt my skin burn with humiliation as I led my mom through the familiar halls of Rex's house and into his plush bathroom. Taking off my winter coat, I stripped her naked and got her into the shower. I was almost on autopilot to get her dressed and ready for bed in the place I had been staying for the past two weeks.

"Alexei," my mom murmured as I put her to bed in my room, and placed a bucket near the bed in case she was sick again. Rex had a full maid service, but I didn't want to take advantage of them. He was doing more than enough for me.

Rex was directing the maids to put my stuff away when I came back downstairs, my hands stuffed deep into my pockets. He offered me a smile and then held out a glass of scotch. "Drink?"

"Yes. Thank you," I said, draining my glass in one go. The scotch burned as it enveloped my palate with a warm, smoky embrace, leaving behind a symphony of flavors that danced on my tongue.

Rex laughed, his eyes wrinkling at the sides. "Fuck, man, you scared the shit out of me last week."

"Sorry."

"Don't worry about it," Rex replied, walking over to his massive couch. "I'm just glad you're okay..." He sat down and sighed. I sat beside him, toying with my empty glass. There was so much I wanted to say, but I couldn't push the words through my throat.

Rex was my friend in one of my engineering classes, one of my few close friends other than Evans who knew about my situation and what was going on with my mother. Both of his parents were doctors and traveled a lot for work, which meant Rex spent a lot of time at home alone. "So, everything's all set..." Rex continued. "They'll come tomorrow to take her. Just don't be surprised if she hates you for it."

She always hated me. I thought. *Or else, why would she choose to do drugs?* I held out my glass for another drink and Rex refilled it for me. As I sipped my drink, I savored the scotch. The taste of oak and toasted grains unfolded, delivering a rich and satisfying experience. It was the good stuff. Leave it to Rex to be as pretentious as possible. Rex's eyes were on me, soft and hooded, and he licked his dry lips, tugging on his woolly grey turtleneck that hugged his torso in all the right places.

"Sounds good," I replied.

"Look," Rex said, inching toward the edge of the couch. "You can stay here as long as you need to, okay? I have more than enough space for you, or at least until you get back on your feet."

Tears stung my eyes before spilling down my cheeks before I could stop them. Fuck, I was an emotional wreck. I dug the heel of my hands into my eyes and took a stuttering breath, while Rex reached over and gently patted my back. "Shit, man. Sorry."

"Don't be," Rex said, his deep voice softening. "You've been through a lot. Why don't you get some rest? I'll take care of everything here."

I really couldn't thank him enough. Everything he's done for me in the past few days was more than I ever deserved. "Thanks, and Evans—"

"He called," Rex interrupted. "Shit man, I didn't know what to tell him, so I just made some shit up. I spread the rumors like you said, but at first, I didn't think he believed it."

He'll believe now. I thought, trying to cringe at the text message I sent him a few days ago.

I'm fine. Don't look for me. We aren't friends anymore. If that didn't smash our friendship to pieces, then I didn't know what would.

6

LOCKER ROOM SECRETS

ALEX MAY

Evans wasn't the type to push too hard. I knew whatever I said he would accept it, no matter how badly it hurt. And it fucking hurt. But it was for the best. There was no way he could go to the NHL with his loser best friend and crackhead mother dragging him down.

"Thanks." Now I was sounding like a broken record, and Rex laughed.

"Get some rest, man. I'll see you in the morning."

I stood, placing my glass on the table, and went back upstairs. Exhaustion made my body slump, but I wanted to check in on my mom before I turned in for the night. Opening the door, I saw that she was blinking awake, wiping away the grit from her eyes. "Alexei…" she murmured.

"I'm here, Mom," I said, then I went to the bathroom to get a drink of water. "Here."

She gulped it down and then ran a hand through her sodden hair. I knew she was just coming down from a high, and sooner or later she'd be itching for her next fix. However, I would not let that happen. "Sleep. I'll see you tomorrow."

"Wait," she said, grabbing my arm. "Where am I? Don't leave me."

"You're safe. I'll be right next door. I promise."

Her eyes narrowed into pinpricks, but before she could say anything, her body lurched and she groaned, rolling onto her side. I let her be, not wanting to witness it for another second. My mom had been like this for years. By now I should be used to it, but every time I saw her like this, it was like a punch to the gut.

She chose this life. Over me. It took many years to finally accept it and ask for the help I needed. Placing the glass near her night table, I closed the door. Normally, I would have stayed with her through the night, making sure to keep her upright so she would not choke on her own vomit, but tonight I went to the guest room across the hall. *I am done with it.*

All of it. I couldn't take care of her anymore. I didn't want to. The anger and bitterness were coiling deep within me like a poisonous vapor and I knew if this continued, I might grow to hate her.

Maybe I already did.

Laying down on the bed, I stared up at the ceiling. Evans' face flashed before my eyes, kind and gentle like a rushing stream. By now, he would have been cracking jokes about the Maple Leafs or the Detroit Red Wings while making my favorite pumpkin spice cookies. We'd be in front of the TV, watching the game and screaming until our lungs were sore and our stomachs ached with laughter.

Then I'd be warring with myself about whether or not to kiss him.

Or tell him I've loved him since we were kids.

No. It's better that I'm here. Surrounded by stainless steel and chrome, with my mother hacking out her lungs in the next room and Rex trying his best to pretend not to notice. It was better than facing Evans and seeing his rejection all over his face. Zara was the right choice.

The safe choice. We both knew it, especially if he wanted to succeed in his hockey career. Not with me. I thought about his gasp. The way his mouth fell open when I took his cock into my mouth. Evans' head flung back as he canted his hips, chasing his release. *Fuck, it wasn't fair.* I finally had him and I knew he wanted me to, only to have it all ripped away.

I dug my nails into my palm, trying to hold back a scream as it tried to claw its way up my throat. *We can't be together. I won't allow it.* That night, I bound my heart tight in barbwire.

Evans would move on. Be great. Play the game we both loved.

While I lingered in the dark caves of misery under neon lights. I would reject the earth between my toes, and the wind on my skin, and settle for a life of compliance. A black sinking nothingness where I was destined to be. I'd get my mom clean. Get back on my feet to study my degree and we'd both go our separate ways. Our relationship was a missed pass on the hockey rink of life, with our cross blades never quite syncing in a perfect play.

And I was good with that.

I had to be.

***

SUNLIGHT SLICED ACROSS my vision, rousing me from sleep. In the distance, raised voices pierced the air, and I yawned, struggling to comprehend the unfolding chaos. "Don't touch me!" my mom's shriek jolted me awake, and I leaped from the bed. My head spun as I dashed out of the bedroom, finding several men from the Addiction Prevention Rehab Society attempting to subdue her.

"Mom!" Shit. They were here earlier than expected, and my anxiety surged. A doctor stood beside Rex, her hair neatly tied in a tight bun, her expression strained. "Let me explain to her what's happening," I pleaded with the doctor.

She turned to me, her eyes narrowing. "Are you Mr. May? We thought she'd be fully informed before we attempted to—"

"Please, just give me a moment to talk to her," I snapped, moving past the doctor and rushing to my mother, who was on the bed. Vomit stained the front of her shirt, soaking it through, and her eyes were wide with fear and confusion.

"Alexei, what's happening? Who are these people, and what are they trying to do?"

I held her trembling hand, struggling to find the right words to explain the situation. "Look, you need to go away for a while. They're going to help you get better—"

She laughed. High-pitched and manic. "I knew it. Last night you—you kidnapped me! I know my rights! You fucking faggoty piece of shit! How dare you—"

"Mom, they're going to take you to rehab," I cut off her tirade, all too used to it by now.

"Rehab? I'm not sick. Do I look sick to you, boy? You need to get your eyes checked. I'm perfectly fine. Take me home. I want to go home."

Home. Where the fuck is that? We've never had a home. With each word she spoke, my anger intensified, a fiery tempest building within me as I struggled to maintain composure. "They're taking you for twelve months. You can come back when you're better."

Pain exploded against the side of my cheek, and I staggered back, staring at her in shock. Then men were on her in seconds, grabbing her flailing arms and trying to hold her down as she screeched like a banshee. "You betrayed me! You're just like your father! How can you betray me? Alexei! Don't let them take me! I'm not sick! Baby, it's me. Your mother—" They hauled her out of the room and all I could do was stand there, stunned.

She'd never hit me before.

Not even when she was high out of her mind. A throbbing ache pulsed through the side of my face and temple, and then Rex was grabbing my arm. "Are you okay? Fuck, I didn't think things would be this bad."

I swallowed hard and touched my burning cheek. "I'm fine."

"Do you need ice or anything? Here." He signaled to the maid to grab it for him and took me to the edge of the bed to sit down. "Fuck, she got you good." The maid handed him the ice pack, and he pressed it to my cheek.

"Mr. May?" the doctor from earlier spoke. "I'm Doctor Alisa Reeds and I'll be your mother's attending physician at the rehab center. Did you have any questions before we head out?"

"Visiting," I croaked. "When can I see her?"

"While she's settling in, we ask that visitors wait a few weeks. Here's my card." She reached into her pocket and handed it to me. "You can call me anytime and we'll set a time to discuss everything."

"Thank you." We shook hands and Doctor Reeds headed out the door. I went to the window and watched them haul my mother away in a white Mercedes minivan.

Rex stood beside me and placed a hand on my shoulder.

It was done.

***

Rex and I sprawled on the couch, the dim glow of the TV illuminating our faces as we watched the entire Fast and Furious franchise. The room was quiet, the high-speed chases providing background noise, but my mind was far away, lost in thoughts of my mother before she struggled with addiction. The adrenaline-pumping stunts of the movie played out on the screen, but I barely paid them any attention.

Rex sighed and huffed a laugh, staring at the screen. "Man, this shit is terrible. I never realized it before, but it's like Vin Diesel is made of wood, and his range of emotions is a two-inch plank."

I burst out laughing. I laughed so hard it hurt. I laughed until I felt like I might crack a rib. "I hate these movies. The only thing that moves faster than the cars in Fast and Furious is how quickly I change the channel when it's on TV."

"Then why didn't you say anything when I put it on?" Rex laughed.

"I don't know. I wasn't paying attention."

We both stared at each other and then collapsed into a fit of laughter. Fuck, it was so stupid, but it felt good to laugh. "Do you know what would make this movie even better? Vodka."

"Sure, man," I replied, leaning back in my seat. Rex grabbed us a few glasses, and we sipped them while watching the movie. A subtle tingle danced along my skin as the alcohol's gentle buzz wrapped around me, making the world feel a little lighter. "Dude, this shit is fucking absurd. Cars vs. trains, cars vs. submarines. What's next? Cars vs. nuclear missiles?"

"That was in the last movie. You missed it, bro," Rex laughed, slapping my arm. "And the laws of physics? Who cares about that? As long as they get to blow shit up and we get to see some half-naked girls."

"Who needs gravity when you have Vin Diesel?"

Rex choked on his vodka, laughing so hard that some of it dribbled down his chin. "Dude, don't kill me. I'm dying. Shit, I got it!" Rex snapped his fingers. "Cars vs Vin Diesel's hairline?"

I nearly fell off the couch with laughter. "They lost that race already!"

We were howling by the next movie and so drunk we could barely see straight. Rex kept the jokes coming and I was reminded once again why he was one of my closest friends. It was deep into the night when Rex decided to make some cookies, and then sank in a seat beside me, breathless.

"I thought you didn't know how to cook?" I asked, feeling light-headed. With each sip, a soft warmth radiated from my core, like a cozy fireplace on a chilly winter evening, and I felt a sense of relaxation settle in.

"I don't." Rex ran a hand through his chestnut hair. "How hard could it be? Turn on the oven and go right? A no-brainer. Besides, cookies aren't rocket science. You just throw it all in a pan and go, right?"

We stared at each other before we burst out laughing. "Nah, I'm sure you'll fuck it up."

"I probably did already," Rex replied and sighed. "What a day. I can't believe you have to go through that shit on the regular. Cheers to you."

"Thanks," I laughed. "She wasn't always like this Evans usually—" I stopped myself. Evans wasn't here. "He'd just tell her a bad joke or something to get her to calm down."

"Yeah," Rex said. "You should call him. He's worried about you."

"I can't," I spoke, keeping my voice low.

"What happened? You two were like this," he said, crossing his fingers.

"I fucked it up," I slurred. Maybe it was the alcohol thrumming through me, but I felt raw and achy. I needed to tell someone, anyone, what happened.

"It couldn't have been that bad," Rex replied, tucking a stray hair behind his ear.

"What do you know? You're straight," I muttered.

"I believe I said I was bi-curious."

"Sounds straight to me."

Rex laughed at the jib and didn't seem to mind it like other guys did. "Fine. Don't tell me. I'll figure it out soon enough anyway," Rex turned to me, his black sweatshirt stretched nicely over his broad chest. My heart rate increased, and I felt my face burn when his dark eyes landed on mine.

Rex and I met in our engineering class and became fast friends, and a part of me hoped we'd stay that way. The alcohol flowed through my veins like a warm, comforting embrace, dissolving the edges of reality into a hazy, pleasant blur. Rex's eyes flickered down to my lips, and I was tempted to lean in and taste him, but I held back.

"I should—" I cleared my throat. "Head to bed."

Rex's didn't move. His eyes nailed me to my seat, and I felt my face burn hotter. "Sounds good. Yours or mine?"

I laughed shoving him off. "Mine." Brushing off some crumbs from my shirt, I sniffed the air, smelling smoke. "Bro, I think your cookies are ready."

"Shit!" Rex jumped up and ran to the kitchen, then cursed. Laughing, I followed him and I saw him throw a tray of charred cookies into the sink.

"I knew you'd fuck it up."

"It's harder than it looks," Rex pouted, his shoulders slumping. "Whatever. I'm useless in the kitchen."

I bit back another laugh and waved him goodnight. "See yah to-morrow."

"Night," Rex muttered.

I climbed the stairs three at a time, feeling relaxed and fluid. I sank into the welcoming embrace of my bed, the weight of my worries slowly dissolved, carried away by the gentle lull of the night. The room around me became a comforting cocoon, shielding me from the world's demands and uncertainties. I closed my eyes, allowing the darkness to wash over me like a soothing tide.

***

THE WEEK WENT BY QUICKLY. With Rex at school, I didn't have much to do during the day besides mope. It took a while, but I went to the local library and they helped me put my resume together so that I could apply for another job since I had lost my last one. I knew I couldn't stay with Rex for too long; the holidays were coming up, and I knew his family would be back home and I'm sure the last thing they wanted was to find out Rex paid for my mother's rehab and then let his homeless friend live in one of the guest rooms. Besides, I was done taking handouts from people. *I relied on Evans for years. I need to stand on my own two feet and become my own man.*

I rummaged through my bags, looking for something suitable to wear to job interviews only to realize I didn't have much besides some ratty jeans and a few long-sleeved sweaters. I didn't have the money to go shopping, and I didn't want to ask Rex to lend me clothes, either. *Whatever.*

I'd just have to make do with what I had. I called Doctor Reeds to set up a time to visit my mother and then went about calling places to set up job interviews.

I spent several days bouncing from one disappointing job interview to another, each one more disheartening than the last. The fast-food chain interview at Burger King felt like an exercise in absurdity, and I couldn't help but wonder how my life had taken such a detour. As I walked away from yet another rejection, I passed one of the main hockey arenas, the home of the Detroit Red Wings.

A sign caught my eye: "Janitorial Position Available." The prospect of working in the very arena where I'd watched countless hockey games filled me with a sense of hope. I entered the building, determined to inquire about the job.

Approaching the lady at the front desk, I inquired about the janitorial position. She pointed me toward the back of the building, where I encountered a man in a cleaning uniform, sporting a sizable belly and a receding hairline.

"Hi, I'm here for the interview," I announced. He squinted at me for a moment, then offered a friendly smile.

"Hey there, son! Oh, great timing. I was just about to wrap up, but I can squeeze in one more." Handing him my resume, we entered his office. "Do you have any cleaning experience?" he asked.

"No, sir," I replied, "but I have a deep love for hockey, and I'm more than willing to work as long as you need me."

"It says here you're a student. What's your name, kid?"

"Alexei May, but people just call me Alex, sir."

He waved me off. "Call me Able. Are you aware that this is a full-time position?"

"Yes, I'm aware," I replied. "But I'm currently facing some financial challenges, and I can't return to school just yet."

Able regarded me thoughtfully. "Well, how soon can you start, son?"

7

SKATING ON THIN ICE

ALEX MAY

Entering the rink, I inhaled deeply, embracing the familiar aroma of cold steel and crisp winter air. *This place felt like home.* "Ready?" Able asked, handing me a broom. Maybe not my ideal way to spend time, but hey, I was amidst the things that I loved. The day of work felt endless as people streamed in, game after game, mostly kids and juniors hitting the ice. My task involved cleaning the restrooms, concession stands, and any spills in the main foyer. The charcoal-gray uniform clung uncomfortably to my broad frame, but there were no other sizes available. Ignoring the giggles of passing girls, I focused on my work, cleaning up a spill near the bathroom, lost in my thoughts.

I tackled my cleaning duties around the bustling hockey arena and I couldn't help but feel a twinge of frustration deep within. Watching all those guys out on the ice, living my dream, made my stomach clench with longing. But deep down, I knew I needed to get back on my feet before I could step onto the rink with confidence. I had to rebuild my life from scratch, starting with a job and a place to live. My tasks were a mix of scrubbing, sweeping, and tidying. I cleaned the restrooms, ensuring they were spotless for the fans. The concession stands required constant attention, wiping away spilled soda and popcorn remnants.

The main foyer often endured enthusiastic fans, and I was there to mop up any mess. It was demanding work, but I took pride in it, knowing that I was contributing to the arena's overall experience.

As I worked, I couldn't help but steal glances at the players on the ice, yearning for the day when I could join them once more. But for now, I had responsibilities and a journey ahead of me, inching closer to the day when I'd be back on that rink, giving it my all.

During my lunch break in the backroom, Able and I engaged in a conversation that eased my initial hesitation about the job. He shared stories of his twenty years working in the arena, but most of them were of his son's antics on and off the ice.

"Your son must be a big fan of the game," I commented, hoping to learn more about his connection to the sport.

Able's eyes lit up with pride. "Oh, absolutely! He's a die-hard Central Michigan fan. Started playing as soon as he could walk, and now he's a defenseman on their team."

"Really? I used to play at the University of Michigan. What's his name? Maybe I know him?"

"Kyle Mathis?"

I checked the name over and realized I didn't and shook my head. "No, sorry. It doesn't sound familiar."

"That's okay, son," Able replied. "I started working here just to be closer to the games and support him. But this place, these people, they become a part of your life."

I nodded, understanding that while my path had diverged from the dream of playing professionally, it didn't mean I couldn't find a different kind of home within the hockey world.

After lunch, Able walked me over to the troublesome ice surfacing machine. "This old girl's giving me a headache," he said with a sigh.

I stepped closer, studying the machine, and asked, "Can I have a look at it?"

Able kinked a brow, handing me a toolbox. "Ah, are you sure you know what you're doing, kid? It would cost my salary and yours if you break it."

Opening the machine, I recognized a few common issues that often occurred with the Zamboni. The blade for ice scraping had worn down unevenly, and there were a few loose bolts in the control mechanism. I grabbed a wrench and a file and set it to work, adjusting the blade and tightening the loose bolts. The machine sprang back to life, and Able stared at me in astonishment.

"Damn, kid," he exclaimed. "What did you say you studied?"

I couldn't help but laugh. "Mechanical Engineering."

Able whistled, his eyes wide. "And you had to drop out? Damn shame."

My smile dimmed. It had always been a hobby of mine, along with playing hockey, but I'd been living in the dream world. The reality was people like me didn't graduate from university or play hockey professionally. We faded into the background, hardly seen by those around us. I was used to it. Evans was the one who should shine. *Not me.*

Able checked the time. "Well, we've got a few hours left. Why don't you clean the locker rooms and then you can head out? And I'll meet you at the same time tomorrow."

"Sounds good, thank you, sir."

I diligently completed my cleaning duties, making sure the locker rooms were pristine. As I worked, I stumbled upon some misplaced clothes and belongings, which I gathered and dropped off at the front desk, just in case anyone came searching for them.

With my tasks completed, I peeled off my grey uniform and packed my bag. The chill of the evening began to set in as I stepped outside. Rex's imposing truck was waiting in the parking lot, its sleek steel exterior gleaming in the fading light. Since I didn't have a car, Rex generously offered to drive me from the arena back to his house. There was no bus service in this area, and I needed to get my car fixed as soon as possible.

"Hey," Rex greeted me with a warm smile as I climbed into the truck.

"Hey," I replied, breathing in the rich and deep scent of his cologne. Rex tucked a brown lock of hair behind his ear and grinned. "Hungry? How about Burger King?"

My stomach rumbled, and I nodded eagerly. "I'm starving. Burger King sounds perfect."

"So, honey, how was your day at work?" Rex said, and I laughed.

"Shit. Absolute shit. Thanks for asking."

Rex winked at me and pulled into the Burger King drive-through. "Have you decided when you're coming back to class? You've only missed a few weeks. I could pull some strings and get you back in."

My hands clenched around the fabric of my winter coat. "Don't. You've done enough. I can't ask you to do anymore."

Rex snorted. "Not this shit again, Alex. We're friends. Of course, I'll help you when I can. I just don't understand why you won't let me. When I was going through that shit with William, you were there for me."

During Rex's junior year, he had gotten into a huge accident. A four-car pile-up on the freeway while on his way to class. Several people were injured, but one person in particular, William, almost died and was put on life support. Although he didn't cause the accident,

Rex felt so guilty that he visited him every day, hoping that William would get better. He didn't and died.

William was only nine years old.

Rex spiraled, thinking he was responsible for his death. He drank. Fucked around his junior year, he didn't care about anyone or anything. Using his money to throw at people when he didn't get his way. Our relationship had been tumultuous, but his self-destructive behavior tugged at my heartstrings. Before I knew it, I was forcing the big lug to study with me and spend his time being more productive. I helped him get back on his feet and he even made the honor roll at school.

"That's different," I replied. "The type of cash you've spent so far…" I didn't even want to think about it. Rehab was the equivalent of one year's salary. There was no way I'd be able to pay him back for this. "I need to find a place for us to live."

"And you can't stay with me?" Rex looked almost hurt, and although he was pretty tight-lipped about his home life, I knew he must have been lonely living in that big house by himself. Pulling up to the drive-thru window, the women on the intercom spoke.

"Hi, can I take your order?"

We ordered two big whoopers and Rex drove back on the highway while he ate in silence. I knew what he was asking, but I honestly didn't want to put that burden on him. Rex was a good person. A great friend, but I had to make my own way in this world. Even since I was young and my mom lost the house, I had always been the sole provider for us. Even though she treated me like shit, I knew deep down she didn't mean to. *It was just the drugs talking*.

My breath hitched at the memory of the sting of her palm against my cheek. *Yes, the drugs.* Even when she let her boyfriends do what they wanted to me. *It wasn't her.* The doctors said so, right? The food turned to ashes in my mouth and I calmly put it back in the bag. I couldn't think about that right now, or else I'd start screaming. Addiction was hard, and I had to be understanding of her wants and needs.

"You're not hungry?" Rex asked, his mouth full of food.

"I'll eat it later."

Rex wiped some crumbs from his chin, using a napkin as he drove. "Look, I'm not saying this to put pressure on you, but if you drop out now, you are less likely to come back, especially if you rent your own apartment. Why don't you stay with me for a bit, and we can figure something out?"

My rage was like a slow-burning fire, constantly smoldering beneath the surface, waiting to erupt. If only things had been that easy. Stay with Rex and let him throw money at the situation to make it all go away. *Yeah, right.* Rex didn't even know half of the shit I had to deal with. *Leaving school was just the beginning.* Not to mention how I'd get my car fixed or return after I lost all my scholarships and I couldn't afford the tuition. "I can't stay with you, Rex."

Rex's mouth thinned. "Why not? Why don't you trust me? You don't have to go through this alone."

I dug the heel of my palm into my eyes, trying not to snap at him. It felt as though I was teetering on the edge of a volcanic eruption. Rex didn't understand. He never would. "I can't leave her."

Rex sighed, his jaw working. "But she treats you like shit, Alex."

I bristled at that. "You don't understand—"

"The fuck I don't," Rex snarled, his massive hands gripping the steering until his knuckles turned white. "She's awful to you. I've seen it. Christ, the level of abuse she throws at you is fucking insane, and all you do is take it? Why not leave her and be done with it? After she's done with rehab, just let her go."

"You think I don't want to!" I exploded. "How many times do you think I wanted to walk away? Let her choke on her fucking vomit? Even when I was a fucking kid, it was all I dreamed about! Do you think I want to get evicted? To be kicked out of my house and have nowhere to go and watch her get so high she doesn't even know who am I anymore? To watch all my years of hard fucking work with hockey and school go down the drain?"

Rex flinched as if he'd been slapped.

"There's no way out of this for me. She's the only family I have left," I snarled. The inescapable resentment I felt towards my mother's addiction was like a shadow that clung to me. I couldn't let her go and I wouldn't. *She is my mother. My family*. Eventually, she'd see that. See me and all the pain she'd caused over the years. I had to believe that.

We drove back to his place in silence. Pulling into the vast driveway, Rex killed the engine, his lips pursed into a thin line. "I'm sorry I said that shit."

"It's fine."

Rex's brow ticked. "It was out of line. I was just trying to help. You have so much potential, Alex, and I hate seeing it go to waste for her. Just think about everything I said, okay?"

"Sure." I wasn't, though. A large part of me was sick of being rescued. First by Evans and now by Rex. *How could I stand on my feet if they kept trying to save me?* I didn't need saving. I was a grown man making my own choices. Rex needed to respect that. We got out, and I strode towards the guest room and closed the door behind me. The room was a temporary refuge from the turmoil of my life, and I needed a moment of solitude. I began stripping off my clothes, shedding the burdens of the day, and prepared for bed. The weeks ahead loomed long and difficult, and I could feel the weight of responsibility pressing down on me.

My phone buzzed, and I saw a message from Doctor Reeds. She mentioned that my mom had settled into rehab and that I could visit her soon. A lump formed in my throat as I thought about facing her. I knew she would resent me for putting her in there, but I had to hold on to the hope that it was the right decision. I replied to Doctor Reeds, letting him know that I would visit my mom after work the next day. I took a quick shower to wash away the day's stress and climbed into bed, ignoring my stomach, which was filling with dread.

***

ICY WIND FELT LIKE DARTS against my cheeks, as I stood on the crowded bus feeling like a packed sardine. After work, I took the nearest bus to the rehab center and Rex said to text me when I was done so that he could pick me up. Shoving my hands in my thin winter jacket, I tried not to shiver. The convenience store flowers I bought with the last few pennies I had were wilted and dried up, almost crushed by the person in front of me. Eventually, the bus stopped and as I stepped out, I was greeted by the imposing sight of the sprawling rehab center. There were windows with curtains, and the gardens around it were well-kept. Red bricks, weathered by time, gave the structure a sense of enduring strength. The entrance looked welcoming, with a courtyard that made you feel like you could find help and start fresh inside. *It better be for almost forty-thousand dollars.* Lucky for me, Rex's father pulled some strings, and they didn't have to pay half that.

A cold shiver of dread ran down my spine, warning me of the troubles to come. Shirley would hate it here. Gritting my teeth, I held the flowers to my chest as I walked inside. A warm blast of air hit my skin, and I went straight to the front desk. "Hello, how can I help you?" a woman asked, her thick-rimmed glasses making her brown eyes look bright.

"I'm here to see Shirley May," I said.

"Sure thing, let me see," she said, her acrylic pink nails clinking over the keyboard. "Mhmm, she's in room 405. Here," she replied, getting up to grab a visitor's pass. "Visiting hours are between 5-8 p.m. and the doctor will be in touch when it's time to start the family counseling. Come on, I'll show you."

I was led down a narrow hallway to my mom's room at the rehab center. The atmosphere was quiet and serene, a stark contrast to the chaos we had left behind. Upon entering, I noticed the cozy furniture, warm colors, and soft lighting that made the room feel welcoming.

My mom sat by the window, her gaze fixed on the distant horizon. "Hey," I said, but she didn't turn or acknowledge my presence. I carefully placed the wilted flowers on the table and approached her. Reaching out, I touched her arm gently.

She flinched and glared back at me; her eyes bloodshot.

Withdrawal. It was almost as ugly as her being high.

The impending sense of dread hung over me like a dark storm cloud, casting a shadow on my thoughts. "How'd you settle in?" I asked, taking the seat across from her.

She ignored me.

"This place looks nice," I said, hoping she would at least talk to me. Ask me how I've been doing. Or how do I plan to deal with the fact that we've been evicted, and I had to drop out of school? Or maybe even comment on how my entire life has been demolished just because she needed another hit.

Anger flared in my chest and I looked away, gritting my teeth. This wasn't the time for that. Mom was here so that she could get better. "What did the doctor say? Are you taking your medication?"

She said nothing.

This continued for the next ten minutes before I finally realized that she wouldn't be speaking to me today. She wouldn't even look at me. Not after everything I'd done to keep her safe or how much I'd sacrificed just to get her here. A cold rage swept through me like a bitter wind. It felt like a pressure cooker on the verge of bursting, with each passing moment escalating the seething ire within me.

Shirley's face was pinched. My heart slammed against my ribcage as acid flooded my mouth.

Sunlight washed her hair in a sea of reddish bronze, and gold, just like mine. Yet her eyes were shrunken, hollow pits, and a part of me hated her to the bone. I lost Evans. My life. My career.

Hockey.

Everything close to my heart for her.

For this relationship, that seemed only to benefit one person. I fled the room then, my heart feeling like it would burst. Rushing out of the dual doors, I ran around the corner feeling that empty part of my chest crack and fissure before breaking apart. Tears stung my eyes, and pain lanced through my chest and before long, a sob ripped through my throat. I crumpled to my knees, falling into a snowbank. Not caring when ice seeps through my jeans. *I had done everything right.*

Been the best son she could ever want, and still she hated me.

The snow cradled me in its icy embrace, and I sat in a trance, the world around me turning surreal and haunting. I had lost everything, and she didn't give a fuck.

8

IN THE SPOTLIGHT

EVANS MULRONEY

"Get your head in the game, Evans!" Coach screeched, and I winced. Vaulting down the ice I shredded past Grayson, obstructing his path for the puck. *What's wrong with me? Why can't I focus?* Jayden intercepted me, the devil in his eyes as he passed the puck to Grayson and they scored.

Crap. These two worked like a well-oiled machine. Irritation sparked within me, and I snarled, going back to my position. My heart was hammering and Chris was giving me strange looks, but I ignored him. I wasn't on my game today.

In fact, I haven't been in the past few weeks.

Not since... *Damn it!* Thoughts of Alex exploded across my vision, and I missed it as Grayson's team scored again. *Fuck, I was a mess.*

"All right," Coach called, giving me the stink eye. "Let's call it quits."

Tearing off my helmet, I panted, berating myself for screwing up so badly during practice. Coach will have my head if I play like this during next week's game. I really couldn't afford to fuck up like this during our next game. More scouts would be there watching and even though it was almost a sure thing, it could still go to hell if I wasn't vigilant enough. I stormed into the locker room, ignoring all the voices there as I changed into my clothes. Bristling with anger at not paying attention during practice. Several of the guys were laughing, and Grayson came up to me, his brow furrowed.

"You okay, man? You seem out of it."

I wanted to bark at him, to let my frustration spill over, but I swallowed it down. "Fine."

"Look ... If you need anything, let me know... don't do anything... stupid..."

His words cut through the haze of my anger, and I snapped my eyes up to meet his. "What do you mean?"

Grayson's face flushed, and he rubbed the back of his neck, his discomfort clear. "You know..."

No. I fucking don't. "Spit it out, Hayes," I forced a laugh. "What the hell are you talking about?"

Grayson's Adam's apple bobbed, and he leaned in closer. "You know ... the crackpipe I saw you with that day... just don't do anything stupid. That's all I'm saying."

All the blood rushed to my face at the memory. *Fuck.* Grayson probably thought I was smoking crack, hence why I've been off during the games. A part of me wanted to laugh, but nothing about this situation was fucking funny. Shirley had left her crack pipe lying around in Alex's bag and I found it there, knowing that his mom would raise hell if she couldn't find it. So, I held it for him, and then when I was waiting for him to return. While I was waiting, curiosity got the best of me. I wondered what all the hype was about, so I pulled it out of the bag and stared at it.

Then Grayson had caught me. There was no way in hell I would jeopardize my hockey career by taking drugs or getting caught with them, so as soon as Grayson left, I threw it out.

When Alex asked about it later, I lied and told him I lost it. It didn't matter anyway, giving it back to Shirley wouldn't do Alex any favors.

"I told you; I was holding it for a friend," I muttered to him. "Don't worry. I'm fine. Just some school shit, that's all."

Grayson nodded like he didn't believe me, but he would placate me all the same. "Sure man, Sarah mentioned a party at her sorority. Are you coming?"

Maybe that was just what I needed. "Sure, I'll be there."

We clasped hands, and then I grabbed my gear and walked out. Grayson was a good friend and a damn good hockey player. When Cricket was here, the three of us had been unstoppable. The icy pavement crunched beneath my boots as I walked out the front door. Each inhale of the crisp air stung my lungs, but I finally reached my car and drove back to the frat house. My phone buzzed in my pocket but I ignored it, looking forward to some downtime before I went to the party tonight.

Zara would most likely be there.

And things between us had gotten a lot better since that night I spent with her after Alex. I was still planning to break things off. I planned to tell her either tonight or tomorrow that things between us were over. Rage still coiled in my gut at Alex's text message, but a large part of me knew he was just trying to run away from what had happened. I didn't know what I was feeling, but I was sure what happened with Alex had been a one-time thing. A few guys I knew had sexual experiences with men and never considered themselves gay. Maybe I was one of them. I couldn't deny the thought of fucking Alex turned me on, but I didn't think I could muster those same feelings with anyone else. Besides that, Alex never told me he was gay.

Then again, there were a lot of things Alex never told me.

Biting into my lower lip, I hated when pain flared in my chest. We've been best friends since we were fucking three. *How could he treat me like this? Like I was fucking nothing to him?* It cut me straight to the bone. Pulling into the driveway, I parked my car, grabbed my stuff, and got out. The house was empty when I opened the door, so I walked right up to my room and threw my stuff on the bed.

Taking out my phone, I flopped down on my mattress. Too tired to do anything but scroll through Instagram. *Babe, are you coming tonight?* Zara's text message read.

Sure. What time? I replied.

Ten, okay? Harpreet's coming too. She responded.

I laughed, thinking about the last time I partied with Harpreet. Man, I loved that guy. *Sure*, I texted back and threw my phone on my nightstand. Running a hand through my sodden thick blond hair, I sighed through my nose. My thoughts went back to Alex, and I wondered where he could be. Snowflakes danced outside my window, their delicate descent clashing with the biting gusts that swept through the desolate streets. *Was he safe?* My throat constricted at the thought.

It was the only thing I needed to know.

Aside from all the fucking bullshit, I just needed to know if Alex was safe. If he were here, he'd be lying next to me. With a head of reddish bronze hair that seemed to dance like the firelight as it spread out on my sheets. Alex's fox-like eyes would stare at me, shaded in dark brown and guarded with more secrets than a well-worn journal. Those pink lips would pull into a wry smile that hinted at a joke I could never quite grasp as I yammered on about my day and practice.

Alex listened. He understood me in ways nobody else did.

To everyone else, I was Evans. Larger than life. A defenseman on the hockey team and one of the best players the Michigan Wolverines have seen in a long time. I was rich. Popular. Had more friends than I knew what to do with, but none of them were mine the way Alex was.

He needed me. I'd looked after him most of my life, and I considered him to be my brother and the possibility of us becoming more never once crossed my mind. However, when I thought back on it, maybe I was the dumb one between us. *Alex had looked at me.*

But not like a brother.

There was a hunger there. His eyes gleamed with a ravenous desire; a primal hunger that stirred something dangerous within me. For how long, I had no clue. Alex always held back when it came to his own desires. Over the years, I'd given up on trying to introduce him to someone, mostly because I knew he would never let anyone get close to him. Once they found out about his mom, he knew they'd be gone.

A part of me had been glad, to keep Alex to myself all these years.

Well, that was until Rex, but from my understanding and from what Rex said, they weren't friends anymore. Sighing, I closed my eyes and felt the edges of sleep pulled at me, before dragging me under.

***

THE MUSIC PULSED THROUGH my veins as I arrived at the party in full throttle. Future's drawl echoed in my ears, matching the DJ's trap music that reverberated through the walls. The place throbbed in time with the infectious beat. Scanning the room, I quickly spotted Zara on the dancefloor, her hypnotic sway setting the dancefloor on fire. She wore a sleek black leather skirt, knee-high stockings, and a matching crop top that left little to the imagination. Damn, she looked incredible.

Clutching my varsity jacket, I acknowledged a few friends with nods and then made my way to the kitchen for a drink. There, I found Sarah, drunkenly leaning on the keg, with Ian valiantly attempting to keep her upright. I couldn't help but laugh at the scene.

"Sarah, you good?" I asked with a grin.

"O-Of course, I'm good," she slurred, her words saturated with alcohol.

Ian shook his head, looking exasperated. "Let's get you home before your parents kill me for being a bad influence."

As they stumbled away, I poured myself a drink from the keg. "Hey, man," Harpreet greeted me, slapping me on the shoulder. He was adorned with glow sticks, and his breath reeked of vodka and tequila. "Why are there two of you?" he asked, confusion etched on his face.

I chuckled at Harpreet's befuddlement and replied, "I've been working out, man. Gained a little extra bulk."

Harpreet squinted at me, then burst into laughter. "I see! The secret's in the jacket, huh?"

"Absolutely," I deadpanned. "This jacket adds at least 20 pounds of pure muscle."

He held up his neon glow stick bracelet like a trophy. "Well, I've got my secret weapon too–the Sith Lord of the Glow Wars!" He began waving it around like a lightsaber and I cringed.

"Yeah, how about you put that away before you hurt someone," I said, grabbing onto his flailing wrists. "Where's Zara, anyway?"

"Who? That betrayer of worlds! She ditched me an hour ago to go dancing," Harpreet pouted.

"How long have you guys been here?" I asked, then without waiting for a response, Harpreet pulled me to the dancefloor where Zara was gyrating on one of her girlfriends. "I believe this belongs to you," I said, shoving Harpreet into Zara who ducked with exceptional speed out of the way, causing Harpreet to almost fall flat on his face.

Zara laughed and flung her arms around my neck, kissing me on the lips. "Baby! You came!" She was wasted, too. Great. Now I had two people to take care of tonight. Getting drunk and forgetting about all my worries just went out the window. Not that I minded. It wasn't so much the drinking, but who I was drinking with that matter. Zara turned to stare at her brother and gave him a dirty look. "Get lost. I want to spend time with my boyfriend."

Harpreet rolled his eyes. "Be careful about that one. She doesn't even know how to cook Dal. Believe me, friend, if you marry her, you'll starve to death. You've been warned."

Zara smacked him upside the head, but Harpreet ducked away, disappearing into the crowd. I laughed, staring after him. "Does your brother not know that I can cook, too?"

"Ignore him," Zara purred. "He was dropped on his head as a child. He won't be in our way, I promised."

Siblings. If it were me and Kateryna, I would have had her in a headlock by now and body slammed to her on the floor. *Ah, good times*. But my mind went back to the issue at hand. Harpreet drinking at a house party was a dangerous combination.

"Should I make sure he's okay?" I asked Zara, grabbing her narrow hips. There was a loud crash behind us, followed by several curses that sounded suspiciously like Harpreet.

"Nah, he's fine. Dance with me?" The beat of rap music pounded from the speakers, matching the hypnotic sway of Zara's hips. Her eyes were captivating, framed by smoky black eyeliner, adding to her allure. My lips curled into a smile as she moved, a spellbinding force striking every onlooker. I couldn't help but feel a surge of pride. Zara was undoubtedly the hottest girl in the room.

I held her waist, our bodies moving in perfect harmony with the rhythm. I mouthed the lyrics as the music enveloped us, making our bodies tremble with its pulse. Beads of sweat trickled down my spine as we danced, and I spun her around, pulling her close to my chest. I noticed every guy nearby straining their necks to catch a glimpse of her. With Zara in my arms, I felt like I was on top of the world.

But it didn't last long.

Zara turned, gyrating her firm backside on my cock, grinding hard enough to make me moan, and my thoughts whirled. I thought back to the sauna. To Alex's perky ass and how it looked clasped in that white towel. What I wouldn't give to take it off. Bend him over and fuck him raw and deep. My cock swelled and throbbed, pressing against the zipper of my jeans. A gnawing guilt settled in the pit of my stomach, like a jagged stone.

Using her like this was wrong. "I'm thirsty," I lied, draining what was left of my drink in my hand. "I'll grab another."

Zara nodded, and as I left, another one of her friends pulled her into a dance. I went to the kitchen to pour myself another drink. Once my glass was full, I got ready to head back to Zara, but my gaze snapped up and my breath caught in my throat. Jayden and Grayson stood in the far corner at the end of the stairs, their bodies molded together as Jayden whispered seductively into Grayson's ear, his palms sliding beneath the thick folds of his varsity jacket.

Fuck. My throat went dry watching them. A smile curled Grayson's mouth. Slow. Secretive. While Jayden's black inky hair looked glossy, the tattoos made his skin look pale and endless. There weren't many gay guys on the team, and very few were out when it came to hockey. I stood there watching, my feet rooted to the floor. Jayden's mouth ticked up, and he pressed a kiss underneath Grayson's earlobe before his tongue darted out, and he sucked it into his mouth. A laugh startled from Grayson and he pressed a firm hand to Jayden's chest, almost warning him not to go further.

But I knew that look.

Jayden was like the devil. His hand snaked out before Grayson could stop it, cupping the growing bulge in his jeans. A wave of dizzying arousal shot through me, and I couldn't believe I was having this type of reaction just by seeing my two close friends go at it. What the fuck was happening? I wasn't gay. At least, I never thought I was. Shit. Why am I so confused?

One minute I'm okay with what Alex and I did and then the next I want to rip my hair out. Running a palm over my face, I went to grab something strong. I poured some vodka in a cup, my throat working before I drank it down. I didn't want to face the facts.

Maybe I was gay.

My father would kill me if he found out. They'd never accept it. Much less if it is with Alex. Even though we've been friends for all our lives, that didn't mean my parents wanted me to be gay. Shirley's addiction had shaken the community to the core. So much so that my parents wanted me to stay away from Alex growing up, but I never listened. Over the years, Alex grew on them, and now he was considered part of the family.

My gaze darted back to them. Grayson had pinned Jayden against the wall with his tongue down his throat. *Fuck.* My cock twitched and I couldn't look away. Jayden's Adam's apple bobbed, and the veins in his arms protruded as he clung to Grayson's jacket as if attempting to swallow him whole. Grayson growled, dominating Jayden with a brutal kiss that left even me breathless. Jayden looked like he wanted Grayson to take him there and then, but Grayson chuckled, his throat moving as he cupped Jayden's cheek, his eyes filled with such adoration that the hair on my arm bristled.

They were in love.

It was a slap to the face. All this time I thought they were fucking, but as it turned out it was much more than that. There was softness there. Behind the crinkles in Grayson's eyes and Jayden's heavy-lidded gaze. I flinched away from it. Heat burned my cheeks, and I downed another drink before heading for the front door.

Fuck. I cursed, walking into the brusque night air, not caring that I left Harpreet and Zara behind. The frigid air pierced through my coat, gnawing at my exposed skin as I trudged through the wintry cold. Everything had been such a fucking mistake. And now Alex was gone, leaving me to work through all of this shit on my own. *What the hell did it mean?*

For most of my life, I considered myself straight. I never once thought of guys like that. Except, maybe Alex, but that was when we were teenagers. I groaned, feeling like my head was going to explode. I can't handle this. Not with my hockey dream within reach.

Zara was fucking perfect, and I felt nothing for her.

Alex was a goddamn nightmare and the only thing I cared about was if he was okay. Was he hurt? Safe? Did he need anything? Taking out my phone, I stared at the message that Alex had sent several weeks ago. *I'm fine. Don't look for me. We aren't friends anymore.* My heart slammed against my ribcage as I read the words until they were branded onto my skin.

Alex's decision to cut me out of his life felt like being pierced by a sharp blade.

Fine. Maybe it was time I did the same.

9

POWER PLAY PASSION

EVANS MULRONEY

Tossing my duffle bag over my shoulder, I waved to some of the guys leaving the frat house before jumping into my hulking truck. It was that time of year and I was eager to get the fuck out of here. I texted Kateryna earlier to see if she wanted to carpool, but she said she was coming later after she finished a few of her assignments for class.

Gray skies loomed overhead as I embarked on my journey home for the holidays. I merged onto the freeway, cranking up the heat to combat the winter chill, and tuned in to the Maple Leaf's game highlights. Usually, Alex would have been right there with me, fiddling with the radio controls and discussing our expectations for the next season. My heart ached with the memory, but I pushed it aside for now. The holidays had always been a bittersweet time for us.

Yet Alex should have been here. With me.

I could feel the pressure building, like a dam straining against the force of a river. *Damn him. What the fuck was his problem dumping me like that? What the hell did I do to deserve his hatred?* It was so fucking confusing, this push-and-pull game he was playing and a part of me wanted to find him just to yell at him. The faint vibration of my phone was a welcome distraction, but when I checked the screen, I saw Zara's name pop up.

How are you? The text message read and my phone was situated on the hand-free device on my dashboard. I ignored it, knowing I'd have to deal with her sooner or later, but now wasn't the time, especially since I was driving. I sped past familiar landscapes, the old pastures, and landmarks that signalled my return to Ann Arbor, a city known for its charm and vibrant college culture. Upon reaching my destination, I pulled into my parents' three-car garage, ensuring I claimed my spot before my sister Kateryna had a chance to snatch it. Stepping out of the car, I gathered my belongings and used my key to unlock the front door.

"Mom, I'm home!" I hollered, the inviting scent of freshly baked kolach wafting through the air.

With her long blond hair cascading down her back, my mom was busy baking Pampushky while chatting animatedly with my grandmother on the phone, their conversation flowing in Ukrainian. "Так, обов'язково прийду наступного року—"

Sneaking up behind her, I planted a quick kiss on her cheek, and she playfully swatted me away. Her gesture was clear: it was time for me to tackle the dirty dishes. I groaned inwardly but was quickly won over by the mouthwatering aroma of kolach that made my stomach growl.

"Hey baby," my mom said once she was finished speaking to my grandmother, she rolled onto the tips of her toes to kiss my cheek. I laughed at how short she was and how I was towering over her. "Where's your sister and Alexei? We promised to finish our chess game!" My mom's blue eyes flickered over my face and my stomach knotted. It was as if a swarm of bees buzzed inside me, their collective annoyance growing louder with each passing moment.

"Alex isn't coming this year."

She blinked at me like I'd grown a second head. "Impossible."

I thought so too once. My frustration rose like a relentless tide, rising higher and higher within me. Avoiding her gaze, I went back to cleaning the dishes. Her hand touched the lower part of my spine. "Are you alright? Did something happen?"

"I'm fine Mama. Let's just forget about it."

Her brows knitted, but before she could say anything, my father came waltzing into the room. My dad was a tall, broad-shouldered man with classical American features, a strong jawline, and salt-and-pepper hair. He and my mom had met when she immigrated from Ukraine to America several years ago.

My Dad clasped my shoulder. "Good, you're here. I've got the equipment I want you to try out once you're done."

"Jesus." My mom rolled her eyes. "No hockey for the rest of the holidays! I honestly can't stand it anymore!"

We laughed at her. Everyone in the house played hockey except her. My sister was a fanatic, and my dad was even worse. It drove her up the wall. I hurried to finish up the dishes and followed my dad down to his massive den. The room had a black, sleek TV screen that took up the entire left wall, along with a spare room where Alex used to sleep and a large sectional leather couch.

"Where's Alex?" my dad asked, brow furrowed.

"He's spending Christmas with his mom this year," I lied, and my dad's mouth pulled into a frown.

"What? Since when?" he demanded. "Is he in trouble? Why didn't you say anything?"

Each question was like a falling brick on my fucking head, adding another layer to the growing mountain of my irritation. "I don't know! Am I his keeper? He's not here. Get over it."

My dad's jaw dropped, and I felt my face heat with shame. *Crap. I've never spoken to him like that.* "Sorry. I'm just... stressed with school and hockey."

"I can see that," he said, but his voice was calm. He shoved his hands into his slacks and stared at me. "Look, I said this before, and I'll say it again. Don't get sidetracked. You're on the cusp of greatness, Evans, and you're about to reach new heights that nobody could ever dream of."

Anger flared in my chest, but I nodded. I was so sick of his damn speech. Every year it was the same thing, but I knew what he was telling me without ever saying the words. My father always thought Alex was a burden to me, a red cross I had to bear.

"How's everything else?" my dad continued, walking behind the massive bar and pouring us both a drink of coke. "How's your girlfriend Zara? She was so lovely. Why didn't you bring her?"

The same girlfriend I've been ignoring for the past few days? I wanted to scoff but didn't respond. Taking the glass of coke, I drained it and sighed around the fizzy soda as it glided down my throat. I didn't want to talk about my life. "What did you want to show me?"

My dad's eyes narrowed at my evasion, and I knew he wasn't going to let it go, but for now, he did. "Check this out."

He led me to the garage and opened the door, revealing a vintage hockey stick once played by Bobby Orr. The stick was a weathered, brownish hue, its blade showing signs of the countless goals it had scored. My jaw dropped, and my stomach tightened.

"No way! How did you get this?"

My dad laughed, patting me on the back. "You know I have connections. Just consider it your official welcome to the NHL next year. Your spot is secured, and I'm so proud of you, son."

"This is amazing! Alex will go ape-shit—" I choked on my words, feeling the name of my ex-best friend making me feel like I was being strangled alive. *Fuck. Alex wasn't here.* My happiness died in my throat and bitterness swept over me once the realization settled in. Clearing my throat, I forced a smile. "Thanks, Dad, I appreciate it."

"What's wrong with you?" my dad asked, piercing me with his brown eyes. "Did something bad happen? Alex is like your shadow and the fact that he isn't here is telling me a lot. Is he in trouble? What does he need?"

"Don't act like you care," I spat before I could stop myself. "You never really liked him—"

"So? You like him. That's what matters. You're right, I don't think he's a good influence on you, but that doesn't mean I want to see him hurt or in trouble. He's still a person, Evans."

My throat constricted, and I looked away. We were practically the same height, with my dad a few inches taller than me, but I knew he wasn't going to let this go, especially if would interfere with my hockey performance. "He—doesn't want to be friends anymore," I admitted finally.

"Oh." Running a hand through his salt and pepper hair, he frowned. "Wow. I'm sorry to hear that. Do you know how or why he came to that conclusion?"

"I don't know anything," I gritted out. "He won't talk to me. Blocked my number. Dropped out of school. I haven't seen him for weeks. I don't know where he is or if he's hurt or dead or—" My heart clenched so hard that I thought it'd stop breathing. Finally, all my fears began pouring out of me like a dam and my eyes stung with tears. *Where was Alex?* That was all I wanted to fucking know. My hand curled into a fist and I bit back the pain threatening to overwhelm me.

"I'm sorry." Placing a hand on my shoulder, he squeezed. "I know how much you cared for him. You guys were like brothers, but I can tell you this was a long time coming."

"What do you mean?"

My dad stared at me. "Shirley was never going to let him live a normal life. You should have known that. He was doing good for a while with the scholarships, but the demons she carried would always transfer over to him. It might be best to leave him be for now until he can figure his life out."

"But dad, what if he's hurt or—"

"If he decided to end the friendship and drop out of school, then you need to believe he has his reasons for that. It might have nothing to do with you. Try not to take it too personally. He's your friend, so trust me. I think he'll come around."

And if he doesn't? I wanted to demand, but the sound of the front door opening and Kateryna's voice made me stop. "Come on," my dad said. "I don't know about you, but that kolach is starting to make my stomach grumble. Let's head back upstairs. We can talk more later."

We headed back upstairs to find Kateryna in the kitchen with my mom, dressed in a white and red hockey jersey, recounting tales of her latest game, knowing it would annoy my mother to death. I playfully shoved her shoulder aside and entered the kitchen, lured by the delightful aroma of fresh bread. Hunger gnawed at my stomach. "What's up, pumpkinhead?"

Kateryna shot me a dirty look. "Go to hell. Where's Alex? I'm all set to kick his butt in Call of Duty again. He's not getting away this time."

Crap. Our Christmas tradition was a marathon gaming session, but Alex was absent. "He's not coming."

Kateryna stared at me in disbelief. "I'm sorry. What? I think I just went deaf for a moment. Did you say Alex isn't coming?"

I shrugged, and my mom began serving slices of warm bread. "No way. Impossible. So where is he? Why isn't he here?"

"Grab some bread, and we'll discuss it later," my mom redirected her, giving Kateryna a meaningful look. The topic was temporarily shelved, but I could tell everyone was disappointed.

***

"Bro, I don't know what the hell is wrong with you," Kateryna said as we huddled around the TV, our wireless controllers in hand, ready for an intense Call of Duty showdown. The flickering screen displayed a war-torn battlefield, and we were about to dive into the action.

We chose our teams and geared up, faces determined and eyes locked on the screen. The game started, and we both got lost in the virtual chaos. Bullets whizzed by, explosions rocked the digital world, and our characters darted for cover.

"Watch out, Kat! Behind you!" I yelled, moving my thumb sticks.

She responded with a burst of gunfire, taking down an opponent. "Got 'em! Nice save, big bro!"

A hail of bullets erupted on the screen, and my character went down. "Fuck, Kateryna! Revive me!" I implored.

She laughed, dodging enemy fire. "Sorry, bro. You'll respawn soon enough."

"Damn pumpkinhead," I sneered, but the match raged on.

She snorted. "You still didn't answer my question." She snarled after her character fell to my relentless onslaught of bullets. The game was in its final moments, and the tension was palpable. "Alex follows you everywhere. I can't believe he's not here. Did something happen?"

My irritation reached a boiling point. I couldn't bear to discuss Alex any longer. The holidays should be about enjoying the moment, right? I shot her character down, ending the game, and then finally responded, "Isn't Alex his own person? Why does everyone act like the world is ending because he's not here?" Maybe because it feels like it is.

"No. You guys share a single brain cell," Kateryna replied, her face filled with disgust. "No. Seriously, what happened? Is Alex okay?"

I went quiet for several moments. "I don't know."

"What do you mean?"

"He won't talk to me and ended our friendship after we..." I swallowed and stared at my hands. Kateryna and I had always been close. There were things that I could tell her that I knew she would never repeat and I had to get this off my chest.

"After we what...?" Kateryna probed. "God, don't tell me you slept with him." Heat burned my face, and I turned away. Kateryna's eyes widened. She leaped out in front of me and got to her knees. "You did? You slept with Alex?" she shrilled.

"Keep your voice down!" I hissed at her.

Kateryna threw her head back and laughed. "Shit. I called that last year! I knew it. The way he looked at you was like you hung the moon!"

"Shut up!" My heart hammered at her words, and knew that it was possible they were true.

"So, what was it like? Who topped who?" Kateryna said, her eyes gleaming. "Don't tell me you're a bossy bottom. I knew it!"

"We aren't discussing this," I responded, shoving her off.

"Come on, you can't drop a bombshell like that and walk away," Kateryna said, nearly vibrating on the spot. "Tell me. What happened?"

My mouth filled with lead, and my face burned with the memory of his touch. This was uncharted territory for us, but when it was done, what happened between us felt so right. Groaning, I slapped my hands over my eyes. "Fuck, it was a mistake ... I... he just made a move, and I didn't..." I sighed. "I didn't push him away."

"Wait, so you let him make a move on you?" Kateryna repeated, her eyes wide. "And now he won't speak to you?"

I nodded, my head down.

"And what about Zara? Have you told her?"

"No. I can't bring myself to. Fuck Kateryna, I'm not gay. I never have been. Alex was just—I don't know what I am. It's so fucking confusing."

"Auntie Olenna thought she wasn't gay, but ten seasons of the L word later she's a completely different person, and now look at her. I think Shane can turn even the straightest girls gay," Kateryna pointed out.

"So?"

"So ... maybe you should just do some research. Nobody is completely straight. People are fluid. I think Alex is just scared you'll reject him. He'll be back, trust me. The way he looks at you..." Kateryna's expression turned dreamy. "Damn, I wish someone would look at me like that."

I wondered exactly what she saw that I didn't. I never noticed Alex looking at me in any kind of way, but I had been dense for all these years. Maybe to everyone else, it was obvious. To me, Alex was just Alex. With fox-like eyes and a sly smile curling his lips, and his hair the color of molten bronze. He was my best friend. I scrubbed my face again. "What do you mean by research?"

"Well, first you need to break up with Zara. I told you before she was way too good for you," Kateryna replied. "Then I'd suggest signing up for a subscription service... if you know what I mean."

Breaking up with Zara was a must. I knew I couldn't continue like this anymore, but the subscription services seemed kind of dicey. Plus, everything was free online now. Why would I pay?

"Evans, just figure out your shit, bro," she said, nudging my arm. "If Alex is the one you can't live without, then you need to fight for him and make it clear."

"How..." I started and then licked my dry lips. "Do you think Mom and Dad will react? Do you think they'll disown me?"

"I will if you keep playing like this for the next game," Kateryna muttered. "Nah, they might be a bit shocked but Alex is already part of the family, so I don't think they'll care. I mean, I don't. In fact, I don't particularly want to know where you stick your dick."

I laughed, shoving her away. "Thanks. I mean it."

"What are sisters for?" She shrugged. "Now, are we playing or what? Don't worry, I'm feeling generous today. T'is the season after all."

"Funny coming from someone whose head is the inspiration for Halloween decorations."

Kateryna's face flushed bright red. "That was one time!"

10

BREAKAWAY HEARTS

EVANS MULRONEY

Alex was naked. Biting into my bottom lip, my eyes roamed under my lids in a sleepy haze. Although I wasn't exactly asleep, I felt as though I were floating in a wonderland. Fuck. I cursed, my throat going dry as images flashed inside my mind of us back at the sauna. This time Alex was laid out on the bench, his gaze beckoning, his cock filling with need. He lay there, legs spread, his cock hard and dripping with precum, his lips red like the skin of an apple. Droplets of sweat trickled down the corners of his mouth and onto his jawline.

My heart pounded. All the blood rushed to my head, and I watched as Alex's hand slithered down his body to grasp his aching cock. Liquid honey eyes pierced my soul. Desire stabbed at my chest, hot and thick, as I stroked myself languidly.

I wanted to bend him. Break him. Chain him. Fuck him in different ways, and I wanted to make him cry. To see the tears of release stain his cheeks. Alex spread his legs wider, giving me a full view of his glistening hole, which was covered in sparse, auburn hair. His eyes were heavily lidded, curving in mocking laughter before his wet finger dipped in. My heart almost stopped, sweat pooled on my bow and I reached beneath my pajamas to stroke my aching cock.

My breath hitched when a blast of cold air touched my skin. I imagined Alex pumping into his fist, fucking himself with wild abandon. I groaned, my hips jerking on their own accord, Alex's name on the tip of my tongue. Things shifted and contorted. Then Alex was above me, straddling me, riding my cock, canting his hips in a way that made me see stars. *Fuck, baby, take me.* He moaned. Tough, and gritty, Alex falling apart under me.

Pleasure licked down my spine, curling hot and low in my belly, before I spilled my hot release into my hand. I cried out through my release. The skin on my arm bristled, and my vision whited out as thoughts of Alex fucking himself on my cock filled my head.

"Shit," I hissed, staring at the puddle of my release soaking my silk pajama pants. It was never like this with Zara or any of the other girls I dated. Licking my dry lips, I adjusted my now-sensitive cock and tried to regulate my breathing.

Alex. *Was I in love with him?* The thought made my skin heat. He knew me better than anyone, but it always felt deeper than that. "Christ," I sighed, taking a few slow and measured breaths. I didn't know where he was or what he was going through, but I sent a silent prayer to heaven, hoping that he'd be kept safe. My phone gave off a muffled buzz on my night table. Reaching over, I grabbed it, only to freeze when Zara's name came up.

Look, I don't know what I did wrong or why you aren't responding, but I need to talk to you. The message read, and I slumped back on the bed. Shit. I had to deal with this. The longer it went on, the worse things would get for us in the future. Besides, Zara didn't deserve this. She was amazing, the best girlfriend any guy could ask for. She just wasn't for me.

Sorry, I texted my reply. *I got busy during the holidays. We'll talk when I get back.* I pressed send and then turned off my phone. I'd deal with it when I returned and not a day sooner.

***

THE HOLIDAYS BLURRED in a series of love and laughter. Kateryna and I made do with Alex's absence, filling it with spending time with my parents, Carol singing, doing charity work, and other things my mom had planned. By the time I was heading back to campus, I felt renewed. As if I had finally made a decision. First, I'd find Alex and speak to him. If he still didn't want to be my friend, I'd accept it. For the past few weeks, I'd been struggling with my sexuality, but Kateryna made me realize something. Sexuality was fluid. Meaning I didn't need to be defined as straight or gay. I could be whoever I wanted. Driving down the winding roads, my phone buzzed in my pocket, but I ignored it.

Hockey practice was starting soon, and I didn't want to be late. Striding into the hockey arena, I bumped my fist with a few of the guys who were coming back from the holidays. Jayden nodded to me, and Grayson patted my shoulder. "You look good, man. Did you do your makeup today?"

"Fuck you," I laughed, shrugging him off. Then I changed into my gear. Heading onto the ice, my lungs filled with renewed energy. This year, this would be different. I had so many things to look forward to and I couldn't let what I was feeling get the best of me. Alex and I would talk.

We had to, and I'd show him I really cared. It was just like Kateryna said; he was probably ashamed of his actions and feared I'd reject him.

With every stride, I felt the power of the ice propelling me forward. The puck was an extension of myself, and I could almost see the net calling my name. The practice had taken on a new intensity, and my determination to prove myself was unwavering.

Darting past defenders, I controlled the puck. The goalie tracked my movements, but he couldn't predict the shot's destination. As I wound up, the arena held its breath. The slap of the puck echoed through the rink as it sailed past the goalie's glove, finding the back of the net.

One goal, then another, and another. I was on fire.

"Damn Evans!" Jayden called. "Save some for the rest of us!"

"Do you want it? Come and get it," I laughed when he snarled, but I was on a fucking roll. For the first time in a while, I would bring my A-game. Next week, we'd be playing the Arctic Avalanche at the Detroit Red Wings arena and I was ready for it. My teammates cheered as each goal was scored, and I reveled in the thrill of the game. The puck became an extension of my will, and it danced at my command. With each goal, I silenced the doubts that had haunted me for weeks.

"Good work, Evans!" Coach's voice cut through the rink, and I felt a surge of pride. It wasn't just about the goals; it was about proving to myself that I could rise above the challenges, on and off the ice. This practice had been a turning point, a reminder of why I loved the game and the sense of accomplishment it brought. After practice, I grabbed my gear and started heading toward the locker room. A group of my teammates stayed back, still discussing the upcoming game.

"Bro," Chris said, nudging my arm. "I heard the Arctic Avalanche demolished their last team and the scouts will be there to pick for the draft."

I nodded because my dad had already prepared me for it. "Yeah, I heard they have crazy dangles."

"Yeah, man, it's so hard I can't wrap my head around it. My dangles are for shit."

"Bro, my left nut dangles better than you," Jayden said, shouldering past Chris and laughing when he tried to swat at him.

"Whatever Taylor. Yo, how's my Justin Bieber mixtape going? I expect "Sorry" to be number one like you promise!" Chris hollered after him.

"You're gonna make a great coach someday, Chris. The worst players always do," Jayden ripped on his way out the door with Grayson laughing on his heels.

"Yeah, fuck you!"

I barked a laugh at Chris' furious expression, but as we approached the exit, I stopped dead in my tracks when I saw Zara standing there, looking stunning in her winter attire. She was standing near the dual door entrance, wearing a pure white winter coat, knee-high black boots, and winter stockings.

Crap. Checking the time on my wristwatch I realized I had a class in twenty minutes.

A few of the guys couldn't help but whistle at her entrance, but I ignored their remarks and walked over to her. However, Zara's expression was anything but welcoming. Her brow was furrowed, and there was a heaviness in her eyes that I couldn't ignore. I knew we needed to talk, and it was clear she felt the same way. The weight of the impending conversation bore down on me, but I straightened my spine and stride towards her, my long legs eating up the distance between us.

Zara's voice was tight, her arms folded across her chest. "We need to talk."

"Can't it wait? I have class in twenty minutes."

She didn't budge. "No, it can't wait, Evans. We've been avoiding this for too long."

Fuck, she was right, but I didn't want to deal with this right now. I had to focus on hockey and nothing else; I knew putting it off was just delaying the inevitable and I sighed through my nose.

"Fine." I followed her out of the rink, and as soon as we were away from prying ears, she turned to me, her eyes heavy with concern.

"What's going on? You've been ignoring me for weeks since you left me and Harpreet at the party. Did something happen?"

Running a hand through my hair, I tried to figure out what I should tell her. Something did happen, and I didn't want to lie to her. "Look—Ah—things are just getting too serious for me too fast and I don't think I can do this anymore."

Pain flashed in Zara's eyes and I felt like a jerk for hurting her. "What do you mean?"

"I ... I just realized something about myself and I don't think I can do this anymore. I'm sorry."

Zara's eyes narrowed into pinpricks. "Do what? Is this about Alex?"

My breath caught. How did she know this was about him? "Well ... fuck." I rolled my eyes to the heavens and leaned against the brick wall. "Yes and no, we—it's complicated, but I don't think I should be with anyone right now."

"Evans—"

"You're great," I pressed on. "Perfect, but Alex, he's..." I laughed, not sure what I was babbling about. "I just realized I might actually like my best friend and it's fucking me up."

"Like ... what do you mean?"

Swallowing around the knot in my throat. "Like—I want to be with him."

Zara looked at me like she'd been slapped and I felt my chest tighten. God, I was such an asshole. "I'm sorry, I'm a jackass. I didn't know I felt this way until he was gone and then—"

"Wait," Zara said, raising a trembling hand. "You and him? How long?"

Fuck. This wasn't coming out properly, but Zara wasn't an idiot. Of course, she would know something had been wrong. But I had to tell her. She deserved to know that I was fucking scum, and she deserved someone far better than me. "Since the day before he left."

Zara took a step back, pain flashing in her eyes before they filled with tears. Shit. I took a step toward her, but she kept inching back like she wanted nothing to do with me. "I'm sorry. It just happened. It was a mistake and I—"

"And you realized you had feelings for him," she finished, resigned. Tears welled in her eyes before spilling over, and then I pulled her into my arms, hugging her tight. *Fuck, everything was a mess.* I had destroyed everything, but she couldn't be with a guy like me. *I wasn't worth it.*

"Evans—" she cried, clutching my jacket.

"I'm sorry. Fuck, I'm so sorry. I never meant to hurt you. I swear."

"No," she said, taking a stuttering breath before peering up at me. Her hazel eyes were shimmering like the dappled sunlight filtering through a forest canopy. "I missed my period."

I felt like I'd been doused in ice-cold water. Shockwaves of disbelief coursed through me, freezing me in place. *I must have gone deaf.* That's it. Because that's the only way to explain the sharp ringing in my ears and the world falling from my feet.

"I'm sorry. *What*?"

***

PACING THE ROOM, I tried to focus on breathing and not the hot bile searing its way up my throat. Zara sat on my bed, nibbling on a few crackers. Tears had stained her cheeks but she was much calmer than before. *Pregnant.* My stomach swooped. *God, I'm such an idiot. How did I screw up so badly?* But there was nothing I could do. Zara missed her period and we wouldn't know until she took the test. My heart slammed against my ribcage and my palms began to sweat.

A father. At twenty-one? What about hockey? My vision fractured into fissions. I itched to grab my phone and call Alex, begging him to tell me what to do. Zara seemed just as conflicted. We never talked about having children. We never planned it. What would her family think?

"What—Ah—" I cleared my throat. "What do you plan to do?"

Zara's gaze snapped to mine. The word abortion hadn't been spoken, but it sat like a jagged rock in my throat. We were both studying to be lawyers and having a child would disrupt all of that. I knew it would for her way more than it would for me. Zara would probably have to drop out and who knows when she'd be able to get back. My family was well off, so I could still support her and continue my career, but my heart ached when I thought about what she'd be giving up to have my baby.

My child. Acid sloshed around in my stomach, and I tried to breathe through the burn.

"I don't know ... Baba would kill me," Zara said, then burst into tears. "I don't know. My career. Everything I worked towards would be gone."

I knelt before her, taking her hands. "Don't worry. Please. I'll take care of everything that I can. I'll get a place off campus. We can hire babysitters and private tutors to help you finish. You will become a lawyer. I promise."

"But will you love me?" Zara asked through tears. "Will we be a family?" I flinched at her words. "Or will you be with us just thinking about him?"

My eyes slipped closed. *Fuck, I couldn't answer that because I didn't know*. All I knew was that I would be there to provide for her, but loving her and being in a relationship with her was something I couldn't do.

"I need to think about it," she whispered finally, and I opened my eyes. "I need time. Please."

"Take whatever you need and whatever you decide, I'll be here for you. I promise."

We held each other in that quiet, tearful moment, a mix of emotions swirling around us like the stormy winds outside. The weight of Zara's question lingered in the air, heavy and uncertain.

For a while, we simply clung to one another, seeking solace in each other's arms. My mind raced, pondering the path ahead and what it meant for us. I knew that things would never be the same, and the complexity of our situation weighed heavily on my heart. The future was uncertain, but one thing remained resolute: my commitment to Zara.

After Zara left, I found myself alone in my room, the silence bearing down on me like a heavyweight. I sank onto the edge of my bed, my thoughts in turmoil. The events of the day had left me emotionally drained, and I needed time to process everything that had happened.

I rested my elbows on my knees and buried my face in my hands, trying to make sense of the whirlwind of emotions that had engulfed me. The news of Zara's pregnancy had been a shock, one that had sent ripples through my world, leaving me grappling with a mix of fear, uncertainty, and the guilt of not knowing how to respond.

My heart ached as I thought about the decisions that lay ahead, the choices that Zara had to make, and how they would affect both of us. I couldn't help but feel the weight of responsibility, not just for Zara, but also for the life growing inside her. Fuck. What the hell was I going to do? I thought about calling my mom, but knew I wasn't ready for them to know yet. Zara had to take a test.

Then we'd know for sure if she was pregnant. Fuck, I was going to be a father. I couldn't wrap my head around it. My stomach growled, and I realized I hadn't eaten since practice. Heading downstairs to grab a quick bite to eat, I saw one of my fraternity brothers in the kitchen. His name was Eli, and he was a friend I'd known for years. He gave me a scrutinizing look, clearly concerned.

"Bro, what's up with Alex?" Eli asked, his brow furrowed. "I tried to say to him earlier, and he straight-up ignored me."

My heart stopped. "Alex? You saw him?"

"Yeah, I did. But his attitude was wack, man. I don't know what's going on, but he's gotta be careful with that kind of behavior."

Alex was here. He was safe. Relief washed over me, but it was short-lived because I needed to know where Alex was. "Where did you see him?"

Eli shrugged his broad shoulders. "At the Detroit Red Wings arena. He was dressed in a janitor's uniform. I guess he works there now. Honestly, I have no clue about the details." With that, he walked away, leaving me stunned and unsure of what to do next.

Just because he was there didn't mean he wanted to speak to me. Right? Alex's words rang in my ear, his last text message severing our friendship for good. He got a job, that's why he dropped out, probably to support himself and his mother, but why didn't he just fucking tell me? My hands curled into fists, but I knew storming into the arena wouldn't do us both any good. I had a game coming up there next week. I'd talk to him then and if Alex still didn't want to meet me, I'd let him go.

For good. Besides, I had other things to worry about.

The shitstorm was just beginning.

11

THE COACH'S DILEMMA

ALEX MAY

As I wiped down the counter, my mind wandered, disconnected from the bustling activity around me. Absently, I grabbed the "Caution Wet Floor" sign and positioned it near the spot where a child had spilled a can of Coke earlier. The soft fizzing sound of the mop echoed in my ears as I efficiently cleaned up the sticky mess. All around me, the air was charged with anticipation for an upcoming game, but I willed myself to remain detached from such distractions. I had a job to do.

Conversations buzzed with excitement as people chatted animatedly, and the arena was adorned with bright yellow streamers to celebrate the arrival of a new team. But none of that held any significance to me anymore. Hockey was no longer a part of my life.

Once I'd finished cleaning, I made my way to the back room, where Able was completing his tasks for the day. "Are you done?" he asked. I nodded and headed to my locker to retrieve my coat.

Able cleared his throat and, with a hint of hesitation, tossed me a high-quality Grey Goose jacket that likely cost more than my entire paycheck. I frowned, perplexed by the gesture. "What's this for?" I inquired.

Able scratched the back of his neck, his eyes filled with a mix of emotions. "Well, you and my son are about the same size. He doesn't wear it anymore, so I thought... well, there's no point in letting a good jacket go to waste. Now, get out of here. You'll miss your bus."

I glanced at the price tag that Able had forgotten to remove and remained silent. Replacing my tattered old jacket, I embraced the warmth and comfort of this generous gift. Tears threatened to well up in my eyes, but I only nodded my gratitude to Able before hurrying out the door. There were only a few people in my life who had ever shown me such kindness.

A few teachers noticed my neglect and called Child Services on my mother. Some neighbors saw me wandering the roads late at night and brought me back home, only to call the police after seeing my mother passed out in her own piss and vomit.

And of course, Evans.

No matter what time of day or night, he would open his window and allow me to crawl into his bed. Even after I was raped by one of my mother's boyfriends. We never spoke about it. Evans helped me clean up the blood, fed me Cheetos, and tucked me into bed, allowing me to sob into his neck.

There was always Evans.

Until there wasn't. A bitter breeze swept through the streets, causing my breath to materialize in the frosty air. Despite the harsh cold, my new coat proved to be an impenetrable fortress of warmth. Due to Rex's classes, we agreed that I'd take the bus near campus and then he'd pick me up when he was done. My car was still stuck in the parking garage near my old complex, and I had no idea when I'd get the money to fix it. Everything was crashing down on me and my anxiety spiked at the thought that it may take me a few months to afford a new place and get my car up and running.

I didn't have a few months. I didn't even have a few weeks. The holidays were over, but at some time, Rex's family would return to their house and the last thing they needed was to have some homeless guy sleeping in their guest room. I couldn't do that to Rex.

Especially after he pulled some strings to get my mother into rehab.

My mother, who still wasn't speaking to me. Pain flared in my chest as I recalled the last time I saw her. Shirley looked ten times better, her skin was no longer ashen and there was even a little color to her cheeks, but the moment she saw me, her expression went cold.

What did I do? I honest to God wanted to fucking know as I swallowed around the dagger of bitterness in my throat. The convenience store flowers I bought several days prior were thrown into the trash, along with whatever treats or Christmas candies I could afford to bring her during the holidays. My chest felt hollowed out at the memory, and thought of last year when I spent Christmas at the Mulroney's. Kateryna was probably pissed I missed our annual Call of Duty marathon, along with Ruslana, Evans' mom, for our chess game. Rubbing my eyes, I groaned, feeling like such an idiot. I didn't think when I sent that text message to him. A part of me just wanted to be away from Evans, so I completely forgot about his family and what they meant to me. Pulling out my phone, I checked the message Kateryna had sent during the holidays.

You're an idiot. Talk to my brother else Call of Duty will seem like child's play.

I barked a laugh, reading it again. Kateryna was too much sometimes. Slipping my phone back into my pocket, I sighed as the bus pulled up to the curb. I got in and dropped a few coins into the slot before taking a seat near the back. Slumping down in the chair, I rested my head against the window, peering at the remnants of the holiday lights, wishing I had spent it with Evans and not wallowing in misery stuck inside my room. Rex didn't stick around much during the holidays. He had family nearby that he went to, and since I didn't know them, I didn't want to impose. The bus drove into campus, and I saw Rex's truck in the distance waiting for me. The winter chill nipped at my cheeks and sent a shiver down my spine as I walked to his car and quickly got in.

"Hey," Rex said, his mouth tugging into a smile. The scent of his cologne filled my nostrils, and I sighed, leaning back into the leather seats. Rex's earthy patchouli cologne lingered in the air, wrapping us in an embrace of masculine allure.

"Hey," I replied, breathless from the cold. "I think my nuts are going to freeze off if I keep having to take the bus."

Rex laughed, the deep timber sending shivers down my spine. "Yeah, bro. Fuck, we need to get your car fixed. If you want, I can get you in touch with a guy. He's affordable and don't worry, I won't stick my nose where it doesn't belong."

"Sure, send his information over I'll call him. I really need my car back up and running."

Rex nodded. "So, what do you want to do tonight? I heard there's a big game coming up and a party at the sorority a few blocks away."

"Women and booze?" I scoffed. "Nah, I'll pass. Besides, I'm dead fucking tired, bro. My shift was crazy."

Rex shrugged. "Okay. We can do a night in again."

I felt bad for not wanting to go. "You can still go. I mean, I'm sure the guys on the team will be there." The guys I told him to spread lies about me too. "You should go."

"Nah," Rex replied. "I don't really get along with them, anyway. Besides, why do that when I can hang out with you? We have more fun together, anyway."

My mouth curled into a smile. "Careful. I'm a gay man. I might take everything you say the wrong way."

Rex laughed. "Too late for that. Besides, would it be so bad if I wanted you to?"

My breath caught, and I nearly choked on my own spit. "What?"

Rex slanted his eyes toward me, giving me a sly look. "Bi-curious. Remember?"

"Well, it's not like you ever let me forget," I said laughing, but heat crawled over my cheeks. "What does that even mean anyway?"

"It means I've never had sex with a man, but I'm open to it," Rex explained while he pulled into the driveway to his house. "Most of my sexual encounters have been with women, but if I find a guy I'm attracted to, I think I'd be down for it."

My throat dry clicked as I swallowed. There was a reason everyone called him Rex. Large hands gripped the steering wheel, while his brown hair flopped over his brow. He was a fairly big guy, but easygoing in a way that I needed. If anything happened between us, I knew Rex wouldn't be the type to make a big deal out of it. Getting off with him would just be a no-strings-attached arrangement and a part of me was desperate to let off some steam, but my heart lurched when I thought of Evans.

Of how long I waited to be with him.

How I wanted to save myself for our first time together. Everyone else paled in comparison, no matter how attractive they were. Rex was great, he just wasn't him. Licking my dry lips, I tucked a stray hair behind my ear and looked out the windshield. Rex killed the engine before he turned to look at me.

"Did I make things weird between us now?"

"Nah, man. I'm just tired," I lied.

Rex rubbed the scuff on his chin. "Good, but if I wasn't clear enough," he said, his hand sliding to rest on my thigh. "No pressure. I know you're going through a lot, but if you ever need ... a break. Come find me."

Shit. This was getting out of hand. "Ah—I don't know Rex," I responded. "I'm in a bad place right now and I'm just focused on surviving. Not really getting my rocks off or anything. I mean ... I don't even have a place to live."

"Fuck." Rex jerked his hand away like he'd been burned. "Shit, man, that was totally insensitive of me. I'm sorry."

"It's okay. We'll just leave it there." Unbuckling my seat belt, I got out of the car and trailed behind him as he opened the front door. I went to my room to shower and wash up, then immediately collapsed onto my bed. What the hell was up with Rex today? Ever since I moved in, he's been acting weird and I wasn't sure if I was comfortable with his behavior. He knew the mountain of shit I was going through. Why was he making passes at me? It reminded me too much of my mother's boyfriends before they got violent. That wasn't something I wanted to deal with, especially from someone who was paying for my mother's treatment. *I need to get out of here. The question is: how?*

The cool comforter felt amazing on my cheek, and my limbs began to unwind as my breath evened out and sleep claimed me.

***

WALKING DOWN THE STERILE halls of the rehab center, my heart throbbed as I followed Dr. Reeds into the counseling room, where I was about to have my first session with my mom. This was a part of her rehabilitation program, and it was something I had been secretly dreading. Throughout all the years of her drug use, my mom only stayed clean for a few months at a time, even after she got fired and we lost our house. I had begged her countless times, but she never attempted to stay clean. It was only now, through force, that she was finally receiving the help she needed for her addiction.

Dr. Reeds led me into a room with a comfortable, plush couch and took a seat across from me. "Coffee?" she asked, her mouth curving into a welcoming smile. Her brown hair was neatly pulled back into a severe bun, but her brown eyes were kind and comforting, a far cry from the first time I had seen her. I nodded, and she poured me a cup. "Cream? Sugar?"

"Black," I replied. She prepared the coffee as instructed and then fixed herself a cup of tea. "Your mother will be in shortly, but I wanted to talk to you first and see where your head's at. This will be our first session, and I know it can be tough, but I want you to know that this is a safe space. Rehabilitation isn't about shaming anyone but bringing people together."

Questions burned at the tip of my tongue, but I held them back. There was only one thing I wanted to know. "Will this cure her?"

Dr. Reeds gave me a sympathetic look. "Unfortunately, there is no cure for addiction. The best we can do is help her regain some semblance of normality with the use of medication, but, of course, that won't work if she decides to start using again."

Resentment festered within me like an unhealed wound, as my mother's addiction continued to cast a dark shadow over my life. "For now, this is just the engagement stage. We'll work on building trust and improving your relationship, and then we'll move on. How does that sound?"

Awful, I thought but refrained from saying it aloud.

"So..." She stared at me expectantly. "How are you?"

Shit. I dropped out of school for this. "Fine."

"You're working now? I thought you were going to school?"

"We got evicted, so I had to drop out," I replied, shifting in my chair.

"Who pays for the bills in your household?"

"Me."

The questions went on like that for several minutes, and by then anger was fizzling in my core. I don't know if they were meant to rile me up, but I was already pissed at having to provide for everything and to make it worse she wanted me to rehash everything for her, to better understand my mother.

"Would you say your mother struggled with co-dependency growing up?"

"My father's name was Alexei, and that's all she calls me. I know she does it for spite." She hated me. Although she never said it aloud, in my mind, how could she treat me like this if she didn't? Doctor Reeds jotted my responses down in her notebook, then glanced at the time.

"Okay. Let's have your mom come in and we can begin."

As we waited for my mom to join us, my heart hammered in my chest. Then the door opened and my mom walked in wearing a simple hoodie and some gray sweatpants. Her hair was pulled into a ponytail, but she didn't even look at me as she took a seat on the far side of the couch.

A heavy silence settled over the room. Dr. Reeds tried to break the ice, her voice gentle and compassionate. "Shirley, it's wonderful to have you here. We'd like to start by getting to know you better. How have you been feeling since you arrived at the center?"

My mom remained silent; her gaze fixed firmly on the window. My heart sank. It was the same shit since she got here, ignoring me and pretending like I didn't exist. Even around the doctor, she acted like

I wasn't even in the fucking room. I clenched my fists, my frustration and disappointment growing. Dr. Reeds continued, undeterred. "We understand that seeking help can be difficult, but it's a significant step forward. What are your goals for your time here in rehab? What would you like to achieve?"

Still, there was no response from my mom. I could feel the tension in the room, and it was like a knife stabbing through my chest. How could she treat me like this, especially after all I'd done to help her? Did she know what it took to get her here? How much it fucking cost? Or how I had to drop out of school and hockey just to fucking be here?

Dr. Reeds shifted her approach. "Shirley, I know this process can be challenging, but it's crucial that we communicate openly and honestly to make progress. Can you tell me what your relationship with your son means to you?"

My mom's stony silence remained unbroken. I glanced at her, my eyes pleading for some kind of acknowledgment, but she kept her gaze averted. *Nothing.* I thought, swallowing around the thistle lodged in my throat. *It meant nothing to her. That's why she couldn't bear to look at me.* Not even now.

"Perhaps we can start with something simpler. What are your hobbies or interests outside of your addiction? What used to bring you joy?" Dr. Reeds continued with patience.

Joy? I scoffed. I once watched her eat her own vomit off the floor after getting high. This woman knew no joy. *Fuck.* Running a hand through my hair, I felt my anger begin to boil within me. Still, my mom refused to answer, and the room seemed to close in on me. I couldn't understand her obstinacy, and it hurt more than I could express. *I had to get out of here.*

"Shirley, we're here to help you regain control of your life and build meaningful relationships. This includes reconnecting with your family, especially your son, who cares deeply about your well-being."

But my mom's unyielding silence echoed through the room, leaving me with a sinking feeling that this journey toward recovery might be even more challenging than I'd feared. A burning anger built within me as I struggled to contain my frustration at her apathy.

"Shirley—"

"Why don't you fucking say anything?" I exploded, rounding on her. Tears burned my eyes, but I didn't care. "Don't you know what I've done to get you here? Don't you know all the shit I've been through just so that you could be here?"

"Yeah?" My mother turned then; her brown eyes hard as steel. "And whose cock did you have to suck to get me here, Alexei? Enlighten me."

I felt each word as if I'd been slapped.

"How many guys fucking bent your faggoty ass over and rammed you hard enough so that I could walk through this damn building? Was it my first boyfriend? My second boyfriend?"

Bile rose hot and thick in my throat, and I grabbed my jacket and fled the room. My heart slammed against my ribcage as tears welled and spilled down my cheeks. *She knew.* Everything blurred as I stumbled out of the building, a sob clawing its way through my throat. It was all wrong. None of the times her boyfriends slept with me had been consensual, but she was too doped out of her fucking mind to remember. Panic welled up as my breathing became labored, and I gasped for each breath, feeling as though the world was closing in around me.

Fuck. Winter's grasp seemed unyielding, and the cold air threatened to penetrate my clothing as I walked aimlessly. There was no way out. And a part of me knew that it was all I was good for. Even Rex wanted a taste, and it was only a matter of time before my mom's rehab treatment needed to be repaid. A feeling of worthlessness washed over me like a tide and it took everything to keep my knees from buckling in the snow. *I never even told her I was gay.* She just knew and used the words to stab at my heart. *I hated her even more.*

It twisted and warped like black tar bubbling from my throat before strangling me alive.

12

FACE TO FACE WITH DESTINY

ALEX MAY

"Fuck, you look like shit, man," Rex said, staring at the tears streaked on my face when he came to pick me up. "Was the session that bad?"

I didn't speak. Just rested my forehead against the window, watching the scenery go back. Rex's voice felt distant as the snow fell with an eerie silence, muffling the world around me and creating an unsettling disconnect from reality. I was trapped in a nightmarish dreamscape, where fear and desperation were my only companions. Rex pulled into the driveway and I got out before he could kill the engine, sprinting into the house and grabbing a bottle of whiskey from the cabinet. I took several large gulps before Rex was wrenching it out of my gasps, his face blazing with anger. "What the hell is wrong with you?" he spat, then slammed it against the granite countertops. "What the fuck happened? Jesus, talk to me, Alex. You look like hell—I—"

I claimed his mouth in a harsh kiss, shoving him so hard against the counter that he cried out. Taking advantage of his mouth opening, I slipped my tongue in, licking the seams of his mouth. Tasting him. Rex felt firm, yet smooth all at once. The taste of spiced whiskey danced on my tongue and scorched my throat. Rex's nostrils flared. His hands came up to cup my face, drawing me closer, fisting the baby hairs on the nape of my neck. Kissing me hard, he groaned low and deep in his throat, thrusting his tongue into my mouth and holding onto me in a white-knuckled grip. "Fuck!" He yanked off my lips, sucking air between his teeth. "What are you doing?"

"This is what you want, right?" I asked breathlessly, my palm massaging the bulge in the front part of his jeans. I tracked the way his large Adam's apple bobbed as he looked at me, conflicted.

"Alex—"

"How long have you wanted me?" I demanded, pressing up against him. Unzipping his winter jacket, I ran a hand over his firm chest, feeling the fabric of his clean and white cotton sweater. Rex's chest rose and fell rapidly, his face flushing when I leaned in closer. "Was bicurious your way of telling me you just wanted to fuck me?"

Rex gave a dry laugh, but it hitched when my thumb brushed his nipples. "Stop, Alex. You're obviously not okay. I don't want to take advantage of you."

"I'm pretty sure it's the other way around," I replied, my mouth curving upward.

Rex's hand shook as it came up to brush a few tendrils of hair away from my forehead. My hair was longer than before. Long enough for locks of reddish bronze to fall over my eyes. Leaning into him, I brushed my tall nose against his and licked his lips. "How long? Tell me. It makes my dick hard to know."

"Fuck," Rex moaned. "Since the day I saw you in junior year."

I laughed but felt nothing. "*That* long?"

"You have no fucking idea, I—" A heated red flush seared Rex's cheeks as he gazed into my eyes. "I've always wanted you."

"Then take me."

Rex growled in his throat, capturing my lips in a bruising kiss. Deepening the kiss, Rex's hands were all over me, clutching my waist before dipping down to squeeze my firm ass. He swiped his tongue into my mouth with skill and precision, mapping out the planes of my skin with his enormous hands.

Rex was a full head taller than me, so I had to roll on the balls of my feet to reach his mouth. His lips were chapped, but soft, slick, and faintly tasted of mine. A deep fog of his cologne wrapped around me, and I swallowed down the bile burning up my throat. My mind disconnected from my body, falling into a numbing void in which I resided. Breaking the kiss, I got onto my knees, working his belt buckle and zipper until his cock sprang free.

"Fuck—" Rex cried out, his other hand coming up to fist my hair. "Fuck. Alex—"

My vision swam as I took him into my mouth, down my throat like I did Evans a few weeks ago. Squeezing my eyes shut, I didn't look at him. I didn't relieve in the taste and feel of his thick cock head jamming at the base of my throat. My chest clenched with nausea. Sweat dripped down my brow and dampened my sweater. I felt myself jerk and retch, almost coughing up a lungful of precome, bitter bile, and whiskey.

I swallowed it down. My hands hooked onto his pants loops, dragging him closer. Rex was withering above me, thrusting his hips so that I was forced to take him deep. His hands drifted to my shoulders; meaty palms kneaded into the hard knot of tension along my shoulder blades.

I gasped and then my mouth was flooded with come. Rex shook. His entire body exploded with tremors as he erupted, wave after wave of milky coming all over my face and mouth. I drank every drop greedily, licking and sucking what I could, making sure to nuzzle him deeper.

"Alex," he chanted my name and went limp against the countertop. I stood on shaky legs, tucking him back into his pants and zipping them up. Rex's forehead was drenched in sweat, his mouth was pressed into a hard lard, and his touch on my hip was loose, tender. "Why..." He tried to catch his breath. "Why did you do that? Alex—"

"Because it was fun. Didn't you say we could have fun together?"

Not like this. His gaze spoke volumes, and I felt the stinging pain of his hand on my shoulder as if he were trying to bleed warmth into my frostbitten heart. Rex didn't speak. He cupped the back of my scalp, kissing down my neck as if I were the most precious thing to him in the whole world. *I let him.*

Let him peel off my winter jacket, and watch it land with a flop on the kitchen tile floor.

Let him kiss down my body, before pausing at my sharp hipbones, tonguing the skin there.

Let him open my jeans and zipper. My cock wasn't hard, but Rex worked me to fullness with a handful of expert strokes. Let him take me into his mouth, his moist cavern hot and blistering against my skin. It lasted for hours. Seconds. Then I was coming hard, gritting the shock waves of pleasure against my teeth. My knees threatened to buckle, and my lungs cinched tighter and tighter until I thought I might burst.

Rex drank it all down.

And I let him crawl back up my body, kiss me hard enough to taste my spend.

Taste the mistake that felt like a knife in my chest. Shirley was right, after all. *How many guys did you need to fuck to get me in here?* She'd asked.

Just one. I thought bitterly.

Just one.

***

"You still never told me what happened," Rex said, breaking the silence between us while we lay on his bed half-naked. My pants were still open, the cold making me shiver as I stared up at the ceiling. After we got each other off in the kitchen, Rex got hard again and we went up to his bedroom so that he could rut against my thigh. Come was pooling on the sheets, and my clothes felt like they were sticking to my skin.

"Nothing happened," I lied.

Rex turned onto his side and stroked my cheek. "You seemed upset when I picked you up…"

I pulled away from him and got up. "It doesn't matter. It's over now. I just need to figure out a way to get my car up and running, and then find a place to stay."

"You don't want to stay here?" Rex asked, perplexed.

My mouth curved into a smile. "Your parents will be back soon. Besides, I don't want to overstay my welcome."

Rex's throat moved. "I see … so what was all that earlier?"

"Having fun like you said," I replied, then inched off the bed, tucking my flaccid cock back into my jeans. I stood, wincing at the ache in my thighs from being held down.

"Oh." Rex didn't move, and I didn't care. This was what he wanted, after all. "Look, you don't have to—our friendship isn't transactional, Alex. I care if you're going through something. You can count on me."

For how long? Until you get bored of fucking me? I wanted to ask but swallowed the words back. I threw a smirk over my shoulder and winked at him, causing his face to flush. "I'm going to shower. I'll see you later."

"Later, man," Rex replied, and I shut the door with a click. The minute it closed my smile waned, and I strode my room and fell on my bed, my eyes still stinging with tears. Now I knew what my mother really thought about me, and I realized that maybe she was right. No wonder she took drugs and hated me so much. I ruined her life. I stole her boyfriends. Even though they'd never taken no for an answer. A laugh erupted from my throat. After all these years, of dealing with her abuse and neglect, even now I was still considered the bad guy. Witnessing her addiction's destructive power stirred a turbulent outrage within me, like a storm of emotions that I struggled to weather.

But there was nothing I could do about it.

Shirley hated me, and I had no choice but to let her.

***

YELLOW AND RED STREAMERS and confetti burst around me as the hockey game began. The Ice Panthers were up against the Michigan Wolverines. It promised to be an exciting game, but I couldn't afford to watch a single second of it. Engrossed in my cleaning duties, I moved around the arena, trying to remain invisible, paying no attention to the players or the cheers from the crowd. Some of the guys on the team noticed me and attempted to strike up conversations, but I brushed them off. I was burdened with shame, but I couldn't let their opinions affect me. My focus was on securing a stable future for my mom and myself.

The arena buzzed with energy as the game kicked off, and even Able, my supervisor, was caught up in the excitement, despite knowing that post-game cleanup would be a daunting task. I laughed at his enthusiasm, briefly savoring the warmth it offered. Still, my chest felt heavy, and I found myself scanning the stands for a familiar mop of yellow hair. Evans. He was the star of the night and likely attracted attention from scouts. Zara was probably in the crowd, proudly cheering him on. I genuinely felt happy for him. Yet, a part of me longed for that spotlight.

During halftime, I occupied myself by taking out the trash from the concession stands. The brisk wind tugged at my uniform as I discarded the bags into the dumpster. When I turned around, my heart froze.

Evans.

Fully geared up in his hockey uniform, including the jersey, shoulder pads, and knee pads. The only thing missing was his skates, which had been swapped for a well-worn pair of black Timberlands. My heart skipped a beat and my throat went dry. Each inhale of the crisp air stung my lungs as I drank in the sight of him. It had been weeks. Blond hair curled around his ears and forehead, nearly touching his shoulder. His gaze was as hard as a glacier's edge.

I swallowed around the blockage in my throat and forced a smile. "Evans. Good to see you. I must have missed a spot. Did you need me to take out the trash anywhere in the locker rooms?"

Evans' face twisted in annoyance and before I could blink, he was advancing towards me, his long legs eating up the distance between us. "Evans—you—"

"What the fuck, Alex?" Evans barked in my face. "You think you can disappear after weeks of ignoring me and start telling jokes?"

I stared back at him. "Who said I was joking? This is my job now. Or can't you read the label on my overalls?"

"Enough of this shit," Evans spat. "What the hell is going on? Why are you acting like this?"

"Like what?" I replied, but my irritation was rising. He was the only person who knew me, who could read through all my bullshit and see who I was. "Don't make trouble for me. I need this job."

Evans' eyes narrowed into pinpricks. "Why do you need this job? What happened to your apartment? Where the fuck is Shirley? You better tell me, or else the entire team will know what happened to you in seventh grade."

My smile dropped. "You wouldn't."

"Try me," Evans said, his blue eyes icy.

"Fuck you," I said, baring my teeth. "We aren't friends anymore. So, you can fuck off—"

"We're not friends? Then why are your hands trembling?" Evans stepped closer, his nose brushing against mine. "You know, I could forgive the fact that you gave me a half-ass blow job and then ran away—"

Half-assed? I made an indignant noise in the back of my throat.

"I can accept the fact that you don't want to be friends," Evans barreled on. "But what I can't fucking *stand* is you standing in front of me, homeless and brittle, while acting like you aren't scared out of your fucking mind. Like you aren't falling apart at the seams, Alex."

Each word was like a falling brick over my head. Pain exploded into my heart and I stared at him as if he'd doused me with cold water. Tears welled in my eyes before spilling over, and my knees nearly buckled. *Evans fucking knew. He knew it all.* Even before I said anything to him, he knew I had been evicted. Even when I tried to have Rex spin the story and make it seem like I was just a jackass to him and everyone else, Evans already knew.

"Don't," I snarled, but anguish nipped at my heels.

"Hockey. Mechanical Engineering. Christ, Alex, we were both set to graduate this year. Two semesters left and then we'd be gone," Evans breathed, his minty breath washing over my cheeks.

God, I wanted to let it all go. Fall into his arms and hug him tight. Beg him to take me away from this nightmare and I knew he would. Evans would leave this game if I asked him to, ruin his career for me and I couldn't allow that. "Go to hell. I don't want anything to do with you!" My voice shook. Each word came out battered and broken.

Evans' mouth tugged into a wry grin. "Hell would be too cold without you."

Fuck, my chest cracked open, agony juddered up my spine and more tears fell from my eyes. "Evans—you don't know what you're saying—what you're asking me to do—"

"I'm asking you to come home with me," Evans said, his hands coming around my bicep. Grounding me. My knees nearly gave out at the warmth bleeding from his palm. Blood roared in my ears and my heart slammed against my chest. Evans didn't have long, sooner or later the game would start and he needed to get back. I couldn't be the one to delay him. I couldn't be the one that made him lose his chance.

Forget me. I wanted to say, but I was just too fucking tired. *I loved him*. Desperately. I needed him so much right now, as the world was falling all around me. I couldn't continue to sleep with Rex. I didn't feel comfortable staying with him after everything had happened between us, but Evans had a girlfriend. He didn't need me around to destroy his life.

"Stay with me," Evans whispered, his voice urgent now. "Lean on me. Let me be your bridge across this raging river."

My knees buckled then, but he caught me and I fell into his arms and then his eyes. A sparkling, icy hue of the first frost on a clear winter's morning. *The Force is not a power you have. It's not about lifting rocks. It's the energy between all things, a tension, a balance, that binds the universe together.* Luke Skywalker once said. And I felt that now, the force that tied our hearts as one.

13

DOUBLE OVERTIME

EVANS MULRONEY

O pening my bedroom door, I tossed my gear to the side, next to my closet. Tearing off my jacket, I sighed as I dropped it into the growing dirty laundry pile. I cracked my neck and stretched before I got to work cleaning up some of the papers on the desk, ignoring the pounding of my heart as the door clicked shut behind me and Alex stood there, wringing his backpack between his hands. *Why wasn't he doing anything?* It unnerved me. Usually, by now, he would have made himself at home. Instead, he stood with his back pressed against the wooden door as if he planned to bolt. Turning to face him, I saw that his face was still tear-streaked, his long brown lashes trembling. Windswept hair, a captivating blend of red and bronze made my breath catch. Even in the dim lighting, it was like a fiery sunrise captured each strand.

"I can't stay here," he spoke, and my gaze dropped to those pink lips. I was imagining what it felt like to have them wrap around my cock. Fuck, what the hell was wrong with me? Alex was my best friend. I never thought about him sexually until a few weeks ago. "I have to get back—I need to—"

"Go where?" I gritted out, hands curling into a fist. I knew Alex. He was probably staying at some fucking shelter in the city. "Fuck, why didn't you just talk to me? Why didn't you just—"

"Because I don't need you to recuse me all the damn time, Evans," he spat back, and the hairs on my arm bristled. "I need to get my shit together without you."

Without you. Each word stabbed at my heart. Alex has never been without me. Those words seemed foreign. It didn't make sense. I couldn't be without him, but I understood where he was coming from. I had a lot of shit going on with the NHL draft coming up, and then with Zara.

Fuck, Zara. I completely forgot about her. A migraine loomed at the back of my head. "I understand, but this is different. We're like family. You should have told me. I want to help Alex." I stared back at him, watching the light dim in his eyes before they curved slightly.

"Family. Right." Alex's throat bobbed, and he ran a hand down his dirty gray overalls.

"Shut up and go shower," I said to him. "We can figure everything out later." I got the spare bedding from my closet that was reserved just for when he came over to sleep. I heard Alex's boots slap against the hardwood floor before the door to the bathroom slammed shut. Rearranging the bedding, I took my time to see if I stocked my mini fridge with snacks and checked our Call of Duty stats to make sure everything was just like how I left it. Alex would stay here for the foreseeable future, and I wanted to make sure he was comfortable.

I'd have to speak to the landlord. The possibility of him saying no was high and if he did, it meant that Alex and I would have to get our own place, which I didn't mind doing at all. We'd talk about it for so many years. It was just I couldn't put up with Shirley and Alex was adamant about not leaving her.

But if she was in rehab, then for the time being, we could get a place together. Steam from the bathroom flittered from beneath the door, and I turned on the TV to watch a few of the game highlights, snuggling down into the blankets. Ten minutes later, Alex came out of the shower wearing nothing but one of my towels and my throat instantly went dry. His skin was lick, wiry with muscles and his pink lips pulled into a sly smirk, his foxlike eyes were hooded and the color of rich autumn leaves that made me feel like I was being yanked under.

"Do you have anything I can wear? Or did you want me to stand here all night naked?" Alex asked, brow raised.

"Maybe that's exactly what I want," I told him, then grabbed a fresh pair of sweats and some underwear, handing them to him. I made sure my lips were close to his ear. "That blow job you gave *was* half-assed."

"Fuck you," Alex whispered, but his cheeks blazed.

"Yeah," I responded, staring deep into his eyes. "Wouldn't you?"

Pain flickered over Alex's face and he turned away, fleeing back into the bathroom to change. I knew what I said wasn't exactly fair, but he needed to know that I was onto him. I didn't want to dance around this subject anymore. We were both adults. Alex sucked me off without warning after being my best friend for over twenty years. *Something was going on with him.* How long was he feeling this way? Why didn't he tell me he was gay? I flopped back on the bed and then the door opened again and Alex came out in a pair of my sweat pants that hung low on his narrow hips. My cock twitched, taking in his lithe but strong muscular build. He was nowhere near my size or bulk, but his body was sensual. His v-cut abs jutted from my tight white beater as he stalked forward.

Alex stood in front of me, but there was a strange anguish in his gaze. "I'm sorry. You're with Zara and I shouldn't have—"

"Shut up," I said, then my hands came to rest on his hips. Alex took a stuttering breath when my thumb brushed against his v-cut. "I wanted it. You knew I wanted it."

Alex's throat dry clicked. "That still doesn't make it right."

No. It doesn't. It was so fucking beyond shitty. Especially to Zara who had no clue. What does it mean? Am I gay? I thought about Jayden and Grayson and how seeing them together turned me on, but not in the way that seeing a naked woman did. My dick was hard, sure. *But my heart ached.* It yearned for Alex. "I don't understand these feelings, Alex," I said, my voice rough. "A few weeks ago, I was sure Zara would be it for me, and now..."

"She still could be," Alex reasoned. "What happened between us doesn't need to change anything. I'll still be your friend. We can still talk."

"What language are you speaking? Cause it sounds like bullshit," I muttered to him. "Zara and I broke up."

Alex stilled. "What?"

"I told her what happened," I replied, staring up at him. Then I encircled my arms around his waist and nuzzled my face into his stomach. "Alex. How long have you been feeling this way? Why didn't you tell me?"

"I couldn't," Alex responded, then gently pulled out my arms. He walked around my king-size bed and got into the covers, turning his back to me. Annoyance flared in my chest. I hated when Alex avoided the conversation, but then again, it was late and I had class tomorrow. Turning off the lights, I got into bed, but instead of facing away from him, I grabbed Alex by the waist and hauled him against my chest. Alex yelped, his arms flailing, before I clamped my arms around him and held him close.

"*Evans*—what are you doing?"

"Sleeping."

Alex gave a throaty laugh but didn't pull away. "Fine, but if your dick touches me, I can't be responsible for what happens next."

"Don't tempt me," I replied, taking in his cool scent. Desperation clawed at my chest. I hated being away from him. It felt like a hole had been punched through me. Alex left without saying a word, leaving me to panic for weeks, wondering about his safety. I needed to know what caused it. Even though I could guess, I still needed to know. "What happened? Tell me."

"I fucked up."

"How?"

Alex sighed. "I lost my job. Then things started piling up. School. Hockey. I couldn't handle it and Shirley was ... well fucking Shirley. We were already a few months behind the rent, so missing one more was just the icing on the cake. They kicked us out."

The injustice of life weighed on me like a leaden cloak, suffocating my every thought, and anger festered deep within my core. "Why didn't you tell me? I could have helped with the rent—"

"You've been paying the rent for the past six months," Alex snarled, his teeth bared. "Did you think I wouldn't notice? The only reason we got evicted is because I told him to start taking it out of my account."

The alarm shot through me like a bullet. "Alex—"

"I don't need your charity, Evans," Alex said, squirming in my arms. "I don't want it. You're about to go fucking pro. In a few months, everyone's eyes will be on you. I couldn't stomach it if your chance got taken away because of my crack addict mother."

My heart slammed against my ribcage. *He was right.* Once the draft happened, the media would be all over me like flies to shit. My dad was finding me a PR agent and once it hit that I was going pro, that meant everything would change. I could no longer do the things that I loved.

I would become a public figure. "That won't happen," I said, but my voice felt weak.

"You don't know that," Alex responded, his voice fierce. "The media, they dig for this shit. Any kind of dirt they can pin on their players."

"So, what are you trying to say?" I said, and my throat constricted. *What the fuck was he getting at?* Just because he had so many problems, we couldn't be friends anymore? That he would leave me again because of that? The mere thought of Alex leaving sent waves of apprehension crashing over me. Alex went quiet and my pulse throbbed as I waited for bated breath for what he was going to say next.

"I don't know ... I just think for now it's better if I keep my distance."

"No," I snarled, holding him closer. "I don't give a shit about that stuff Alex—"

"Well, I do. How many times have we talked about making it? Now it's finally happened. I don't want to be the reason everything goes to hell. I've had enough of that in my life."

Fuck that. Alex wasn't going anywhere. An icy grip clutched at my heart as the thought of Alex walking away consumed my mind, leaving me paralyzed with the fear of abandonment. We lapsed into silence, and then his breath evened out. I lay awake for several moments before my eyes started to droop and sleep beckoned me.

***

SUNLIGHT GENTLY FILTERED through the window, rousing me from slumber with a contented groan. Outside, delicate snowflakes danced in the morning light, and I relished the warmth of having Alex by my side. His hair resembled a fiery bronze halo, and his pale skin shimmered, making me wonder what it might be like to kiss those luscious, cherry-red lips.

There was a palpable shift in the air between us; an unspoken understanding that we were teetering on the edge of something more than friendship. Alex's desires were clear, and my heart soared with the possibilities, but I couldn't disregard the concerns he had expressed yesterday. He was right. With the spotlight of the media on me, I needed to ensure I had a clean record before venturing into the NHL.

Brown eyes peeled open, and my breath hitched as I peered into a polished amber, almost like the first rays of dawn. "Morning," Alex croaked, his breath raspy.

"Morning," I replied, inching closer. "How did you sleep?"

"Good. Better."

I cupped his cheek, leaning closer to him. I wanted to kiss his lips. Taste his skin and my cock throbbed in my sleep pants. Alex was moving closer too, his hand gripping my bicep hard as if he were restraining himself from lurching forward. We have never kissed before. Not even after his lips were around my cock. It was uncharted territory, and I was just about to seal my mouth over his when a piercing blare interrupted us. Alex winced, and I laughed, pulling away. "Sorry," Alex said, then reached over to the night table to check his phone. "Shit." He shot out of bed and hurried to put a sweater on. "Shit."

"What happened?" I asked, sitting up.

"Fuck I forgot about—" His mouth slammed shut, and he hurried to get dressed. "Look, I need a ride or let me borrow your car."

"Let me come with you," I said. "My class doesn't start until noon."

Alex ran a hand through his hair, his mouth pulled into a hard line. We hurried to dress and ran out the door. A crisp wind slapped against my cheeks as we jumped into my truck, and I turned on the heat, waiting for the car to warm up and for Alex to tell me where we were going. Alex took out his phone and punched in an address in the GPS. I recognized the address immediately, and I frowned. "Rex? What the hell? Is that who you've been staying with?"

Alex avoided eye contact with me and nodded. Jealousy seared through my veins like molten lava, scalding my insides with an irrational, all-consuming heat. "What the fuck Alex? You went to him and not me—"

"He was the easier choice," Alex muttered, keeping his head low. What the hell was that supposed to mean? Why didn't he just tell me what was happening? I would have helped. Rage burned through me, but I didn't want to argue, so I revved my engine and tore out of the driveway. I gripped the steering wheel, my knuckles white as I raced through the city streets. The engine roared in sync with the turmoil in my chest, every sound of the car's powerful heart mirroring the anger that consumed me.

My mind raced with images of Alex and Rex together, their laughter echoing in my head like a taunting soundtrack to my pain. *What did he have that I didn't? Why did it have to be him?* During junior year, Rex and Alex had become close after Rex got into a car accident that claimed the life of a child. If Alex wasn't with me, he'd most likely be with Rex but something about him always rubbed me the wrong way, and still to this day I couldn't pinpoint it.

I pressed the gas pedal harder, urging the car to go faster, to carry me away from the tormenting thoughts. The city lights streaked past, blurring into a sea of colors, much like the whirlwind of emotions inside me. Nothing was making sense. I thought Rex implied they had a falling out. Or did he just say that shit so that I wouldn't ask any more questions? A cold realization washed over me, and I shot my gaze at

Alex, only to see him shrinking in the seat next to me. They planned this. To keep me in the dark, while Alex stayed with Rex and tried to piece together his life. *Why?* Pain stabbed at my chest, and I couldn't understand why he wanted to cut me out so badly. *What did I do?*

"So, what Rex said about you screwing him over on the assignment, was all of that bullshit?"

Alex didn't respond. Gritting my teeth, I bit back the fury rising in my throat. We reached Rex's house and pulled into the sprawling driveway of his mansion. I had been here a couple of times for a few parties he had. Alex got out first and I followed, shoving my hands deep into my pockets while he used a key to open the door. *Since when did he have a fucking key?*

"Rex?" Alex called out, toeing off his timberland boots and walking into the foyer.

"Where have you been? I came to the rink to pick you up, and they said you left with—" Rex's words died in his throat as he rounded the corner and saw me standing there. "Shit."

"Yeah. Shit," I said through clenched teeth. *What the fuck?* Rex knew I was so worried about Alex that I even wanted to go to the police and file a missing person's report. The bastard let me do it, knowing Alex was safe and sound. *Was this just a joke to him? Or did Alex not want me to know anything?*

Rex fiddled with his grey sweater. "Sorry, man. Alex, ugh—can we talk?"

Alex nodded and Rex led him into the kitchen, while I strolled around the living room, taking in the plush furniture and bay panel windows. I tried to keep my gaze from wandering to the kitchen, but I wanted to hear what they were saying to each other so I inched a little closer, pretending to be examining the family photos on the wall.

"What happened last night? I was so worried," Rex whispered, but his hand rested on Alex's elbow. "Why did you leave like that? I thought—" He cut himself off. "Did something happen?"

"Yes. Evans came to the rink ... look, I'm going to be staying with him for the time being. I can't thank you enough for getting my mom into rehab, but I don't think I can take advantage of your hospitality anymore."

Damn, Alex always knew to hit people where it hurt, and even though I didn't like Rex, I knew what he must be feeling right now. It was the same way I felt. Betrayal. Hot and scathing, like touching the stem of roses, not realizing you had been pricked until a blistering red haze filled your vision.

14

A NIGHT IN THE PENALTY BOX

EVANS MULRONEY

R ex stared at him as if he'd been slapped. "Take advantage? I have six rooms in this house. You're more than welcome to stay."

"I can't," Alex replied. "I still have to get my car fixed and ... my life is a mess, Rex. I just want to get back on my feet again. You understand right?"

"Is this about the other night?" Rex lowered his voice. "I'm sorry. If I did something wrong..."

Alex's mouth pulled into a rueful smile. "You didn't. I'm just not in a good place."

Rex looked unsure, but there wasn't any more he could say. He nodded and they went upstairs to pack the rest of his stuff. I lingered in the living room, trying to make sense of what I just heard. Did something happen between them? The thought made bile rise in my throat, but who the hell was I to get jealous? Alex wasn't mine. I had no right to feel this way, especially since after Alex got me off in the sauna, I slept with Zara shortly after. *Fuck Zara!* Pulling out my phone, I saw that I had several missed calls and two text messages from her.

Hey, didn't see you after the game but call me when you get home. We need to talk. She texted last night.

Hey, call me, please. I think we should take a test in a few days. A pregnancy test. A wave of dizziness washed over me, and I swallowed around the knot growing in my throat. *This was happening.* I made it to the NHL but all of it would be blown to pieces if I was about to become a father.

Alex and Rex came down the stairs with his stuff, and they loaded everything into the back of my truck. I jumped in the car, ignoring Rex completely, but watching them say goodbye through my rearview mirror. Rex said something, causing Alex to laugh before he pulled Alex into a tight hug. Damn, Rex was a beast towering over Alex, and I nearly growled when the hug lasted longer than necessary. Rex's thumb brushed Alex's lips causing me to see red, and then he walked away, his hands shoved into his pockets as he fought off the bitter high winds. *Bastard.*

Alex got in and I sped out of the driveway. "I'm sorry," Alex spoke. "I was a coward. I just ... you deserve this chance, Evans. I don't want to do anything to jeopardize it."

So, you fucking lied? Cut me out of your life? Fabricated a story to make it seem like you were a jackass so I couldn't ask questions? That would have been fine, fucking dandy if I didn't need him so badly. Zara might be pregnant. I might be a father and all I wanted to do was confide in my best friend and tell him what the hell I was going through. Each breath I took felt like inhaling shards of ice, my lungs burning with a bitter cold that mirrored the icy resentment in my heart. But there was nothing left to say. What's done is done. I said nothing as we made the trek back to my frat house. The minute we stepped inside, I started packing up my textbooks for school, feeling Alex's eyes burning a hole in the back of my head. "I need to go to class," I said, stuffing my books inside my backpack. "You can take my truck to work and I can walk back home. The campus isn't far. Just text me when you get home."

"Evans—"

"The fridge is fully stocked. You can use my credit card to order food or something. I should be done around six."

"I'm sorry," Alex said, his brown eyes singed my flesh.

I barked a laugh. "You're not sorry."

Alex twiddled his thumbs. "No, but I'm sorry you found out this way. I was trying to do the right thing. I hope you can understand that. I thought you'd be better without me."

Fury burst through my chest. The intensity of it felt like the biting winds of a blizzard, sharp and unforgiving, cutting through any semblance of calm like a relentless snowstorm. I slammed my backpack against the ground causing Alex to jump. "For who? God, Alex you—you sucked me off in a sauna causing me to question my sexuality! Then you tell me you don't want me to be friends anymore, all the while staying with someone who I thought hated you? I've been going through hell worried sick about you. Did you ever stop and think about how I felt? Or what the hell was happening to me? You're best my friend. How could you treat me like this?"

Alex flinched as if each word had struck him like a dagger. "Evans…"

"Zara might be pregnant," the words burst from my throat and I shouldered past him. "That's how the fuck I've been without you."

***

I STORMED INTO MY CLASS, my heart pounding, and finally took my usual seat near the front. Zara followed shortly after; her eyes filled with concern. I shook my head to reassure her as she settled into the seat next to me. Before I could ask if everything was okay, the professor entered the room, and our law studies began. I forced myself to focus, diligently taking notes and preparing for the upcoming exams. I knew that law school was still an option for me, even if I went pro, but my decision depended on which team drafted me.

During the lecture, Zara gently touched my arm and gave me a sweet smile. "Can we talk?" she mouthed, and I nodded. After class, I followed her to the cafeteria, ignoring the playful jeers and hollers from our other friends. We found a secluded spot to speak.

"How are you feeling?" I asked, trying to be considerate. I knew that nausea was a common pregnancy symptom, and I wanted to make sure she was okay. Was she feeling sick right now? Should I be feeding her crackers? Crap. "What can I get you? Ginger? I heard ginger is good for nausea—"

She laughed. "I'm fine, besides it's too early to tell. I think after we take the test, then we'll know. I might just be late for my period."

Right. "So, what did you want to talk about?"

"Harpreet," Zara said, tucking a stray hair behind her ears. "I told him we broke it off, and he wasn't happy about it. I don't think he'll bother you, but just don't be surprised if he does."

Harpreet? Shit. I scrubbed a hand over my face. We were friends, and I knew he'd been pissed about me just dumping his baby sister. "I'll talk to him."

"You don't have to," Zara laughed. "He's just being an ass. We hadn't even been together that long, and he was acting like we were going to get married already. He had my wedding saree planned out and everything."

I laughed at that, and her hand found mine. "I'm scared, Evans," she said, swallowing. "I've always wanted to be a lawyer and I can't—I don't know what I'll do if it's positive. I—I'm sorry, but I don't know if I could keep it."

The world fell away from my feet. I knew she was being honest and that it was her choice, but the thought of her terminating the pregnancy made my stomach swoop. It was what was easier. For both of us. We weren't going to be together, and although I would be with Zara no matter what, I wouldn't be her boyfriend or provide the comfort only a partner could.

"Just—think about it. Promise me?"

Zara ducked her head, biting her lower lip, and nodded. "I will. I promise."

It was the most I could ask for. It was Zara's choice, but I wanted to let her know that she wasn't alone in making it. Zara cleared her throat, wiping a few stray tears, and got out her law textbook. "Help me with the homework? I'm stuck on question twenty-four."

"Of course." I forced a smile and together we got to work.

***

A COLD WIND SEEPED into the folds of my jacket as I walked back to the frat house. The streets were dark and quiet as nighttime descended over the area. I thought about Zara and everything she said. I wasn't exactly sure what I was feeling, but I felt raw. My chest ached. Too much had happened in such a short amount of time. A part of me wanted to go home and fall into my mother's embrace. Striding inside the house, I saw that my bedroom light was on. I opened the door and noticed Alex standing there in grey sweatpants and a tight red t-shirt that stretched across his chest.

"Hey," he whispered, a smile tugging on his lips.

"Hey," I said, my voice gruff as I peeled off my jacket and threw my stuff into my closet. A tantalizing scent coming from the table made my stomach growl, and I stepped closer, my eyes taking in the dinner Alex had prepared for us. Two very large roasted beef sandwiches lay before me, topped with mustard, mayo, and ketchup. The warm, golden-brown bun cradled slices of perfectly cooked beef, its savory aroma filling the air and making my mouth water. Crisp lettuce, ripe tomatoes, and red onions added freshness and crunch to the sandwich. There was also a selection of cheeses, each one a melting promise of creamy indulgence. Beside it were two sad "I'm sorry s'mores". The graham crackers were perfectly toasted, topped with gooey marshmallows, and squares of rich chocolate. "Do you think you can buy me with food?" I asked, brows raised.

"Yes," Alex replied. "You're a slut for a good meal. We both know it."

I laughed at that. He wasn't wrong.

"But..." Alex continued. "I am sorry. I mean it. And to prove it to you..." He grabbed the remote and pressed play. The Star Wars theme song filled the room and I burst out laughing at his wiggling brows. "How about some Return of the Jedi?"

"You had me at hello." I nudged his arm, and together we sat down on the floor with napkins and the sandwich between us while the movie played. I loved Star Wars. Ever since I was a kid it was one of the movies I replayed over and over again until I had every word memorized. Alex was sick to death of watching it, and all I could was laugh at his sour expression. "It can't be that bad."

Alex let out a playful groan. "Man, watching this so many times should be considered a form of torture. I mean, how many times can we witness the same plot holes and cheesy lines?"

"It's a classic, even with its quirks. Besides, it's our tradition. Can't break it now."

Alex smirked and took a bite of his sandwich. "True, I can't argue with that. May the Force be with us through these billion more viewings."

"Whatever," I muttered. "The movies are a masterpiece. You're just jealous."

Alex threw his head back and laughed. "Bro, you know Luke could've just Force-pulled the lightsaber out of the Rancor's hand in Jabba's palace."

I chuckled and took a bite of my sandwich. "Yeah, but where's the drama in that? It's more exciting when he gets to wrestle the giant monster."

"That's not even the worst of it. And what's with the Ewoks taking down the Empire? Little teddy bears with sticks somehow defeat the Galactic Empire's finest troops. Classic."

I laughed. "And the Emperor, he's just sitting there, watching it all unfold. No backup plan, nothing."

"Dude was chilling like a villain, but then he's shooting lightning from his fingertips, but Vader just throws him down a pit, and that's it. The galactic emperor was defeated. No plan as to what's going to happen next, or who takes over what? Then Luke fucks off to nowhere and the war is just done? Come on, you have to admit that could have been done better."

"Nope. The emperor shooting lightning from his fingertips was badass as shit. That scene always gets me, not to mention Luke's epic battle between good and evil, following in his father's footsteps or breaking away and becoming his own man, that was epic bro. Always will be in my books."

Alex scoffed, but he ate his food and watched the movie. It was epic. The movie went on and I found myself enthralled with the universe once more. Rebellion plots. Imperial starships. These were all the things I loved from my childhood.

"Obi-Wan once thought as you do. You don't know the power of the dark side. I must obey my master."

My mouth pulled into a smirk and I turned to look at Alex, only to see he was stiff beside me, his face pale.

"Search your feelings, father. You can't do this. I feel the conflict within you! Let go of your hate!" Luke Skywalker begged.

"It is... too late for me, son. The emperor will show you the true nature of the Force. He is your master now."

"Then my father is truly dead."

Tears brimmed Alex's eyes, and he turned his face away. I knew the last line would hit close to home. It always did when we sat down to watch this movie. Alex told me once he felt his mother was drawn to the dark side and as a child, he did all he could to bring her back to the light. Credits rolled on the screen as the movie ended. I yawned and stretched my legs out in front of me, checking the time.

Alex cleaned up the mess. He'd gone uncharacteristically quiet during the movie and I watched him move about the room for several moments. The sweatpants he wore hung low, his ass looked plump and round, and his thighs muscular. I imagined what it would be like to have him under me, my hands mapping out his skin. He was my oldest friend and yet a fire burned in my core.

Heat pooled, low and deep, stiffening my cock and before I could think better of it, I stood and walked over to him, pressing my chest against his firm back, his ass flush against my cock.

"Evans..."

"I want—" I swallowed around the knot forming in my throat, mouth brushing against his earlobe. "What's happening between us, Alex?"

"Nothing."

The word stabbed at my chest, and bitterness threatened to consume me. "Alex—"

"Nothing can happen between us," he said, turning to face me. "Like you said, Zara might be—" His Adam's apple bobbed. "Fuck, is she pregnant? Why didn't you tell me?"

"I would've if I could find you," I snapped at him and then forced myself to calm down. "We don't know yet. She wants to take a test in a few days."

"Fuck," Alex hissed.

"Yeah." I didn't want to tell him how badly I fucked up. How I slept with her after he sucked me off because I had been so confused. All my life, I thought I was straight. I never questioned it and now all these emotions were rushing through me, and Zara said she was on the pill, but shit happened. I was a dumbass. "It doesn't change how I feel about you."

Alex stared at me incredulously. "How do you feel about *me*?" he spat the words at me. "You just got drafted to the NHL. You might become a father and you're still worried about me?"

I felt a spark of irritation. "Why is that so hard to understand?"

"Evans, look at me. I'm a mess," Alex said, then choked on a sob. "My mother hates me for trying to get her clean. I have nowhere to live. I—I can barely think because I've wanted you for so long. I've loved you for so long and I—everything is fucked!"

Loved me for so long? How long? I wanted to demand. I wanted to know everything he was thinking and feeling. Kateryna said maybe Alex had feelings for me for a long time and now he confirmed it.

Alex loved me. Probably since we were kids. I grabbed the back of his neck and hauled him into a bruising kiss. Alex made a noise in the back of his throat as I slammed him against the wall, the force of it rattling my bones and causing him to cry out. Gripping his waist, I barreled forward, no longer able to control myself as I rutted against him, clawing at his shirt as I kissed him with everything in me.

Brazen fire licked down my spine. Alex grunted, kissing me back with equal intensity. The room swam with heat as I slipped my tongue into his mouth. Alex groaned, canting his hips, his voice like a scalpel cutting open my chest. I kept him pinned, knocking his knees open so that I could slide between the space there, I thrust my hips and felt his cock harden in his sweatpants.

Fuck, Alex feels amazing against me. Firm muscles, taut and tender flesh as I ripped and swallowed each moan from his throat. Alex shivered in my arms before he fisted the fabric of my shirt. Tears burned down his cheeks as he jerked his hips, chasing his release. I tasted the s'mores on his tongue, the gooey marshmallows, and savored the warmth and laughter falling from his lips as I spun us around and pushed him onto the bed. Alex bounced before I crawled over him, far too impatient to get him out of his clothes. I'd seen him naked a dozen times, but this was different. My chest expanded to the point of pain, my lungs cinched as I kissed him harder and deeper, pressing him into the mattress. Alex shuddered, a whine escaping from his lips as he gasped for air. It was a flurry of arms and limbs. A frenzy of molten heat that felt desperate and aching.

I broke the kiss, my pulse throbbing, and stared down at him, wishing to keep this moment in my memory forever. "Alex," I rasped, seeing the color rise to his cheeks.

"Don't talk. I'm done talking," Alex whispered, his eyes shining with more than just tears. "Make love to me, Evans. I need you."

Sweat dripped down his temple, and his bronze hair was the color of embers. It struck me then that Alex was like brazen fire. Memorizing and hypnotic from far away, but once I got too close, I'd be singed alive. A dazzling display of beauty and destruction.

That would soon turn everything to ash.

15

ALL-STAR ALLURE

ALEX MAY

Evans' eyes drew me in like a whirlpool, and I helplessly surrendered to the captivating waves of their oceanic allure. I shivered against him, my hands braced against his massive shoulders, his bulk pressing me down further into his delicious heat. Evans licked his dry lips and turned his face away, red blossoming across his cheeks. "I don't know how."

My brain short-circuited. What? I stared at him incredulously before I felt my face warm. Oh. He'd never done anal sex, and neither had I. Well, shit. "I've seen some videos…" I said, avoiding his probing gaze. "It doesn't look that complicated."

Evans rested his elbows by my face and nipped at my cheek. "I don't want to hurt you…"

"You won't," I said, breathless from the heat between us. "Please. I need you."

Evans growled and then reached into his night table, pulling out a pack of condoms and some virgin coconut oil. I burst out laughing when I saw it. "Why do you have virgin coconut oil?"

"It's for my hands, okay? I like the way it makes my skin feel soft as a baby," Evans replied, then sealed his lips over mine. "Besides, you love my baby soft hands. Don't lie. We both know you get off on that shit."

"You caught me. Why are you even studying to become a lawyer? You should become a detective instead," I deadpanned.

Evans' laugh was belly deep and then he kissed me harder, his dick swelling in his jeans. I moaned and took in a shaky breath when his hand slid up my thigh, giving me a gentle squeeze. "Don't worry, I'll finger fuck you good with my baby soft fingers."

"Please stop talking about babies," I said, then gasped when his hand wrapped around my cock, which was thickening in my sweatpants. Evans gave a firm stroke as he kissed me, licking into the seams of my mouth before his other hand flew to my throat, pinning me there. Evans groaned, rolling his hips hard enough for our cocks to brush as a spark ignited through me. "Evans," I cried out.

Evans grunted, stroking me in time with his hips. Pleasure licked down my spine, curling hot and low in my belly. Fuck, I was close. Evans' hands grabbed the base of my shirt before he pulled it off, and I did the same time. While he worked on his jeans, I peeled off my sweatpants, exposing myself to my best friend. We chuckled when his pants got caught and he had to kick it off, before he crawled over me again and kissed me deeper.

"Fuck, you're beautiful Alex," he whispers against my lips, before claiming my mouth again. I couldn't breathe. I couldn't see anything that wasn't Evans. Desire roiled through me, and I ran my palms over his massive chest, taking in his pecs and biceps that rippled beneath my touch. Evans' skin was fair and sun-kissed. His mop of blond curls fell over his brow. Swallowing around the knot in my throat, the words 'I love you' got stuck there. It was way too soon, and so many things could go wrong. I was better off just enjoying this moment for what it was and never wishing for more. Tucking a stray lock of hair behind his ears, I stared into his mesmerizing shade of cobalt blues and found myself effortlessly swept away by the currents. I felt like a rock battered at sea, trying to cling to the s only to be swept under.

Evans' cock was hard and aching, flushed an angry red as it ruts against my thigh, leaking precum down the slit. Reaching for the coconut oil, Evans spread some over his fingers before running them along the seams of my thigh. He paused then, his throat bobbing before he leaned down and kissed and bit at my collarbone. I'd never felt this way before. Tears stung my eyes, but I held it together for him as his finger pressed against the crack of my ass before pressing in.

It was strange. Wet. The coconut oil made everything slippery, and I wasn't sure what I was supposed to be doing with my hands. I claimed his lips, trying to distract myself from the doubt building up inside me before his fingers brushed a bundle of nerves that forced me to wrench away from the kiss with a shout.

"Fuck!" I hissed, pleasure rippled through me and it felt like tiny bubbles on my skin.

Evans' cocked a brown and gave a wicked smile. Now I knew I was done for. Evans laughed then went back to kissing me with a savagery I'd never known, his fingers thrusting in and out so hard and fast my gaze nearly went white. Evans growled, hooking his arm under my knees and spreading my legs wider. "Fuck—Evans—" I cried out, now on full display for him. I stared down at my flushed cock. The head was leaking while Evans had his fingers knuckle deep in my ass. Evans' mouth dragged into a smirk and then his fingers curled. "Fuck—shit!" I nearly screamed. Blistering sparks of pleasure wracked through me, my back bowed and my vision fractured as he kept hitting that spot. "Baby—I'm gonna come—" I grasped, feeling my balls draw taut, ready to burst, but then he pulled out, laughing.

I wanted to sob at the emptiness and I shot him a dirty look, but Evans pinched my cheeks, then reached down to the condom and rolled it onto his dick. My lungs cinched as his length disappeared beneath the latex. His girth was wide and thick, impressive. And the thought of all of that going inside me made my throat dry. Evans positioned himself between my legs. Hitching my thigh over his hip, he stared deep into my eyes. "There's no going back after this," he breathed against my lips. "You've ruined me for anyone else. I was a virgin gay before you corrupted me."

I laughed, but something inside my chest cracked open. Our hands found each other's beneath the covers and my throat constricted when he kissed me slowly on the lips. *I love you.* But I didn't dare speak the words. Evans splayed his hands over my sharp hips, holding on for purchase before he grabbed the base of his cock and pressed the head against my gaping hole. I grunted when he pushed through the first ring of muscle, pain flared through my spine like a dagger and I gritted my teeth against it before he finally bottomed out. "Fuck," I whispered, feeling a throb start low before thrumming through me.

Evans groaned. "Fuck, you're so tight. Are you okay? Did I hurt you?"

Tears burned my eyes, but I shook my head, and Evans touched my cheeks, his fingers coming away wet. "Shit, Alex—should we stop? Does it hurt too much?"

"Don't you dare," I snarled. "Just—fucking move, alright?"

Evans nodded and began with a slow, methodical thrust. My breath hitched; the world spun as pain gave way to pleasure, as he fucked into me. I arched my back, moaning when his hand slithered down my body and grasped my cock. "Fuck—Evans—" I jerked while he drove his hips in time with his thrusts. Sliding his massive palm over my length and down the sensitive head, I cried out. A burst of pleasure shot through me like I'd touched a live wire.

Evans cursed and my cock twitched, dribbling precum down the long length. His thrusts were short and quick, shallow at first before he built up a brutal pace. Then he was fucking me hard into the mattress. The headboard slammed against the wall, and the legs screeched against the wooden floors in protest as he drove his hips deep. A scream clawed its way up my throat, but it was swallowed by his mouth on mine. Evans growled, ravishing me. Drowning us in the taste of each other. His tongue. His breath in my lungs and mine in his. *Fuck.* I spread my legs wider and hooked them to cover his hips, digging my heels into his ass to drive him closer. Desire lanced down my spine, making my toes curl as heat pooled like molten lava in my belly. A strangled cry tore from my lips, as milky white spurts of come erupted all over his stomach. Golden lightning forked and split across my vision. My back arched, and I felt his hips stutter as he came deep within me.

"Alex—fuck—" Evans snarled before he collapsed on top of me, crushing me with his weight. Blood roared in my ears, my cock was still twitching and sputtering come, and a shiver rolled through me. I closed my eyes, feeling the pain pulsing there like red-hot needles. Evans kissed my cheek, my tingling lips before he pulled his cock free. I let out a strangled whimper as he pulled out of me, my asshole spasming and raw. "I'll clean us up," he said, then headed to the bathroom to grab a washcloth to wipe me down. Once he was done, he settled beside me and brought me into his arms. "How are you? Are you hurt anywhere?"

My mouth dragged into a smile. "Yes, my ass stings like a motherfucker but I'm..." My breath caught. "I'm good. Thank you."

"Only you would thank someone for fucking you," Evans responded, kissing my temple. "I finally swiped your Gay V-card, I should get more than a thanks."

"Greedy fuck." I tried to shove him off, but he brought me back. "What more could you possibly want?"

"Your heart," Evans' voice turned serious.

Heat flared across my cheeks and I felt like I couldn't breathe. "What? Evans?"

"I love you," Evans responded. "If you couldn't tell. This isn't a game to me, Alex. Or some fucked up experiment. I want you. I love you."

My throat closed like a straw, sucking in too much air. *What could I say? I wanted the same thing, but it was too complicated. What about Zara? What about the NHL?* He was about to become a pro athlete. All eyes would be on him. *How could he even consider someone like me?* Fear mounted with each breath, and I couldn't bear to see the hurt in his eyes when I told him it wouldn't work and that he should leave me, but then I realized that wasn't what I wanted.

I wanted Evans.

I loved him too. He had all of me. Why was I trying to fight it? *You must unlearn what you have learned.* Yoda once said. All my life my mom had taught me I was worthless and never meant to have love, but Evans had seen my worth since I was three. He'd always seen the best in me.

"I love you too," I said, the tears brimming in my eyes before finally spilling over. "Fuck I love you, Evans." His mouth claimed mine in a brutal kiss, and I shuddered into the kiss, wishing I could stitch our souls into one. So much was happening around us, but I knew we'd get through it together.

***

WE MADE LOVE DEEP into the night. And the next night. *And the next night.* We were fucking so much that I considered quitting my job so that I could be home just to have Evans bend me over whenever he saw fit. Eventually, we had to peel away from each other and get back to our daily lives. A few days later, I was hit by the scent of freshly cut ice as I entered the rink, mingling with the tang of leather equipment and the sharp, invigorating aroma of cold air. Resting my hands on the boards, I watched the guys on the team run scrimmage. *Evans was like a god.* Vaulting down the rink, his skates slicing through the ice like a knife through butter. He intercepted a shot from Chris before going straight for the goal. It was a tough game, and I longed to be with them. My hands itched for my stick, but those days were long gone. I couldn't go back to the team, Coach had made it clear after I dropped out.

Besides that, they were all graduating soon and none of the sponsors were interested in a half-ass player who barely showed up for practice, but Evans was different. Tearing off his helmet, Evans' blond curls were sleek with sweat, glistening in the light as he laughed at what one of the guys said. He spotted me and waved, skating down the rink. Those powerful thighs made my head spin at how sexy he looked.

"Hey!" Evans said breathlessly as he nearly crashed into me, his face flushed with heat and exhilaration as he leaned over and kissed me firmly on the lips. "They're all going over for drinks later. You down?"

It was time I faced them. Ever since I dropped out of school, I had been avoiding the team, but they were like family, and it made my chest ache. "Sure."

"Fuck, you look sexy," Evans laughed, kissing me again. "I'm tempted to say screw the drinks. We can just go home and have our own fun."

"Don't you have that game coming up?" I chuckled. "Nah, it's just a few hours, and then we can leave. Besides, I want to talk to the guys again."

"They've been asking for you, especially Grayson," Evans responded. "Okay. I'll get changed and meet you out front?" His lips found mine, softer this time, and a few of the guys started hollering.

"Why is Evans trying to maul Alex's face?"

"Are you trying to kiss him or eat him, Evans?" Grayson chirped.

I laughed, tearing my mouth away. Evans flipped them off, then skated away, trying to hit Jayden with his hockey stick. *God, I missed them.* Shoving my hands into my pockets, I waited by the door, feeling slightly nervous about seeing the team again. A few minutes later, they all filed out one by one, looking surprised to see me again.

"Alex, damn bro, where have you been?" Chris said, clasping my hand.

"Long story," I replied, and then Jayden and Grayson came up to me. "Good to see you."

"He's got the look of love in his eyes," Jayden said, smirking. "Trust me, I'm an expert. Grayson does this insane thing with his tongue and—"

"Please shut up," Chris said, shaking his head. "My eyes are bleeding from all the flirting you guys do on the ice."

"You know what? If you got your dick sucked regularly, I'm sure you'd be nicer," Jayden preened, throwing his arm over my shoulder.

"Oh, yeah? Is your mom still available?" Chris scowled and then ran away laughing when Jayden moved to hit him. Evans strolled out with Kevin and a few other players hot on his heels. He made a beeline over to me, shoving Jayden's arm off before cupping my face and kissing me gently.

"Oohhhhh!" all the guys screamed.

I laughed, pulling away, my face flaming red. "Shut up or we'll do more than a kiss!" The guys scattered out the door.

"I'm down," Jayden said, shrugging, but Grayson was hauling him away.

Evans chuckled and brought me close. "God, it feels good to have you back here. Ready to go?"

"Sure," I said, then wrapped my arms around his body. The snowflakes kissed our faces with a soft, cold touch as we walked hand in hand. His arms enveloped me, and the wintry landscape felt like a serene backdrop to our shared moment. Most of the guys didn't care if we were straight or gay, and that was what I loved about our team. We walked into the bustling pub, filled with students. I recognized a few familiar faces and exchanged greetings while Evans found us a table towards the back. The guys wasted no time and ordered several pints, Jayden and Grayson squabbling over seating arrangements, and a flat-screen TV played the highlights of a hockey game in the background, providing a lively backdrop to our conversation.

"So, how did you guys get together?" Jayden, always the curious one, chimed in.

I took a sip of my beer and smirked. "A series of unfortunate events."

Jayden chuckled, "Damn, you went off the radar, May. We thought you'd quit for sure. Who knew you were just shacking up with Evans?"

Evans playfully slapped Jayden upside the head. "Don't talk to my boyfriend like that. And yes, Alex was going through some stuff, but he's back now."

The word 'boyfriend' hung in the air, and I could feel my heart racing in my chest. A warm flush crept up my neck, but there was no denying the fond smile that tugged at my lips. Evans leaned in and pecked me on the lips. "He's mine now."

"Maybe you should pee on him and call it a day," Jayden muttered around his cup, and Grayson nudged him, jostling his arm so his beer spilled. "Hey!"

"Shit," Evans said, nearly choking on his drink. A man came charging through the lively crowd, his face etched with thunderous anger as he confronted Evans, throwing a disdainful look in my direction. "Crap, Harpreet — I can explain—" Evans began.

But Harpreet's words cut him off sharply. "There's nothing to say. I see you left my sister to shack up with your teammate." Harpreet shifted his attention to Evans and added, "You were about to starve to death, right? I told you she couldn't cook. Be thankful I saved you from a lifetime of misery."

Evans couldn't help but burst into laughter, and Harpreet's stern expression transformed into a grin. "I meant it, my friend. No hard feelings."

I realized that this was Harpreet, the person I'd heard so much about. Guilt tugged at me as I thought about what had transpired with Zara.

"Hey, man. I'm sorry—" I began, wanting to make amends.

But Harpreet swiftly silenced me, raising his hand as if to block my words. "Do not speak to me, homewrecker. My tolerance is limited," he said, a touch of humor in his voice. "I'm too sober for this. Shots on Evans tonight!" he called out, raising his glass, and the entire group erupted in cheers. Evans blushed, shooting me an amused shrug, and I couldn't help but smile. "Hey—you, bartender! Don't turn away I know you see me! Start running a tab on this guy!" Harpreet pointed at Evans and I couldn't help but laugh at his sheepish expression. Did Harpreet know about the possible pregnancy? Probably not. It was still in the early stages, but I knew his attitude would change once he did. Fuck, I wanted to groan.

It was going to be a long night.

16

THE ROAD TRIP OF LOVE

ALEX MAY

"You're dead meat!" I screamed, frantically jerking my controller as Evans dominated me in a game of Call of Duty. The tension was palpable as we neared the end, and I had just forty-five seconds to eliminate my opponents, or I'd face virtual death. How had Evans gotten so good? I was sure he'd been practicing during the holidays. Just a few weeks ago, I had him completely beaten.

"Eat dirt, May!" Evans hollered triumphantly, effortlessly taking down several adversaries and shattering my high score.

"Dammit!" I yelled in frustration, and then, the dreaded "Game over" message flashed on the screen. I felt the urge to throttle him for this defeat.

Evans flashed me a triumphant grin before leaning in to capture my pouty lips. "Don't be upset, babe. I'm just better than you. That's all."

"Screw you," I muttered, unable to stifle a grin despite my frustration.

"More popcorn?" Evans called from the bedroom, holding up the empty bowl. I nodded and got up, opening his bedroom door, then quietly headed down to the kitchen. It was getting pretty late, and I felt guilty about making too much noise since there were others in the frat house, but we were immersed in our late-night gaming session.

Throwing the popcorn into the microwave, I leaned against the counter, listening to the kernels pop. My thoughts revolved around how I was going to beat Evans in the next game. The sound of the stairs creaking caught my attention, and I assumed it was Evans returning. However, to my surprise, Eli rounded the corner. His hair was styled in a fro, and he nodded to me as he entered the kitchen.

"Alex, where have you been, man?" he inquired. I winced internally, recalling that the last time I saw him, I had ignored him.

"Yeah, sorry about the last time," I admitted, feeling a pang of guilt. "I was going through some stuff."

Eli crossed his arms over his chest and regarded me with a serious expression. "No worries."

I shifted uncomfortably, realizing the awkwardness of the situation. "So... are you, like, living here now? A few of the guys and I are a bit confused. You're here *like all the time*."

His question hit me like a ton of bricks. I hadn't considered that perspective. This was a fraternity house, and everyone paid rent and tuition to be there, while I had essentially been squatting.

"Ah—yeah—I'll figure it out. Sorry."

"No worries, bro. Just curious. I'll see you around, okay?" He slapped me on the back, but I was too busy telling the panic to swallow me alive. Eli wasn't a bad guy and I knew he was just genuinely curious since I had been here a lot. It was against the rules to have people stay here long term, but I had no idea where I wanted to go or if I could go anywhere else. Fuck. Running a hand through my hair, I grabbed the popcorn and went back upstairs. Evans was fiddling with his controls, ready to set up another game when I slammed the popcorn onto his night table, causing him to jump.

"Hey," he said, then got to his feet. "What is it? What's wrong?"

I gritted my teeth against the frustration building inside me. Things between us were great, but that didn't change the reality of my situation and I realized that I had been living in a fucking bubble for the past few days. *I was homeless.* My mom was in rehab. *I couldn't stay here with Evans.* How could I tell him that? My throat closed and I thought about lying, but Evans knew me too well.

"I saw Eli downstairs," I admitted. "Turns out some of the guys want to know if I'll be moving in."

Evans' mouth turned into a thin line. "Shit. I didn't think. I'm sorry."

"They pay rent and tuition to be here, it feels unfair that I get to squat here—"

"You aren't squatting Alex. You have nowhere else to go," Evans snarled and then sighed. "It's fine. We can get an apartment off campus. I've been planning to, anyway. This room is way too small for us. We can start looking tomorrow."

"Evans, I can't afford first and last month's rent, especially with my mom—"

"Let me worry about it," Evans replied, leaning in to kiss my cheek. "I promise."

"What about when you're drafted? We don't know what team you'll be assigned to. Maybe we should wait until then?" I suggested.

"Good idea," Evans said. "In the meantime, I'll speak to the landlord so that I can explain what's going on. If I have to, I'll pay him a little extra so that you can stay here."

"I can't ask you to do that—"

"You aren't asking," Evans replied, staring down at me.

Fuck, I hated when he got like this. Why didn't he understand that I needed to do some things for myself? Taking care of my coked-out mom was my responsibility. Finding a place to stay and standing on my own two feet made me feel like a man. How could he take that away from me? "Fuck off with that," I growled at him. "I need to take care of myself. My mom will not stay in rehab and when she gets out—"

"She can fuck off to hell and back for all I care," Evans exploded. "Jesus, Christ! Alex looks at how she treats you! You dropped out of school and hockey and for what? I know she still treats you like shit because you haven't even mentioned once that you wanted to go visit her."

Rage burst in my chest, and resentment boiled my skin. What the fuck did he know? All his life, he'd had everything handed to him. Evans didn't know the first thing about addiction or treating addicts. "She's still my mom and I won't leave her—"

"She's already left you, Alex. A long time ago," Evans sighed, running a hand through his hair. "I don't want to fight. I know things are complicated, but I love you. I don't want to be away from you because of your fucked up sense of pride. We all need help. I don't see you as less than equal because you can't afford the rent just yet. For fuck's sake Alex, you were studying to become an Engineer. When you finish, I'm sure your income will demolish mine. I want you with me. Always."

My chest tightened. He was right. All I could see were the circumstances I was in right now, but Evans was looking past all of that into the future. I only had a year left so I could finish up my degree in no time, and then I would make the money I wanted to. Throwing my arms around his neck, I hugged him close, breathing in his musky scent and losing myself to his warmth. "I'm sorry. You're right." Tears burned my eyes, but I refused to let them fall. "She fucked me up good, eh?"

"She did, and I don't want her in our lives anymore, Alex," Evans responded, his arms encircling my waist. "I know she's your mom, but some people choose drugs. They choose addiction over everyone else and they don't change. You can still support her. I won't fault you for that, but there needs to be clear boundaries. You're old enough now to let her go."

God, he was right. I had to let her go. The next time I saw her I'd tell her that. Evans pulled back and kissed me on the lips. "I'm gonna shower. It's late, so we can finish the game tomorrow."

Biting my lip, I nodded and watched him disappear into the bathroom. I tidied up the room, knowing if I didn't, Evans would have kept the place a pig's sty. Rummaging through the drawers, I smiled when I glanced at some of the old photos of us at the beach or playing hockey together at the local community center rink. We spent so much of our youth joined at the hip and I knew I never wanted to be anywhere else besides Evans. I was busy packing away the food when I saw Evans' phone buzz. Leaning over, I checked the message and my heart jumped into my throat.

I'm ready for the results now. Let's test tomorrow. From Zara.

Fuck, my heart slammed against my ribcage and I felt the world fall from my feet. *What if she was pregnant? Then what? Would Evans leave me to be with her? What if she demanded it?* Okay, relax, this is the twenty-first century and Evans was gay. Right? He never said he was. I swallowed around the dagger in my throat, wondering what the hell I was going to do. Support him. But then what? We'd have to get a two-bedroom apartment and that would be expensive in the city. I scrubbed a hand over my face as the bathroom door opened and Evans emerged in nothing but a flimsy white towel. The scent of his aftershave nearly made my knees go weak, it was thick and masculine, like pine as it filled my nostrils. of water ran down his smooth flushed skin, and his muscles bulged and tensed as he took out the clothes he would wear for bed, slicking his blond hair back from his face.

"Are you okay?" his blue eyes flashed toward mine and I melted.

I couldn't lose him. Not yet. Closing the distance between us, I grabbed his neck and yanked him down into a bruising kiss. Evans laughed and moaned, his large hands instantly gripping my waist. Our lips met in a clumsy kiss. He responded by opening his lips for me, a hungry groan slipping through when my hands ripped off the towel, exposing his naked body to the cold air. Evans hissed, sucking in air through his teeth as I backed him up toward the bed and shoved his chest.

Evans fell on his back and bounced on the bed before I knelt between his legs, staring greedily at his flushed cock.

"Shit, Alex," Evan chuckled, and I took hold of the base of his cock, giving it one long stroke before I looked up at him. "Fuck, I love you." His hand cupped my chin, fingers scraping against the stubble that had grown there over the last few days. He took quick shallow breaths, the steamy air still floating from the open bathroom as I stroked his cock.

My tongue darted out to taste the head, moaning at the pearls that beaded at the tip. Evans hissed, sucking in air through his teeth, and his other hand came up to fist my hair. I took him into my hot mouth, watching him squirm as I didn't take him in too deep. Evans' chest was flushed red, heaving as he struggled not to thrust to the hilt down my throat. A smile curved my lips, and I swirled my tongue around the head, licking with fast, strong strokes. Evans' breath hitched, his hips jerked, and he cried out when I took him down to the root. "Fuck, baby—" he muttered, straining against the bed.

I groaned, devouring his cock, hollowing my cheeks to take him deeper while it jabbed the back of my throat. Not hard enough to make me gag, but hard enough that tears burned my eyes. Drool dribbled down my chin and Evans grunted, while my hands cupped and massaged his scrotum, salvia pooling on his firm thighs. "Alex—baby—I'm close—"

Yes, come in my mouth. I thought, feeling my cock rise and stiffen at the thought. Evans cried a guttural moan, echoing off the walls as his body spasmed and jerked. Hot come erupted into my mouth and flooded my senses with salty come. I swallowed what I could down and let the rest drip down my throat and neck. Evans' hand held my hair in a vise grip, his blunt nails digging into my scalp as his hips jerked, and his body thrust. I pulled off, and he gasped, sighing through his pleasure, collapsing onto the bed. I laughed and crawled up his body, pressing our chests flush together.

"Fuck, you're going to kill me," he said, stroking my wet chin. "I love you so much."

I smirked and kissed him, allowing him to taste his spend on my tongue. Evans' piercing blue eyes were like deep sapphires, and when I looked into them, I felt myself getting lost in the powerful currents of their ocean-like intensity. *Will you leave me?* I thought, touching the blonde, sparse hairs that covered his chin. His large hand reached between us and found my aching cock. I moaned when heat engulfed it and I couldn't help but jerk into his palm.

"Evans..."

"Call me Luke Skywalker," he whispered, and I laughed, swatting his arm.

"Perv," I chuckled, but it died when he stroked my cock harder. "Ugh—Evans!"

"Yeah, baby. I'll take good care of you—" he rasped before claiming my lips, stealing the breath from my lips. I groaned into the bruising kiss, and Evans slipped his tongue into my moist cavern, licking the seams of my mouth while his hand jerked with me off. Stardust burst before my eyelids and I felt my balls pull taut, my cock twisted and spasmed and my toes curled with pleasure. Heat pooled low in my trembling stomach, and I felt coiled. "Ah—yes—" I groaned, thrusting my hips into his tight fist. Feverish warmth rushed through my veins, my teeth rattled from the crushing blow of his kisses as desire darted through me, ripping my lungs apart with live silver bullets.

Fuck. I came hard. Erupting into his firm fist, a painful bliss soaked the sheets as a blast of color filled my fractured vision. I collapsed on his chest, my body heaving as I struggled for breath. Evans chuckled low and deep in my ear, causing a shiver to crawl down my spine. "Good?"

"The best," I said with a laugh. "But I'm never calling you Luke Skywalker in bed, so you can get rid of that little fantasy."

"That's okay. I know Han Solo is much more your type."

I grabbed the nearest pillow and threw it at his head.

***

STEPPING INTO THE HOCKEY rink, the distinctive aroma of frozen history embraced me—an intricate blend of chilly metal, weathered wood, and a subtle hint of Zamboni exhaust. It was a unique mixture of nostalgia and excitement that was impossible to ignore. I spotted Able near the concession stand, and he waved me over, giving my back a hearty clap.

"Well, don't you look like the cat that caught the canary," he quipped, his eyes twinkling as he observed my sly grin. "Who's the lucky girl?"

I cleared my throat, unsure if I could trust him with the truth, but deciding to take the chance, anyway. "My boyfriend. Evans."

"Boyfriend?" Able's face lit up. "Well, congratulations, son. But we've got a lot of work to do today, so let me show you what needs to be done."

I nodded, and we made our way to the back. Engaging in the tasks of cleaning up the rink and the seating, I couldn't help but let my mind wander to thoughts of Evans and the tender goodbye kiss he'd planted on my lips this morning before dropping me off. I still needed to pick up my car, provided it hadn't been towed already. Tomorrow, we'd begin our search for apartments together. Evans was expecting to hear which team they had drafted him to next week, and the anticipation was causing my heart to race.

As I was just finishing up for the day, I saw Rex coming through the dual doors and the sudden lurch in my chest caught me by surprise. Rex entered the rink, his imposing figure magnified by the winter coat he wore. His face was etched with stern determination as he scanned the room, and his brown eyes eventually locked onto me.

Shit. It was too late to turn around because he had already spotted me. His brown hair looked tousled and windswept, but his eyes were sharp as razor blades. My tongue clung to the roof of my mouth as I stared back at him, shifting from one foot to the other with the broom in my hand. I had ten minutes before my shift officially ended, and I prayed Rex wouldn't make a scene at my workplace.

"Hey," he said, his baritone voice deep. "Can we talk?"

I licked my dry lips. "Sure, I get off in a few minutes. Can you meet me out back?"

Rex regarded me for a moment, his cool eyes drilling into my heart. "Sure. See you soon." Then he walked out, his long legs eating up the distance between him and the dual doors.

Fuck. I ran a hand through my thick hair, wondering what the hell I was going to tell him and if we'd still be friends by the end.

***

I CONTEMPLATED THE IMPENDING conversation with Rex, and a shiver of dread coursed through me, making my stomach churn with unease. The brisk wintry air outside seemed to mirror my internal chill, and I hesitated, taking a deep breath before finally stepping into the cold. Each step I took felt heavier than the last, the weight of my apprehension bearing down on me as I trudged through the snow-dusted path. The gray sky above matched my somber mood, and I pulled my coat tighter around me in a futile attempt to shield myself from the impending discomfort. Rex stood off near the brick wall, his hands stuffed deep into his pockets, his face flushed from the chill.

"Hey," I said and instantly felt stupid for saying that. I was such an ass. Leaving him hanging like that was beyond unforgivable and guilt wracked my insides.

"Hey," Rex replied. "How are you?"

"I'm ... better. Thank you," I said, then swallowed around the knot in my throat. "Rex ... I..."

"It's okay." Rex gave me a rueful smile. "You don't have to explain ... when I think back on it, it's pretty fucking obvious." He laughed, but it was hollow. "You guys were joined at the hip, so ... I guess it makes sense. Besides that, you've got all the tact of a bowling ball."

I rolled my eyes. "Okay. I deserved that. I guess you think I'm the devil too, for sleeping with you and trying to hide my feelings for Evans."

"Well, you do a great job combing your hair. It's impressive how you're able to hide the horns."

"Shut up," I said, shoving his arm and Rex chuckled. "Seriously, I'm sorry and I'll pay you back, I swear—"

"Nah, dude, it's fine. You have already done so much for me with that accident all those years ago. The least I could do was help you out when it mattered."

I sighed in relief, and then Rex pulled me into a tight hug. Wrapping my arms around his neck, his scent filled my nostrils, and I prayed Rex would find someone to love him how he should be. I pulled away, and we both laughed. "So ... the rehab—"

"Your mom can stay there as long as she needs," Rex said, answering my question. "It's already paid for, and my parents don't mind, so we can just call it even."

I chewed on my bottom lip, nodding. "I'll have to thank them when I see them again."

"Yeah," Rex nodded. "Fuck, it's cold as shit. I feel like my balls will freeze off."

"Yeah, same here—I should get going?" I said, looking around the parking lot I saw Evans' large truck waiting for me. "Text me?"

"Of course." We hugged one last time, and a loud horn blared, startling us apart. Rex raised a brow, and I ducked from his gaze. Evans needed to work on his jealousy. I waved goodbye to Rex and sprinted to Evans' car. As I opened the door and climbed inside, the rich scent of leather enveloped me, the polished seats were firm yet inviting, and the scent of Evans' aftershave and cologne made me feel intoxicated. Heat blasted in my face, and Evans' coat pooled around his waist. He sported a tight white Levi sweater that stretched across his pecs and biceps, making him look delicious. Evans leaned over and claimed my lips in a slow and sensual kiss before pulling away.

"Fuck, that guy is too handsy. Why does he always want to touch you so much?"

I laughed, licking my dry lips. "Why not? I'm an attractive guy. Who wouldn't want to touch me?"

"Shut up," Evans muttered, peeling out of the parking lot. "I'll have to drop you at home. Zara texted me so I'm heading to her dorm room…"

Shit. "Is she taking the test?" I asked.

Evans nodded; his mouth set into a hard line. I took his hand into mine, intertwining our fingers. I couldn't imagine what he was going through. Whatever the outcome was, it would change our lives. I never thought about having kids so young, but if it was Evans', I knew I'd cherish them for the rest of their lives. I'd go back to school and work hard to provide them with a decent life, the way I never had when I was growing up. Swallowing around the blockage in my throat, I sat back in the plush seat thinking about how to be there for Evans. Once he was drafted, we'd have to figure out where we'd be going next. And if it was away from his child, then that would be a big problem. Fuck, where would things go from here?

"Do you want me to come with you?"

Evans shook his head. "I don't think Zara would take kindly to see you, especially at a time like this. No, just wait for me at home. I'll let you know what the results are. I promise." A light tremor exploded over his hand, and I stroked his cheek while he drove and placed a kiss on the inside of his wrist. We'd figure it out together. *I won't let Evans go through this alone.*

17

On Thin Ice

Evans Mulroney

I drove over to Zara's dorm, my heart pounding in my chest at the prospect of her taking a pregnancy test. Just as my hockey career was about to take off with a potential NHL draft, I had finally found love with Alex. *How could this happen now?* I tried not to let bitterness take over, but I couldn't help but feel overwhelmed by the situation. *Would Alex stand by me through this? Or would he leave once the child was born?*

A wave of dizziness washed over me, and my stomach sank as I pulled into the parking lot of her dorm. Students bustled about in the bitter cold, and I zipped up my jacket before getting out. Taking the elevator up to her room, I adjusted my clothing, my nerves making my hands tremble. Zara answered the door in nothing but her pajamas, her face worn, and I was concerned instantly. "Everything okay? How are you feeling?"

"Ugh!" Zara made a gagging noise. "I had finals last night and I could barely sleep." She stretched her hands over her head, and her shirt ride up over her plump ass. "I'm tired and I can't wait to get this over with."

I threw off my jacket and sat on her bed, resting my elbows on my knees. "So, you bought the test?"

She nodded, taking it out of a plastic pharmacy bag. "I—Ah—I'm not sure how this works, but I didn't want to be alone in case it was … positive…"

"Of course," I said. "I'm here for you."

Zara bit her lip, her hair was thrown in a messy bun and she wore no makeup today, leaving her face natural. "I'll just—Ah—take it now, I guess." She went into the bathroom and the door clicked shut behind her. My heart raced like a wild stallion, its thunderous hooves echoing in my chest. Fuck, what if it was positive? What the hell am I going to do? How would I tell my parents?

A part of me wasn't sure what the fuck I was feeling: sentiment, anger, but at the same time hope. It unfurled in my chest like liquid heat spreading to the tips of my fingers and toes. A child. I never considered being a father, but something about it was terrifying but simultaneously endearing. I'd be there for the kid. Alex and I would teach them hockey and play with them, giving them the best childhood they could ever ask for. I knew Zara would be a bomb-ass mother, and we'd work out a good custody agreement so that the child could be with us both. Eventually, Zara could go back to law school and take the bar, and we'd figure out a way for her to become a full-time lawyer with childcare.

It could work.

Zara threw open the bathroom door and set the test down on the nightstand along with a timer set for 30 seconds. Her face was streaked with tears and I opened my arms to her, allowing her to crawl into my lap and bury her face in my neck. "Fuck, I can't breathe," she whispered. "I don't know what to do. It's so fucked up, Evans, but my parents will kill me. I don't know if I could go through with it."

"Don't worry," I responded, stroking her tiny arms. "I'll be here no matter what. I promise."

"Evans," she said, looking deep into my eyes. "I can't do this to you. Your whole life is about to change—I can't—I won't be a burden. My Baba's family would disown me and Harpreet…" She took a stuttering breath. "He wouldn't even look at me."

"They could come around after the child is born," I offered, trying to lighten the situation. I didn't know much about Indian families, but I didn't think Harpreet would abandon her completely. Things in life happened, and whoever didn't speak to Zara or cut her out of their life wasn't worth keeping to begin with. My thoughts wandered to my own family and how they would react if they found out. I knew my parents would be disappointed, but they loved Zara and would welcome this next addition to the family.

The timer beeped.

My stomach twisted in a knot of apprehension, churning with unease. Zara and I shared a look, neither one of us wanting to move, but then I nodded and reached over, taking the small white stick in my hand and staring at the single blue line.

"It's … negative," I said, making sure to read it again and again.

Zara sagged in relief and then burst into tears. "Fuck, I'm never having sex without a condom ever again. This shit is what horror movies are made out of."

I laughed and hugged her close. Negative. Fuck. It was good news and yet … Nervous energy surged through me, tingling in every limb like an electric current. *Why did I feel disappointed?* I shrugged off the feeling and lay on the bed, with Zara still wrapped in my arms. Zara wiped her tears and stared at my profile, then she tucked a few stray blond strands away from my brow. "Thank you for being here. I don't think many guys would be."

My mouth tugged into a smile. "Honestly, I was so scared I nearly shit myself but ... I don't know. Having a kid with you didn't seem so bad."

"What about Alex? Aren't you guys booed up now?" Zara asked.

"How'd you know?" I turned to look at her.

"Please, you had your tongue down his throat at a bar. Of course, I knew. Besides, Harpreet saw you, and gossip in our community spreads faster than the scent of fresh samosas at a family gathering."

I barked a laugh. "Damn, but those samosas are *delicious,* though."

She shoved me off. "Trust me, you don't know the half of it. My aunties have a secret talent: they can turn one small piece of gossip into a three-act epic saga."

We collapsed into fits of laughter. Staring up at the ceiling, I wondered how different our lives would have been if we had stayed together. Loving Zara was easy. We had so much in common and her resilience made me believe in a higher power, but she wasn't Alex.

She wasn't *him*.

"Anyways," Zara sighed. "I'm tired, and I need some rest after the near heart attack I just had."

"I'll get going then," I replied, then grabbed my jacket and shrugged it on. Zara walked me to her door and then placed a small kiss on my cheek. "If you ever need anything, let me know. I'll be there."

Her mouth kinked, and I had a feeling that she wouldn't, even if she did. "Sure, goodnight, Evans Mulroney." I waved goodbye and shut the door, knowing deep in my heart that this was goodbye.

***

I DROVE HOME BENEATH the darkening sky and twinkling lights. My mind wandered through the twists and turns of life. The road ahead seemed both familiar and unpredictable. I couldn't help but think about how strange and beautiful it was, and how I had found something extraordinary in the midst of it all. Alex was the anchor in the sea of life's uncertainties, and I vowed to love no one else.

Arriving at the frat house, I parked my car in a hurry and rushed inside. The guys were gathered around the TV, engrossed in their video games. They shouted for me to join, but I had something more important in mind. I bounded up the stairs three at a time, my heart racing with anticipation. Bursting through our bedroom door, I found Alex there, scrambling to his feet. He wore nothing but a pair of grey sweatpants and a tight white beater, looking as irresistible as ever.

All the words I had been thinking on the drive vanished, replaced by the overwhelming desire to hold him close. Life might be strange, but the love I felt for Alex was the one constant I cherished and would cherish for the rest of my life. His reddish bronze hair was washed in the fading sunlight, it ignited a spark in my core. "Everything okay?" he asked, but those wily fox eyes caught my growing grin and then glistened with secrets known only to him.

"Better. Much better." I closed the distance between us, grabbing the back of his head and yanking him into a bruising kiss. Alex's cry bit off into a moan as I gripped his shirt, bunching it up at the sides before tearing it off. The sight of his compact frame had my cock hard in seconds. Sleek, creamy milk skin and taut abs were splayed out before me. Alex laughed when I licked the seam of his mouth, walking him back toward the bed, before pushing him down. My hands roamed every inch of flesh. Small brown freckles and moles dotted his ribs and stomach, and I crawled over him, kissing every inch I could reach.

Taking his nipple into my mouth, he moaned, back arching as I flicked my tongue over the bud, lightly nibbling before my hand ran the length of his sweatpants to his cock. Alex jerked and hissed when I cupped his bulge, wrapping my hand around it. "Evans..." he said breathlessly. "You better have good news or else this isn't going to be very sexy anymore."

"It's negative," I responded, kissing him harder. "Zara's not pregnant." I went to kiss him again, but Alex stopped me with a firm hand to my chest. "What?"

"How do you feel about that?" he asked, his brown eyes wide.

Warmth flooded my heart. He knew me better than anyone. "Good. I was disappointed at first, but I'm not ready for children yet, but this experience made me realize I do want them. With you. So shut up so I can impregnate you," I said, capturing his lips.

Alex laughed but didn't shove me off. I ground my hips into his cock, relishing the spark that tingled down my spine. Gripping his hips, I flipped us over so that he was on top, grinding his cock down into me. Alex gasped, chasing his release when I explored his mouth, sliding my fingers beneath his sweats and grabbing two handfuls of his round, plump ass. He shot me a coy look, then began peeling them off, and we stripped as fast as we could, and then his mouth was back on mine. I grunted into the kiss, feeling a fire pool in my gut as I thrust my dick against his hard stomach.

"Ride me, baby. I want to see you on top." Blood roared in my ears when Alex reached over to the nightstand and grabbed a bottle of lube and a condom. Desire flared within my chest when he held my dick, sliding the condom on with precision. "Fuck, you're so amazing."

Leaning down, Alex peppered kisses alongside my jawline, his tongue darting out to suck a kiss in the hollow of my throat, branding my skin. I wished I could stay in this moment for longer, but then

Alex was moving, rising, and straddling my waist. His cock was hard, slapping against his stomach, and flushed an angry red. My hands gripped his hips, thumbing his v-cut, before reaching out to thumb at his hole. A small bush of reddish bronze pubic hair covered Alex's thighs and backside, and I felt my cock swell even more with need. Grabbing the lube, I slicked up my fingers before entering him. We both moaned when I breached the first ring of muscle, and Alex kissed me hard, sucking on my tongue and bottom lip.

"Fuck," he hissed when I slipped another finger in and then a third. "Uh—I'm so hard for you."

He was ready. Pulling my fingers out, I position myself with him poised over my cock; the head pressed against his entrance. Alex tensed for a moment, but I smoothed my hands down his arms and thighs before grabbing the base of my cock and pressing in.

"*Ugh—Damn, baby—*" Alex grunted, his body lurched forward. He braced his palms near the side of my head while I carved him open with my girth. Insurmountable warmth engulfed my dick in white hot heat and I hissed, grabbing onto his hips until I sunk in. Alex's chest heaved, his eyes slipped closed in bliss, and I shuddered from trying not to come right then and there. A few minutes passed, and then Alex's eyes shot open and he nibbled at my earlobe. "Fuck, you feel so damn inside me. I wish we could stay like this."

"Ugh—" I grasped, and then thrust my hips, plunging myself deeper. I needed to come. My balls pulled taut, and my cock twitched. "Ride me, fucking ride me, baby," I pleaded.

Alex rose on his knees, placing his palms on my massive pecs before he started rolling his hips in such a sensual way that my brain short-circuited. My lungs cinched when his gaze turned hooded, and fire licked across my stomach. He lifted his hips and then slammed down on my cock so hard I was seeing stars. "Fuck—" the words tore from my throat as Alex laughed, fucking himself down on my cock like he was at the Goddamn rodeo! "Shit—" my hands scrambled for purchase, guiding his hips up and down, fisting his round ass that filled out my palms deliciously. "Oh, God—Alex—" I cried out, losing myself to him riding my cock, trying not to spill deep inside him,

Fire streaked across my vision. My cock throbbed with each thrust and before I could stop myself, I was lifting my hips, tearing screams and grunts from Alex as I fucked him hard.

"I-Evans—I'm gonna come baby—" he almost screamed, and I grabbed the head of his swollen cock and stroked it in time with my brutal thrust. "Evans—fuck—" He erupted in my hand, milky spurts of come soaked my chest and his stomach. Alex's back bowed. A flush crawled down his neck as he shuddered through his release. I growled in my throat and flipped us over. Alex bounced before I clutched his hips and forced him onto all fours before ramming my cock into him. A guttural scream tore from his throat, and then I set a brutal pace, my hips snapping so hard against his ass the entire bed frame slammed against the wall. The wooden legs screeched in protest and my heart seized. My lungs could barely breathe past the fire threatening to engulf me.

Alex cried out, coming for the second time all over the sheets. Grasping his shoulder for purchase, I piston my hips like a jackhammer, my balls pulled tight before I could think a blistering white haze filled my vision. My hips stuttered. Brazen fire pooled in my stomach before erupting. Fracturing my vision into a million pieces when I cursed and fucked through my release. A tremor exploded down my legs and thighs as I struggled to maintain my balance.

"Fuck—baby—" My back bowed, and pleasure curled my toes as my cock twitched my release into the condom. "Fuck." I collapsed on top of him, shaking. *Shit.* I gasped and rolled off him, trying not to crush him with my bulk. Alex huffed a dry laugh, sweat covering his face and dripping down his neck. Leaning over, I kissed him on the lips and sighed into it. Alex pulled away and ran a hand through my sodden hair. "That was amazing. I think we need more 'I'm-glad-my-ex-isn't-pregnant-but-kinda-disappointed-sex'."

"No, thank you," I said, chuckling. "Once is more than enough and I'm too young to die from stress." My breathing finally evened out, and I sighed long and deep. "No, seriously. Just knowing that you were here waiting for me ... I didn't think I'd get through this without you."

Alex's mouth tugged into a smile. "That's okay. You were a slippery baby. I mean damn, not wrapping your dick? They teach that shit in grade school."

"Fuck off." I shoved him, shaking my head. "I was ... it happened after we got each other off. Back then, my head was a fucking mess. It was like I was trying to prove to myself that I didn't have feelings for you and that I wasn't gay."

Alex tilted his head. "And how did that work out for you?"

"I'm sure what we just did was pretty fucking gay." I kissed him on the lips. "And better than expected. I love you."

"I love you too," Alex muttered against my mouth. "I—Ah—got a call from Doctor Reeds, the physician looking after my mom, she wants to try again and I don't think I can go alone."

"Sure, whatever you need," I responded, taking his hand in mine. I knew how Shirley could get. She fashioned her words like barbed wire. I hated it growing up and not much has changed since then. Shirley was far too toxic for Alex, but I knew there wasn't much I could do to convince him to leave her behind. It had to be his choice, with no regrets. That was the only way Alex could be free.

18

OFFSIDE CONFESSIONS

EVANS MULRONEY

I winced as Jayden's body collided with mine, slamming me against the boards. Pain shot through my shoulder, but I shook it off and darted down the ice, my stick flicking the puck into the net for the winning goal in our practice game. My team erupted in cheers, while Jayden shot me a dirty look. I just shrugged it off.

Grayson glided over to Jayden, ready to reprimand him for his rough tactics on the ice, but I paid little attention. I felt exhilarated, while Alex sat bundled up in the bleachers, wrapped in a cozy winter jacket. Beside him, several men in sharp black suits caught my attention. Scouts. It could only mean one thing.

"Good work!" Coach bellowed from the sidelines. "Evans, come with me!" I nodded, then left the rink, my stick trembling in my grasp. After quickly changing and freshening up, I stepped into the coach's office. There, my father awaited, dressed impeccably with a wide grin on his face.

My eyebrows shot up when I saw the two other men in the room, also in sharp suits.

"Evans, this is Agent Derek Johnson and Keith Frederickson. They'll be your new agents," my father announced. I shook their hands, my heart racing.

"Great to meet you, son," Derek said, giving my hand a firm shake. "You're terrific on the ice. I'm sure we can get you drafted to a great team."

Keith nodded in agreement. "Right now, we're focused on preparing for the draft itself. The lottery will be a 30-minute stand-alone show from seven to 7:30 p.m. ET, broadcast live on ESPN in the United States, and Sportsnet and TVAS in Canada. It will determine the order of selection for the first sixteen picks in the first round of the 2011 Upper Deck NHL Draft."

My head spun as they bombarded me with information.

"Kid, take a seat before your knees give out," Coach Cornell advised, and I quickly settled into a chair.

"Now, things will happen quickly once we know which team you'll be on, and then it'll be a matter of getting you set up and situated there. It could be in a different state, so we assist with getting our players situated properly and any help they may need with other things," Keith continued. "Think of us as your fairy Godfathers," he laughed at his joke. "But here's my cell." He dug into his breast pocket for his card. "Call me any time of day for anything. We want to make sure the draft goes smoothly and there isn't anything to impede them from choosing you or dropping you from the pick at the last minute."

"Good," I said, taking the card. Then swallowed down my nervousness. "Wow. Okay."

"Don't worry, you'll be fine," Derek said. A dark lock of hair fell over his brow but his gaze was calm and welcoming and it instantly put me at ease. "Now, if there is anything and I mean *anything* in your closet we need to know about it first before the media gets wind of it. So, your dad mentioned you had a girlfriend? How's that going?"

Shit. Clearing my throat, I avoided eye contact with my dad. "We—ugh—broke up." I gave him a sheepish look. "She's studying to be a lawyer and it just didn't seem practical anymore."

Derek nodded. "Fair enough, I've had plenty of short affairs in my life. Was there anything else you wanted us to know? Any special dietary needs? Or things you think might help make things more accommodating for you?"

Fuck. I couldn't tell them about Alex before coming out to my dad first. Fuck. Panic welled up in my throat at the thought of coming out to them. It seemed that for all my bravado when the time came to it, I was scared shitless. *Maybe we could keep this under wraps until after the draft? What if the news broke, and they didn't pick me?* No. That was nonsense because there were several openly gay hockey players. The silence stretched too long as I warred with myself for what to say before my father cleared his throat. "Evans, son, was there something else?"

"No. No. I was just—Ah—" I laughed, feeling my face heat. "Overwhelmed, I guess, I just spaced out."

"Happens to the best of us," Keith chuckled, his green eyes flashing with warmth. "Well, if you think of anything, call me and I'll do my best to help. Whatever it may be." We shook hands, and I stood.

"Thank you. This means everything to me."

Coach Cornell slapped me on the back and then stuck his head out the door. "Grayson! Get your ass in here!" I walked out the door, watching as Grayson jogged toward the room, he shot me a puzzled look and I held back my laughter. *Boy, he was in for a surprise.* I knew Grayson had issues when it came to being captain. The fucker never thought he was good enough, but the way he managed this team far exceeded my expectations. I knew he'd be drafted, and he'd be the best player the NHL had ever seen.

Alex. Guilt gnawed at my insides like a relentless beast, tearing through my composure as I undressed in the somber locker room. Jayden came over to me, leaning against the locker and trying to peer around me as if he could see inside the Coach's room that Grayson was in. "So, what did they say?"

"I got a few agents." I shrugged like it wasn't a big deal, but Jayden's entire face lit up.

"No fucking way!" He slapped me on the back. "So, you're in the draft! That's crazy! Congratulations!"

I laughed. "I didn't get picked yet, but yeah, shit's crazy, man."

"And Grayson?" Jayden demanded.

"I don't know," I replied. "But I'm sure he's a shoo-in. The bastard can play."

"Yeah," Jayden said and his cheeks flushed. "Taught me everything I know."

Chewing on my bottom lip, I stared at him, wondering if he could answer my question. "How do you do it?"

"Do what?"

"Be out and play hockey ... don't you fear it'll backfire?"

Jayden shrugged, his emerald eyes darting away. "Sometimes, but how I feel for Grayson is stronger. I'm willing to give it all up just to live my life with him, and I know he feels the same. If they don't accept us, that's okay. I can live with that, but I can't live without him. I refuse."

"Damn, you're a sap," I said, shoving his shoulder, but Jayden laughed.

"Yeah. He's it for me man, even if I don't get drafted, hockey will still be the game I live and breathe." Just then, Grayson stepped out of the room, his face flushed red as he thanked them all profusely, and

I knew we had both been picked. Jayden still had a few years left of college, but I knew it was a matter of time before he was snatched up. The men strode out of the locker room and into the corridor, and Jayden ran up to Grayson, taking his face in his hands and kissing him on the lips. Grayson laughed, his face bright red as he grinned ear to ear. His eyes found mine, and I pumped my fist.

Fuck yeah. We made it.

***

The atmosphere in the karaoke bar was electric as the guys from the hockey team celebrated our big moment. Excitement buzzed in the air, and the lively chatter of our friends filled the room. As I glanced around at the smiling faces, guilt clawed at my insides. Grayson and I had made it to the NHL draft pick, a dream we had chased for years, but beneath the joy, there was an unspoken truth – I hadn't come out to anyone in my family besides Kateryna.

Jayden and Grayson were already taking celebratory shots, their infectious laughter filling the room. Meanwhile, Chris, brimming with misguided confidence, grabbed the microphone. As the opening notes of Whitney Houston's "I'm Every Woman" filled the air, he launched into the song with enthusiasm, only to be met with booing from the audience.

"I've heard better singing from a malfunctioning car alarm, Chris!" Grayson shouted.

"Chris, you sound like a cat being strangled by a walrus!" Jayden hollered.

"Is it karaoke night or a horror movie, Chris?" another guy said, causing the room to erupt in laughter. Trying to shake off my inner turmoil, I joined in the laughter, clinking glasses with the guys. Alex sat beside me, chuckling, his eyes sparkling with pride and affection. He had been my rock throughout this journey, supporting me without question. But I couldn't bring myself to tell him the truth, not yet. I didn't want to jeopardize my relationship with my father, who still didn't know I was gay.

"Screw you!" Chris shrieked. "*I'm every woman—it's all in me!*" He gyrated his hips and wailed like a banshee and I was tempted to throw my drink at him just to get him to shut up. I stole a glance at Alex. His smile was genuine, his eyes filled with love, but I saw the flicker of concern. He sensed my internal struggle, and I knew I owed him the truth. I wanted to share my whole self with him, but fear held me back. "Everything okay?" he asked when he noticed I was no longer laughing.

"Great." I leaned over to kiss him on the lips and then turned back to the stage, my smile waning. The guilt intensified as I wrestled with my emotions. *Fuck. What the hell was I going to do?* If I joined a team and they had no idea, I was gay and it came out later, they would hate me. I needed to get ahead of it before it got leaked. I wasn't going to hide my relationship with Alex, but at the same time, I needed to tell my parents first. Grayson grabbed the microphone from Chris and shoved him off stage.

"You're welcome," he said to everyone, and the audience chuckled. "Now, for some real talent!" The Bon Jovi song started playing in the background and everyone got on their feet, pitchers raised in the air as he belted out a pitch-perfect version of "Livin' on a Prayer," earning cheers and applause from the crowd. The attention shifted, giving me a moment to collect my thoughts.

Taking a deep breath, I reached for Alex's hand, my voice low but determined. "There's something I need to tell you," I began, my heart pounding in my chest. "I haven't been completely honest with you, and I want you to know everything. But I'm scared, Alex. Scared of losing you, scared of disappointing my dad. I need your support more than ever."

Alex's eyes softened, his grip on my hand reassuring. "Evans ... you made it. You don't have to be afraid," he said, his voice steady and kind. "We'll face this together, whatever it is. I love you for who you are, and nothing will change that." Encouraged by his words, I took a deep breath, ready to share my truth. In that moment, surrounded by friends and love, I found the strength to embrace my identity and face the challenges ahead. "Now come on, I know a Britney Spears song with our name on it!"

"Fuck yeah," I responded, taking his hand and tugging him to the stage.

***

STRIDING DOWN THE HALLS of the rehab center, I trailed after Alex, my mouth thinned into a hard line. I never liked how abusive Alex's mother was. Even though she was getting help now, it wasn't by choice. This woman was so selfish and only cared about herself. One of the workers led us to a furnished room with a large bay window and a couch. Alex sat beside me, but I could sense his uneasiness, and it only intensified when the doctor came in. She smiled at Alex and shook his hand before turning to me. "And who's this? Your friend?"

"This is Evans, my boyfriend," Alex replied. "He's here for support."

"Of course," she said. "I'm Doctor Reeds, and I look after Mrs. May. I thought today we could get some more work done on the communication and healing aspects."

Yeah, right. I wanted to scoff. This woman didn't care about anyone except herself. After all the years watching Shirley treat Alex like shit, I had enough and the minute I was drafted I was taking Alex away from this place so that she couldn't dig her claws deeper into him. There was a knock on the door before it creaked open, and a thin woman walked in. My eyes widened as I took in Shirley's appearance. Her hair was pulled into a tight ponytail, but her face looked fuller, as if she were eating regularly and her brown eyes were bright.

She did look better. Shirley took a seat on the opposite side of the couch, keeping her body away from Alex. She didn't even look at me, and I was just fine with that.

"Good afternoon, Ms. May. This is Evans, Alex's boyfriend," Doctor Reeds explained, but she already knew me, so it was pointless. "Why don't we begin with something positive? Why don't you tell your son what skills you've been working on recently?"

Shirley kept her mouth shut and stared out the window.

Doctor Reeds clicked her tongue. "Come on, Shirley, you said you would try today."

Still nothing. Alex gripped my arm, his blunt nails dug into my skin. Anger tore across my vision, and before I could stop myself, I scoffed. "Don't bother, if it isn't about crack, I'm sure she doesn't want to hear it."

Shirley shot me a scathing look.

"Please refrain from those types of jokes, Evans, or else I will ask you to leave," Doctor Reeds warned, and then turned back to Shirley. "It's been a few weeks since you've seen Alex. Why don't you tell him what you told me in our sessions? Don't you want him to know how much you care?"

Care? I nearly snarled. For years, I watched that woman tear Alex down. To the point where he almost dropped out of grade school because she kept forgetting to *feed* him. It was my family who made sure he had his school supplies, and I watched out for him. In his junior year of university, Alex had taken on two jobs along with his school work just to make sure they could afford a place to live. *What the fuck did she know? All she did was smoke a fucking crack pipe and ruin his fucking life.* My hand curled into a fist when I thought about that time Alex told me to hide her pipe and Grayson saw me with it. *Fuck, if it had been anyone else, my entire career would have been destroyed. Did she care? Did she care where Alex was living or how he got the money to send her here in the first place?*

She never once called him.

And the more I thought about it, the angrier I became. Now she was sitting up here in a lavish place while Alex scrambled to find somewhere to rest his head at night. This woman wasn't his mother.

She was a fucking monster. I hated her, but I loved Alex, so I would never tell him that.

He hoped she would change, but I knew differently. *People like her never changed.*

"Mom," Alex said but there was a slight tremor in his voice. "I bought you those candies you like. Remember when we used to play airplanes together? You used to say I could build anything. That I could even touch the sky." Alex scrambled to reach into his pocket and pulled out two crushed cherry red candies. I didn't know how long he had been keeping them in there, but they looked old and worn. "Evans made it to the NHL. He's going pro. I might head back to school next year. I made it. Aren't you proud? Aren't you happy for me?" Each word he spoke hitched higher and higher, and my heart broke for him. "Mom, please. Say something. Tell me it's working. That we can be a family again."

Shirley looked at him, her gaze like a red-hot blade sinking into my chest. "You never did answer me, Alexei. Whose dick did you have to suck to get me in here?" she spat with disgust. "Whose dick are you still sucking to keep me in here?"

"*You fucking bitch*!" I exploded, jumping to my feet. "Don't you know what he's done to keep you safe—"

"Evans!" Alex grabbed my arm, holding me back from strangling her alive.

"You were evicted from your apartment!" I roared at her. "He's lost everything just to get you here and keep you safe! Why can't you see that? Do you have your head so far up your fucking ass that you can't see how much your son has suffered? How much he continues to suffer because of your addiction!"

"That perversion is not my son," Shirley said, her body tense. "Please leave. I want nothing more to do with you or him. Alexei, don't come here again."

Each word felt like a shard of glass piercing my heart and I turned to Alex and he looked like he'd been slapped. After all of this, she disowned him for being gay. How absurd. "Let's go," I snarled, then grabbed Alex's hand, but he wrenched it free. "Alex—"

"Y-You—" Alex barked a laugh, staring at his mother's stiff form. Tears brimmed his eyes before trailing down his pale cheeks. "Y-You hate me that much. I disgust you that much? How about this? *You disgust me.* Who cleaned up your shit and vomit? Who paid all the bills in the house? Who made sure you didn't overdose and wind up in a ditch somewhere? And now—*you say I disgust you?*" His laugh was hysterical, and I feared he might break.

"Baby, don't," I pleaded with Alex. "Let's go. She's not worth it."

"T-They raped me," Alex continued, his breath stuttering. "For years, and you let them. I've hated you for so long and now you say y-you hate me." His entire body vibrated with rage and sorrow and there was nothing I could do to stop it. "I used to pray you'd drop dead. I begged God for it every day, but you were my mom and all I had left. Then I realized you weren't all I had left. Evans has been there for me the whole time. Like building on the remains of a demolished tower, he lifted me and allowed me to soar." Alex sucked in a hard breath; his chin high in the air. "Maybe I'm not worthy of your love, but you were never worthy of mine."

Shirley flinched, but her eyes remained turned away. "So be it then. You never needed me in your life to begin with."

"No. I guess I didn't," Alex said, then walked out of the room. I raced after him, but just as I closed the door, I watched Shirley bury her face in her palms and crumple into a sobbing heap.

19

SHOOTOUT FOR THE HEART

ALEX MAY

I stared out the window as nighttime descended, the world outside darkening into an eerie stillness. My mother's harsh words echoed relentlessly in my head, each syllable cutting deeper into my consciousness. The night outside seemed to mirror the shadows creeping over my soul, the weight of her criticism clinging to me like an invisible shroud.

"I'm so sorry, baby." Evans' arms encircled my waist, and he pressed his pecs to my back, engulfing me in his warmth. "Fuck, I hate her for saying all that shit to you."

"Don't," I barked, then took a stuttering breath. "You don't get to hate her."

Evans sighed, kissing the nape of my neck. "Baby..."

"She was always like this. I guess I never knew how much she hated me until now," I continued, but more tears brimmed my eyes. "Why doesn't she want to be my mother, Evans? Why doesn't she love me?" I blurted out, but I felt gutted. All the things I've done for her over the years have led to nothing. She hated me. She thought I stole from her boyfriends. That I deliberately allowed them to rape me when I was a child. How sick. How depraved.

"She loves you…" Evans said. "In her own fucked up way, but it's not enough. I fear she loves herself more, and it has nothing to do with you, Alex. You're an amazing man. You've been there for her this whole time and if she can't see that, you're better off without her." Evans turned me in his arms and kissed my cheeks. "You're smart. Gorgeous. Sexy. When I look back, I think I've loved you my whole life. I never aspire to be away from you, Alex."

"Kiss ass," I muttered but allowed his kind words to wash over me.

Evan's chuckle vibrated against my temple and I sighed deep into his embrace. "I love you, Alex. I love this ear." He nibbled on my lobe. "I love this neck." Evans inhaled and pressed a kiss to the hollow of my neck. "I love these arms." He ran his hands down my shoulders. "I love this ass." He moved down to cup my backside, grabbing it firmly. "I love this scent."

My dick hardened beneath his touch, and I moaned when rested his hands on my hips.

"Fuck," Evans hissed, then closed the distance between us. "When you're with me, I swear I will fill the void she left behind with all the love I can give. You won't ever need her love or look for it when you're with me, Alex. I promise."

Tears stung my eyes, and I nodded, fisting his t-shirt tight. It's been like that ever since we were kids. Evans has always been there showering me with all the love and support that I could ever ask for. Tracing my fingers across his firm chest, I circled my finger around his taut nipple causing Evans to shudder and moan. Leaning onto my toes, I kissed him on the mouth, licking the seams with my tongue, working it open. Evans held me tighter; his hands bunched the fabric of my shirt as we kissed deeply. My heart slammed against my ribcage and soon things turned frantic. Latching onto his neck, I sucked onto his collarbone, feeling him arch his neck.

Fuck, he always tasted so good. For years, I had dreams of nothing else besides him. My cock swelled to the point of pain, and then he was walking me back towards the bed. Falling on the mattress, I sighed, staring up at the ceiling while Evans got to work taking off my clothes. He stripped me bare and tears gathered in the corner of my eyes before spilling over.

That perversion is not my son.

Squeezing my eyes, I bit back the wail that threatened to rip through me. After all these years, that's all I was to her. A heavy, suffocating cloud of despair settled over me, making each breath a laborious task as I sank deeper into a pit of hopelessness.

"Stay with me, baby," Evans said, crawling up my body and kissing the tears that slid down my cheeks. "Stay with me."

My throat tightened, and I nodded as he nestled between my legs. A feverish desire flashed through me, and Evans sucked on my neck, bruising the skin so harshly that I cried out. It stung. His tongue swiped over the skin before his hand came up to capture my nipples, pinching it between his thumb and index finger, rolling the bud. I groaned, arching into his touch, thrusting my hips against his jeans. "Why do you still have your clothes on?" I gasped, opening my eyes to stare at him.

"This is just for you," Evans said, a smile tugging on his lips. He claimed my lips again before his hand drifted down my body to grip my aching cock. My breath hitched when he stroked me from root to tip, pleasure fizzling all over my skin like tiny bubbles. I grunted, splaying my hands over his sculpted chest, feeling his heart jackhammer beneath my palm.

Evans was so beautiful like this. Hovering over me, his face caught in rapture as he watched every expression flicker on my face like he was drinking it in. I loved him for that. Dark blond lashes fanned his cheeks, his pink lips parted and he stroked my cock harder and harder. "Evans—" My stomach quivered, every part of me on edge ready for my release. "Fuck—I'm gonna come—"

"Not yet," Evans growled, drawing his hand away from my cock and I almost cried out in frustration. "Not until I say so."

"Cocktease," I said breathlessly.

"You love it," Evans said, nipping my lower lip. When he pulled back, his eyes were an intense shade of deep blue, reminiscent of a boundless summer sky, reflecting the vastness of his emotions. His blunt fingernails ran through my neatly trimmed reddish-bronze pubic hair, and he made a strange sound low and deep in his throat. Spreading my legs wider, Evans just stared at me and a flush crawled up my neck beneath his intense gaze. "I want this moment to last forever," he said, then swallowed my cock whole. I lurched off the bed, my back bowed as I cursed when his hot mouth went down to the root. Evans grinned, and I wanted to slap him, but it felt so fucking good. Fondling my balls, he rolled them between his large calloused fingers, and pleasure licked across my belly.

Now I was going to come.

"Evans—fuck—I'm close—"

He yanked off at the last second, and I groaned in frustration, squirming on the bed while he laughed at me. Evans reached into the night table, and grabbed a bottle of condoms and lube, tossing it near my hip before he opened the front part of his jeans. His aching cock sprang free, and he gave one long stroke before pinching the head, trying to stave off his orgasm. "Shit, I could watch you all day like this."

I laughed, but it broke off into a yelp when he flipped me onto my stomach. Large hands spread my ass open, and he nuzzled in deep. Looking over my shoulder, I arched a brow, watching him lean down before I felt the long stripe of his tongue against my crack. I cried out, not sure what the hell he was doing and feeling open and bare in front of him.

"Relax baby, I'll make it good for you," Evans mumbled, his voice rich and husky. My hands clenched on the edge of the mattress as his teeth came down on the soft flesh of my ass cheeks, sinking deep enough to hurt.

"Fucker!" I gritted out and Evans laughed, then smoothed the area over with a kiss. Evans peppered flowing kisses down my spine to wash away the sting. He repeated the process on the other side, skin taken into his mouth and pinched, tongue lapping at the bite mark even as his lips curved in satisfaction. I felt a knot swell in my throat and a shiver tore through me as I watched him, my neck straining. "Evans..."

"I'm yours..." he replied, then went back to lavishing my ass with kisses and bites. I squirmed with his stiff tongue dancing across my balls, carving a wet path up my entrance. A moist tongue circled the rim, darting out with hard strikes that I gasped, arching into it. To say it was strange was an understatement. But Evans kneaded the plump flesh of my ass, moaning low and deep in his throat, the vibrating making my skin tingle. Evans trailed teased circles across the flesh, and then I felt something hard probe against my hole. He slipped a thick finger in, timing the thrust with his tongue before he curled it.

Stardust burst before my vision and I jerked. "Fuck—" I hissed, sucking in air through my teeth.

I shuddered as his fingers thrust in and out at a languid pause. My balls drew taut. Blood roared in my ears and pleasure made my toes curl. I shuddered as he explored, driving as deep as he could before withdrawing to drag the flat of his tongue over me instead. The contrasting sensations and the delicious ache of being spread sent pulses of warmth to the pit of my stomach in time with the throbbing of my cock, hanging heavy and untouched between my legs. *Fuck, I am about to burst.*

Reaching around my waist, his hand grasped my hard cock and he stroked me slowly, driving me crazy as he fucked his fingers into my ass and stroked my cock at the same time. A wave of dizziness washed over me, and my stomach quivered and tightened, and I was so fucking close to coming my balls throbbed with the need for release.

Then he pulled off!

"*Evans!*" I cried out and spun around to glare at the bastard who was hiding his laughter behind his fist. I took my pillow and threw it at his head.

Evans dodged it, his shoulders shaking. "Sorry, I couldn't resist. Don't worry, I'll let you come, baby, I promise."

"When?" I almost sobbed and Evans crawled over him, his massive weight pressing me down into the mattress.

"When I'm inside you. Trust me, baby."

"Fuck you." He laughed hard.

"Hold yourself open for me," he commanded, and I gritted my teeth, but obeyed. A shift in my stance let me rest all my weight on my chest, freeing my hands to reach back and peel apart my ass cheeks just as he asked. He hummed his approval. "Exquisite. Stay there."

Evans drizzled warm lube down my crack, it dripped down my hole and my balls onto the bed.

He dropped to his knees behind me again, left hand returning to its place ringed around my cock while his right traced the line of stretched skin in the crease between my cheeks, playing with the liquid that pooled there. When he reached my entrance, his feathered touch ran a circle around it once before dipping a single digit in. In the same motion, he stroked his other hand long and hard up my shaft, the twin sensations carving a guttural groan from me.

Fucking bastard planned this!

That wicked grin returned to his lips as he began to spread and pump me before he drew his fingers away and replaced them with the thick head of his cock. "Now, you can come." Evans thrust to the hilt, and I cried out, gripped onto the bedspread for dear life, and he bottomed out, his fat cock spearing me open so hard I thought I'd pass out. Pain stabbed through me, but it quickly gave way to pleasure as he grabbed my hips and began fucking me in earnest. "Fuck—" he bitched. The harsh sound of skin slapping against skin filled the room as he set a brutal pace.

"Uh—Ah—Evans—" I gasped, losing myself to his touch. Pleasure exploded like fireworks before my eyes and I fought to keep my eyes from drifting closed.

"Yeah, baby—come on my fat cock deep inside you—" Evans gritted out, chasing his release. His cotton t-shirt clung to the sweat on my spine, and his jeans chafed against my ass cheeks and, for some reason, it turned me on even more.

Evans sank into me. Agony lanced through me, and it was replaced by a blistering haze of mind-numbing pleasure. Drool dribbled down my chin, and Evans lifted my hips, taking me even deeper. My breath caught with each slam of his hips. Our ragged breaths mingled and the thought of him fully clothed, taking me naked and bare flung me over the edge.

I came with a shout, soaking my chest and the sheets as my vision fractured into a kaleidoscope. Evans thrust home, not giving me an inch of relief as he chased his release, ramming into me hard. He fucked me through my orgasm and before I could think, I was hurled head-first into another.

"Evans—fuck—" I whined. Dark spots danced before my vision as I came for the second time. The air tore from my lungs and I choked on a crushing scream. Evans grunted, his hips stuttering as he lost his rhythm, and he released a long, smooth groan.

"Ah—fuck—fuck—" his hips jerked and spasmed, and then I felt my hole fill with come. *What?* I looked over my shoulder and saw that he had entered me without a condom. A laugh bubbled from my throat as his cock twitched and spasmed before he pulled out. Milky white come spilled from my hole and Evans sat back on his knees and then slapped my ass. "Fuck, that was amazing."

His hair clung to his forehead, and his blue eyes were bright with pleasure. "Did you forget the condoms?" I asked, snickering at him.

"Huh? Shit!" Evans said as he stared at the condoms lying on the bed. "Damn, I forgot."

"Obviously," I laughed and turned onto my back, wincing at the burn in my ass.

"Don't be mad," Evans said, lying beside me. "I was too into it."

I rolled my eyes, not caring either way. We both got tested regularly, so it wasn't a big deal. I kind of like it. My ass squelched when I shifted my hips and I chuckled.

"Give me a minute," Evans said, then got off the bed to grab a washcloth from the bathroom to clean us off. After he was done, he collapsed into a heap beside me and closed his eyes, his breath already evening out. I watched him sleep for several moments and then nuzzled down next to him. Closing my eyes, I let sleep claim me.

20

A HOME GAME FOR TWO

ALEX MAY

I woke to the press of warm lips over my mouth, and I sighed into the kiss. Sleek golden threads of morning light flitted across my vision. "Evans..." I rasped, arching into his touch.

"I'm here, baby," Evans replied, his mouth hovering over mine while he stroked my morning wood. Gasping for air, I felt the weight of desire pressing down on my chest, leaving me breathless and desperate for relief. Evans' mouth sealed over mine, swallowed all the soft kitten moans I made in the back of my throat, while he thrust his tongue deeper. I grunted, jerking my hips into his tight fist, and it didn't take long before I spilled into his hand.

"Fuck..." I whispered, trying to catch my breath. Peeling my eyes open, I flinched from the sun and my gaze waned before it finally came into focus on the person in front of me. Evans' eyes were like two tranquil lakes, inviting and calm, yet concealing the depths of his thoughts and feelings.

"Morning," he spoke, his voice rough.

"Mhmm ... morning," I said, relaxing back into the bed, ready to go to sleep. Checking the clock on the night table, I realized it was after five a.m. so Evans must be getting ready to go to practice. He was fully dressed, his hockey gear waiting by the door and his large winter coat making him look bulky.

"I'll be back after class, but I wanted to talk to you about something that couldn't wait," Evans said.

"What is it?" I asked, then stretched my limbs and yawned.

"I want to come out."

My breath hitched. Confusion warred within me as I struggled to understand what he meant. "Aren't we already out?" I asked.

"To my parents."

Oh. *Shit.* For some reason, I forgot about them. Wiping the caked sleep around my eyes, I sighed, not sure how to respond. The Mulroney's were a whole different ball game. They had such high expectations of Evans and I feared that they wouldn't accept me because of my background. I knew Mr. Mulroney thought I was beneath Evans and has thought that for years. Even our friend had been problematic and now we were dating. What if he didn't accept us? Or worse, what if he thought I turned his son gay?

Fuck. Running a hand through my hair, my heart slammed against my ribcage. "Can we talk about it when you get back?"

Evans' eyes narrowed into pinpricks. "I wasn't asking you, Alex," he said, his voice stern. "You were willing to come out to your mother for me. They're going to announce the draft soon, and I don't want to be on a team and hide who I am."

"And who are you exactly?" I muttered, keeping my eyes downcast.

"I'm bisexual and I'm with you."

I winced at his declaration. Bisexual. Bicurious. *Did that mean he would eventually run off to find a wife once he's had his fun?* I knew Evans wasn't that type of guy, but fear clogged my throat. Coming out to our parents was one thing, but coming out to the world was something different. Once it was done, we couldn't go back. If Evans and I split, he'd always be known as the gay hockey player. *Did he want to define his career like that so early?* He'd be shoved into a box and most people weren't so forgiving. My unease gnawed at me, a relentless presence, as I worried about making a wrong move that could jeopardize Evans' NHL prospects.

I'm a fucking janitor with nowhere to live. *How could he possibly think that this was a good idea?* I looked up into Evans' eyes and knew that he had his mind set on it. *Damn stubborn bull.* Evans wasn't going to change his mind about it. "Okay. Fine."

He brightened, kissing me on the lips. "Okay. I'll pick you up from work later."

"Sure," I mumbled, then watched him walk out the door, slamming it shut. This would be a fucking disaster. My blunt nails dug into the comforter as my hand curled into a fist. Fuck, what the hell am I going to do? A light pain throbbed on my temple and spread down the nape of my neck. Apprehension gripped me like a vice, my heart racing as I imagined how Evans would fuck things to hell and back just by announcing he was gay. On top of that dating a fucking janitor, whose mother was in rehab for a coke addiction. *Yeah, that would go over well with the public.*

I wasn't good enough for him. I should have just ended things when I had the chance.

Blood roared in my ears at the thought of leaving him, and my hands shook as another wave of anguish washed over me. *I can't leave him.* I was too weak now. *I needed Evans.*

Biting my lower lip, I cursed and swung my feet out of bed. Pain lanced down my spine, but I ignored it, storming to the showers. *Fuck it.* I wasn't going back to sleep, anyway.

***

SINKING INTO THE PLUSH leather seats of Evans' car, I gazed out the window, the passing scenery a blur. Soft jazz tunes played in the background, and Evans hummed along while he gently held my hand, navigating the freeway. We were en route to the Mulroney's, and my anxiety had started to build. It wasn't that I didn't want to see them again; I'd missed their annual Christmas party, and Kateryna's persistent texts made it clear that I had some explaining to do. The thought of coming out to them gnawed at me like an impending disaster.

Just a few months ago, Evans had been in a serious relationship with Zara. They might have even been on the path to marriage if it weren't for me. I knew his parents had liked her, and the idea of potentially losing a daughter-in-law and the chance for grandchildren weighed heavily on my mind. They'd likely offer support, but beneath the surface, they might resent the profound changes I'd brought to Evans. The anxiety grew like acid churning in my stomach.

My palms grew clammy with sweat, and I hastily withdrew my hand from Evans' grasp, pretending not to notice the perplexed look he shot my way as he continued to drive. I questioned whether I could go through with this. Maybe if we broke up, Evans would still have a shot at the NHL, and I could find my own place. We could continue to see each other but in secret. He wouldn't have to reveal our relationship to anyone.

"Are you okay?" Evans asked, turning off the freeway.

"I'm fine. Nervous, that's all."

Evans chuckled and then took my hand again. "Don't be. They love you."

They love you, I wanted to say back but refrained. Arguing would just increase my anxiety, so I went back to staring out the window. My heart slammed into my ribcage when Evans pulled into the parking lot. Evans' suburban house was a picturesque sight, with its well-maintained facade and an expansive three-car garage. The manicured lawn sprawled out in front and the exterior exuded warmth and charm, but as we pulled up, my stomach plummeted into an even deeper pit.

I spied Kateryna's BMW in the driveway along with Mr. Mulroney's Mercedes Benz and Mrs. Mulroney's bright red Lexus. The entire place screamed money, and although I used to live in their neighborhood when I was younger, something tightened in my chest whenever I came back. My dad had left us when I was two, running off with some secretary, leaving my mom to take care of their house and me. It wasn't long before bitterness set in and then she started using drugs to quell the ache of losing her spouse. Evans' hand found mine again as he dragged me up the front steps and opened the door.

"I'm home!" he yelled, and the faint, delectable smell of Makivnyk wafted through the air, teasing my senses and instantly igniting my appetite. As I stepped into the kitchen, my eyes were immediately drawn to the Makivnyk, a traditional Ukrainian Poppy Seed Roll, placed prominently in the center of the room. The roll's crust, a beautiful shade of orangy brown, gleamed with a subtle hint of sweetness, creating a captivating contrast with its monochromatic interior. But it was the dark, mesmerizing swirl at the core that stole the spotlight. Finely ground poppy seeds were intricately woven, promising a flavor both unique and unforgettable. This culinary masterpiece beckoned, inviting me to savor not only its appearance but also its delightful taste.

"Surprise!" everyone shouted, sprang up from behind the kitchen counter, almost giving me a heart attack. Evans leaped ten feet in the air, screaming at the top of his lungs like a wild banshee, and I burst into laughter at his shocked face.

"Fuck—I almost shit my pants!" he exclaimed, placing a hand over his chest.

"Language," Mrs. Mulroney said and came around to hug him. "Congratulations baby, I knew you could make it—Ah—my baby in the NHL." Her expression turned dreamy, while Kateryna nearly tackled Evans in a bear hug.

"You made it, loser! Now pull some strings to get me in the women's NHL. Don't hold out on me, bro, I practically raised you," Kateryna huffed, then pulled away. "And you—" She pointed at me before advancing. "Don't think I've forgiven you for ignoring my text messages and bailing on our Call of Duty marathon—" She stalked towards me and I raised my palms, inching back.

"I can explain—it's all really a funny story you see—" I caught her as she jumped on me, laughing when I spun her around as we hugged.

"I missed you, loser," she said against my neck.

I smiled and set her down on her feet. "I missed you too. Don't worry, I'll kick your ass later."

"In your dreams," she muttered, arms crossed. Mrs. Mulroney dragged me into a hug, and I sighed against her floral scent.

"We'll talk soon, Alexei," she said, patting my cheeks.

Mr. Mulroney was busy shaking Evans' hand and congratulating him before his eyes fell on me and he grinned. "Glad to have you back, Alex. Things haven't been the same without you around." We shook hands and Mrs. Mulroney led everyone to the table for a slice of dessert. I almost moan when the rich taste of the dessert flooded my tongue, creating a near oasis of sweetness. Laughter and lively chatter filled the air as we all savored the delicious treat.

"You know, guys, I've been thinking about trying out for the women's NHL," Kateryna said. "I mean, why not? I've got the skills!"

"Yeah, bench-warming skills," Evans snickered and Kateryna slapped him upside the head.

"You just think you're better than everyone because you made it to the NHL," Kateryna huffed.

"First off, I am better than everyone, especially a pumpkinhead like you. Second off, you would never make it to the women's NHL. They don't recruit pumpkins."

"You shut up!" Kateryna seethed and smacked his arm and then mine.

"What was that for?" I asked, trying to hide my laughter behind my fist. "He's right. Pumpkins have no place in the rink."

"Enough with the pumpkin jokes!" Kateryna snarled. "Mom, make them stop!"

"Your head is abnormally shaped, sweetheart." Mrs. Mulroney patted her arm. "Don't worry, we can get you a hat."

Everyone burst out laughing while Kateryna seethed. They exchanged witty banter, and the playful back-and-forth added to the festive atmosphere. "By the way, why are you guys here today?" Kateryna inquired. "I thought we weren't celebrating until March break."

Shit. My heart pounded against my ribcage, and suddenly, the once-delectable cake seemed to lose its flavor, tasting like ash. How could we tell them about our relationship? The mere thought of revealing our secret threatened to disrupt the harmonious atmosphere. Desperately seeking support, I turned to Evans, who calmly took my hand in his.

Evans cleared his throat. "I'm here because I have something important to tell you."

"No way. Are you serious?" Kateryna said, her eyes widening.

"Shut up, pumpkinhead, or I'll put laxatives in your water bottle before hockey practice."

"Jerk," Kateryna muttered, but she was biting back a smile.

"As I was saying… Alex and I have decided to take our relationship to the next level," Evans continued. "The truth is, I think I've loved him for a long time, and we'd like your blessing as we decide to pursue our relationship."

The room lapsed into an eerie silence. My heart jammed into my throat and heat burned my face as I tried to make sense of their expressions. Nothing moved. And as the silence stretched on the more uneasiness filled my core. This was a mistake. A big fucking mistake. They would hate me. Disown Evans just like my mother did me. Tears burned my eyes, and I wanted to beg them to forget everything Evans just said, and that we would break up if they really didn't want me to be with their son. But Mrs. Mulroney stared at both of us in shock before turning to Mr. Mulroney.

"You owe me fifty bucks," Mrs. Mulroney informed her husband. Perplexed, I looked between the two of them as Mr. Mulroney sighed and reluctantly handed over the money.

"Fine. My bet was on Zara," Mr. Mulroney admitted.

"Mom! You bet on us?" Evans exclaimed.

Mrs. Mulroney couldn't contain her laughter. "Of course, I did, you noob. You two were so blatantly obvious. How could I not? It was your father who was utterly clueless about it," Mrs. Mulroney explained. I burst into fits of laughter, but tears sprang to my eyes before running down my cheeks. Evans kissed my temple, taking me into his arms.

"See baby," he whispered against my forehead. "I told you they love you."

How could they? Nobody loved me, not even my own mother. Mrs. Mulroney pulled me into a tight hug and I let myself absorb her warmth, feeling it seep into my bones. "You're one of us now, Alexei. Don't forget. Once a Mulroney, always a Mulroney."

A knot snarled in my throat, and I nodded at her before pulling away and wiping at my tears. "Thank you. I love you guys."

"We love you too," Kateryna said, then her brow kinked. "So, tell me all the dirty and juicy details. Alex, is my brother paying you to be with him? Be honest, he's got a face only a mother could love."

"Brat!" Evans threw a napkin at her face and Kateryna dodged, running behind her dad and using him as a human shield. "This is sibling abuse!" she cried when Evans stormed after her. I laughed until it felt like my sides would split. Being with the Mulroney's always felt like home. And I realized then that it was never about whether they would accept me, but if I would ever accept myself. Staring into Evans' oceanic eyes, I knew that I had.

Beyond a shadow of a doubt.

***

WE ENDED UP STAYING the night when a blizzard rolled through that evening. Evans and I spent the day catching up with the family and talking. Kateryna was still in her junior year, but she was serious about making it to the women's NHL. We played board games and watched all the Marvel movies, followed by an intense marathon of Call of Duty, in which I demolished Evans and Kateryna in one go. My cheeks hurt from smiling so much and eventually, we all went to bed. During the night, Evans and I made love in his childhood room. Evans stifled my cries with his large palm over my mouth while he fucked me into his mattress. I came with a half-stilted yell that we thought woke up the house, only to almost die of laughter after realizing how quiet it was and how everyone was asleep.

We stayed up talking about nothing and everything.

Old jokes. Faded dreams and catchphrases we used to tell each other. Evans spooned me, his face pressed against the nape of my neck, as we basked in the afterglow of our lovemaking.

"I'll never forget when we tried to make our own lightsabers from cardboard boxes and then got pissed off when they didn't glow." Evans chuckled into my shoulder blade. "Fuck, we were so stupid. How did we even function back then?"

"I have no clue," I snickered and sighed. "Those were really the best times."

"Yeah..." Evans said. "Or that time you bought me my first hockey stick and signed it with your chicken scratch handwriting?"

"Hey! It took me a lot of quarters to save up for that." I grinned at the memory.

"For the longest time, I thought it was straight-up gibberish and everyone made fun of me for it, but I didn't care. I loved that stick." Evans pressed a kiss to my cheek. "Just as much as I love you."

I shivered from my touch and I wondered, not for the first time, if we should really come out to everyone. "Evans ... maybe we should hold off on telling your agent about us."

"Why?"

I took a deep breath. "Because I'm not exactly boyfriend material, besides you just broke things off with Zara. Why don't we let the dust settle and see what happens?"

I felt Evans' mouth draw into a frown. "What are you talking about?"

Frustration welled up within me. He knew exactly what I was saying, and I didn't like how he wanted me to spell it out for him. "You know they'll dig into my mother's past. You'll be the first openly gay NHL draft player in at least five years. The media will have a frenzy.

Why don't we wait until your spot is secured that way nothing can go wrong."

Evans' body tensed. "I see. And what other excuses are you going to be coming up with?"

"What?" I turned around to face him, noticing how his brows were knitted. "I'm not making excuses, Evans. I just think we should cool it."

"*Cool it*?" His brow arched. "How the fuck do *we cool* it? We are planning to move in together, Alex. I want you to show up to my games as my boyfriend, not my roommate."

"I understand but—"

"Why are you trying to run away from me?" Evans demanded, his voice gaining volume. "I want a serious relationship with you, and every time you pull away from me. Am I not worth taking seriously? Do you want to leave me so badly?"

"No—I just—Evans," I huffed, not sure why this argument was spiraling. "I don't want to jeopardize your spot on the team."

"And you think who I fuck will do that?" he spat.

"Of course, I do!" I flung the words back at him. "I'm a college dropout with a crackhead mother. They'll dig into my past, and what if they accuse you of taking drugs or performance enhancers—"

"I'm guilty by association," Evans scoffed. "Fuck off with that shit, Alex. No, this is just your excuse to run away again. Do you want to leave me? You think you aren't good enough and you're ready to bolt at the slightest inconvenience. Well, guess what? I'm not. I said I loved you and I meant every word."

Each word was like a slap to the face. Anger tore through me and I staggered out of bed, my heart hammering in my chest. Finding my jeans, I stabbed my legs through them and then grabbed my shirt, shrugging it on. Evans watched me like a hawk on the bed, not moving to stop me. I grabbed my sweater and wrenched open the door, thankful that Evans didn't follow me. We both needed to cool off. I stormed down to the kitchen, poured a glass of milk, and drained it, slamming the glass against the countertop, almost shattering it. The flames of my fury burned white-hot, scorching reason and rationality, leaving only the searing heat of unbridled rage. *How could he say such a fucked-up thing?*

Of course, I loved him. I wouldn't be here if I didn't. However, Evans was naïve when it came to the way the world worked. People weren't as accepting as he thought they would be. They'd ridicule him. Scorn him. Evans' life would be defined by the choices he made now. *What if nobody chose to have him on their team because of his sexuality?* The thought made tears burn my eyes. All of this is for me. *I wasn't worth it.* Maybe he was right. A part of me never felt worthy enough to be with him, but he would be giving up a lot if it didn't work out.

I poured another drink and banged the mug on the countertop again.

"Easy there, what did the milk ever do to you?" a voice said from the shadows, and my breath caught when Mr. Mulroney came in wearing nothing but his pajamas.

"Sorry," I laughed. "I just wasn't thinking."

"Well, that's one of her good mugs so if she finds it broken, you better run." He flashed a grin and went about fixing a snack. "So, are you and Evans all ready for the big day?"

"Somewhat," I replied.

"I have a few colleagues coming through, and some family from out of town for Draft night," he said, popping some chips into his mouth. "Everything should go great, well ... that's assuming nothing goes wrong." He turned then to stare at me, his salt and pepper hair standing stark against his pale skin. It unnerved me when he looked at me sometimes, and through the years I come to recognize what his gaze meant. Mr. Mulroney didn't hate me. Nor did he want me away from his son, but the look in his eyes was something worse. Like he'd done everything in his power to prevent something that happened anyway. Time slowed down, and I felt the inevitable words like a sword to my chest.

"Anything to go wrong?" I whispered. The blood roaring in my ears was deafening.

"You're smart Alex," Mr. Mulroney said. "So, I won't insult you by beating around the bush. I haven't exactly been in favor of this friendship, but it's clear to me now that Evans loves you with all his heart and I know he'd do anything for you. Even if it wasn't the right choice."

My lungs cinched, and I swallowed around the bile searing my throat. "Sir?"

"All I want you to do is help him make the right choice," Mr. Mulroney said, his voice stern, and then he walked out of the kitchen. My knees almost buckled. All the years I thought I could fit in and find a family has led to this. He kept me around because he knew he'd have no choice but to. Mrs. Mulroney, Kateryna, and Evans loved me, but he tolerated me. I didn't know what the fuck was worse. Gritting my teeth against the pain in my heart, I put the mug away and headed upstairs. Evans was fast asleep when I crawled into the space next to him, bitter tears clouding my vision.

Of course, I'd help Evans make the right choice.

If it was the last thing I'd do.

21

LOVE IN THE TIME OF PLAYOFFS

EVANS MULRONEY

Standing on the stage for my first NHL draft, my heart was a relentless drummer inside my chest, thumping so hard it felt like it might burst through my suit jacket. The bright, blinding lights overhead beat down on me, causing beads of sweat to form on my forehead and trickle down my temples. The deafening roar of the crowd echoed in my ears, a cacophony of cheers and applause that made it hard to hear my own thoughts. *Fuck, it was hot in here.* Tugging on the collar of my shirt for the fifteenth time as I tried to calm down. To my left, Grayson sat with a confident grin on his face, his eyes gleaming with excitement. Coach Cornell and several of my teammates from the junior league were there too, offering silent support through their presence. It was a surreal moment, and I couldn't believe I had made it this far.

It was astonishing that Grayson and I were the top pics of the draft and from the same university. The stage was set in the center of a massive auditorium, packed to the brim with hockey enthusiasts, scouts, and fans. Banners of various NHL teams adorned the walls, creating a colorful backdrop for the event. Each team's table was decked out in their colors, logos, and merchandise. It was a sea of jerseys, caps, and waving flags.

My eyes scanned the crowd, searching for a familiar face. I desperately wanted to find Alex among the spectators, but the glaring lights made it impossible to see beyond the first few rows. My palms were clammy, and I wiped them discreetly on my suit pants. *This was it—the moment I had been working toward my entire life.*

"Evans!" The announcer's voice rang out, echoing through the arena

I nearly jumped ten feet in the air, and then the cheers erupted. The roar of the crowd intensified, drowning out all other sounds. Grayson's voice broke through the noise.

"You did it, man! You're on your way!" He slapped me hard on the back, propelling me to move forward. Coach stood up and laughed, wrapping me in a tight bear hug, and then shoving me toward center stage. A representative from the hockey teams walked up to the podium, a jersey and cap in hand. With a congratulatory smile, he handed them to me, and I slipped on the jersey with trembling hands. The team's logo was emblazoned proudly across the front.

"Welcome to the Pittsburgh Penguins, Evans!" The representative patted me on the back, and I nodded, unable to find my voice in the overwhelming moment.

Tears of joy welled up in my eyes as I looked out at the enthusiastic crowd. I had been drafted to an NHL team, and I was one step closer to living my dream. Grayson whooped behind me, and Coach Cornell offered a nod of approval. As I stepped away from the stage and waved to the cheering fans, I knew that this was the beginning of a new chapter in my life—one filled with challenges, hard work, and incredible moments on the ice. And, even though I couldn't see him in the crowd, I knew that Alex was out there, his love and support guiding me every step of the way.

***

EVERYTHING AFTER THAT HAD been a blur. Grayson got drafted to the Tampa Bay Lightning, which made sense since the bastard was light on his feet. Jayden showed up wearing a slick black suit and a black undershirt, his tattoos and slick black hair turning all the heads as he made a beeline to Grayson, who was caught up in a crowd of fans. The devil moved like a panther before planting himself right in front of Grayson, and I watched trying to cover up my snicker as Grayson gave an audible gulp before Jayden's hand came around his neck to cup his head, bringing him into a one-armed hug. Whispering in his ear, I saw the blush spread down Grayson's cheeks all the way down his neck before he pulled away laughing.

They shared a sensual kiss before pulling away, beaming.

Fuck, where was Alex? I craned my head above the crowd, but I couldn't see anything. Jayden and Grayson held hands, and he was being pulled this way and that way, but Jayden remained by his side. My heart hammered in my chest at the thought of having Alex with me, but I couldn't see him.

"Evans!" Keith called me over to him. "Come meet your new Coach Daryl, he'll be the one assisting you when you get set with the Pittsburgh Penguins."

Fuck, this guy was a legend. My throat went dry when the big man clasped my hands. Towering over me, he gave me a broad smile, showing a row of pearly white tight. His suit stretched over his muscular form, but something about it seemed kind. "Evans, good to finally

have some new blood. Don't worry, I won't go too hard on you. Yet."
He grinned and my knees went weak. "I've been following your career
for some time now, kid, and it's great to have you on the team."

"Thank you, sir. You don't know what this means to me," I said,
awestruck. *This was happening.* "I've always admired the Penguins.
Winning multiple Stanley Cups in recent years—seriously, you guys
are like the rock stars of hockey. How do you keep them playing at
such a high level? Jedi mind tricks?"

Coach Daryl laughed. "I wish! Nah, it's a mix of talent, hard work,
and maybe a dash of magic. Seriously though, it's all about teamwork.
These guys know how to work together and have each other's backs."

"Teamwork makes the dream work, right? Alright, you must have
a favorite memory from all those victories," I said, keeping up the
conversation. It's not every day one gets to meet their idol.

"Oh, I have many, but I'd say our first win in 2009 was like winning
the lottery. Seeing the Cup back in Pittsburgh after a long wait was like
a city-wide party."

"Yeah, fuck, I can imagine the celebrations. And then going on to
win it again, you guys were on fire. Do you mind sharing what you did
differently?"

"Well, if I tell you, I might have to put you on the payroll!" Coach
Daryl belted out a laugh that caused several heads to turn. "Kidding
aside, it's about dedication, hard work, and maybe a bit of good luck.
Always give your best and have fun with it."

"Evans," Keith nudged my shoulder. "I want you to meet a few
sponsors that are waiting to do endorsements with you. I have Nike,
Adidas, and Sports Check all lined up for right now."

Wow, that was quick. I nodded, then turned back to Coach Daryl.
"It was a pleasure meeting you and we'll talk soon." We shook hands
and Keith dragged me away to meet another group of people who

would be my next sponsors. To say it was a whirlwind was an under-statement. I kept my smile wide as I spoke to them, making sure to put my best foot forward. This was all part of the game as well, and the more sponsors I could get, the more my popularity would soar. I let Keith pull me this way and that way throughout the night until finally, my parents found me.

"Evans!" Kateryna yelled and clamored over to me. I laughed, catching the little minx in my arms and suddenly my eyes were burning with tears. "You made it, big bro!"

"I can't believe it either," I said, swallowing down my emotions. It was a hard-won victory, but I wouldn't trade this moment for the world. But where the hell was Alex? "Hey, have you seen Alex? I thought you guys were all coming together?"

Kateryna shook her head. "Nah, he said he had some stuff to do before he arrived."

"Oh." What things? I frowned, not sure what she was referring to, but then my parents walked over. My dad slapped me on the back and brought me into a tight bear hug.

"All those hockey lessons paid off," he laughed in my ear and I hugged him back. "I'm so proud of you, son."

"Thanks, Dad, for believing in me."

"Of course. He beamed, cupping my cheeks, and then my mom shoved him away and dragged me into her arms.

"My baby's going to be a Penguin!" We all gave a collective groan. "What? That's the name of the team."

"You're so clueless, mom." Kateryna rolled her eyes but smiled. "So, where's the after-party? Isn't there some gala after this?"

"Ah, yeah, it should be happening in the next room. After the press conference, I think—"

"Evans," Keth said, touching my elbow. "Come on, Molson Coors, Tim Hortons, and Gatorade are all lined up and wanting to meet you, then we'll get you prepped for your first press conference with Derek."

"Duty calls," I said, shrugged, then waved them all goodbye before I was dragged away. Smoothing down my crisp suit, I scanned the crowd again, looking for Alex, wondering why he wasn't anywhere to be found. Where was he? The harsh lights of the stadium made me feel dizzy, but I pressed onward, keeping a smile on my face as I met brand after brand. Most of them were intrigued by my story and interested in getting to know me on a deeper level. It wasn't at all like how I thought it would be. Since these were big brands, I half expected them to be rich assholes, but they were all very nice and cordial. I left with several business cards that Keith immediately swiped. We were about to rush into the press conference room when I spotted Zara several feet away from Harpreet.

"Give me one moment," I said to Keith, then jogged over to her, smiling. "Hey!" Zara grinned up at me. She was wearing a tight white dress that accentuated her curves, her hazel eyes were lined with smoky eyeliner and her hair was straight and cascaded down her back. "You came!" I laughed, dragging her into a tight hug. Zara kissed my cheek and lingered there longer than necessary, and before I could blink, a paparazzo snapped a photo of us. I jerked away, shocked by the flash, but Zara took it all in stride, wrapping her arm around me and posing for the next picture.

"One with you and the pretty girl together!" a man with a camera shouted. "Get close. Closer. Wonderful! Love it—God, you're gorgeous—" the paparazzi man said, before walking away.

"What the hell? Are they all like this?" I sneered after the guy. He didn't even wait for us to give him permission before he started snapping photos. *What a jerk.*

"You better get used to it baby, you're famous now," Zara said, patting my chest. "Wow, look at you. All cleaned up." Her hand touched my smooth jaw. I straightened my Armani suit jacket and crisp black slacks that were neatly pressed. Keith had a stylist cut my hair and sleek it back with gel. My dad had spent a lot of money on the suit and I was glad he did because I felt like a million bucks.

"Mhmm, hello?" Harpreet waved. "What am I, chopped liver? That stupid paparazzi didn't even look at me." I rolled my eyes and dragged him into a tight hug. "Seriously, man, congratulations. You deserved it."

"Thanks, man," I said, patting his back. "Hey, have you seen Alex? I haven't seen him anywhere and the press conference is about to start."

"Oh," Zara said. "I think he was having some trouble getting in at the door. Something about a dress code. I don't know."

Dress code? My brows furrowed, and I moved to head to the front, but Keith tapped my shoulder. "The press conference is about to start. We should head inside now."

Fuck. I couldn't miss it.

"If you see him, let me know and I'll do my best to come out as soon as I can." She nodded, and I followed Keith into the dual doors of the press conference. This was it. What every athlete dreamed. My heart pounded in my chest, but I knew deep down I was ready.

I can do this.

***

A BRUSQUE WIND SLAPPED against my face as I stepped outside with Keith and a few other sponsors, chuckling at a joke one of them said. I felt buzzed from all the alcohol I had earlier at the gala, and my body was tingling from the rush of having my dreams come true. *I finally made it.* Everyone seemed enthralled with me at the press conference and under Keith's instructions, I nailed all their questions, even throwing in a few jokes for good measure.

I shoved my hands into my pocket, fighting off a bitter wind when Keith pointed to the limo that was waiting for us. I scanned the crowds for the last time and felt a pang in my chest when I didn't see Alex. I must have missed him. Irritation sparked within me and I wondered why he didn't just come with my parents. *What was Zara talking about? What dress code?* The limo pulled up to the curb and just as I was about to get in, I saw a flash of reddish-bronze.

My breath caught as Alex stood there amidst the hordes of people stuck in the line outside. What the hell? In his hand, he held a single rose, but then I noticed that his suit was worn and he wore ratty sneakers, the same ones he always had. *Fuck, I'm such an idiot.*

Keith and my father set everything up so that my image would be perfect for when I met with the sponsors, but I never thought about Alex or what he would wear when we got here. I wasn't thinking. Too wrapped up in everything going on. No wonder they wouldn't let him in. *It was a black-tie event, and all Alex had worn his sneakers.*

"I—"

"Are you getting in or what?" Keith laughed, his hand on my shoulder. "Let's go. Those people will swarm us if we don't move. We've got the CEO of Nike right behind us."

Shit. The crowd was bustling, several people screaming at the top of their lungs, and I knew we had to get a move on. I tried to convey my apology with my eyes, but I couldn't wait any longer and got in.

***

"Fuck," I hissed, pacing the confines of my room, wishing I could melt into the floor. It was past midnight and Alex still wasn't home yet. I felt like such a dick when I realized that if he didn't come with my parents, he must have taken the bus to get there. I groaned aloud, palming my face when I thought about him standing out there in the bitter cold in fucking sneakers. What kind of boyfriend was I? And I knew Alex would never ask for help, especially when it came to stuff like this. He had his pride, and I felt like a bastard for not recognizing it.

Tugging off my tie, I threw it in the laundry along with my sleek black jacket. I pulled out my phone and texted him for the tenth time before dialing his number. Cursing when it went straight to voicemail. Fuck, it must be dead. I was just about to grab my keys and head to the local bus stop when I heard my front door creak open. Leaping toward it, I yanked it open and Alex stood there, his face pink from the cold and his thin winter jacket barely covering his wide frame.

"Shit—baby—I'm so fucking sorry—" I dragged him into my arms and hugged him. Alex puffed a laugh, but he was shivering. "I'm so fucking stupid. I completely forgot to give you my keys and I should have just made sure you were riding with us, but I didn't know if I could do that so I didn't ask, and fuck—everything went to shit!"

"It's all right." Alex patted my spine. Then moved out of my arms. "I'm fine. Just a bit cold." He peeled off his coat and toed off his winter shoes, and I stepped into his space again. Taking his hands in mine, I rubbed them together, trying to warm him up. "I'm sorry I didn't get a chance to call. My phone died while I was waiting for the bus."

I swallowed around the dagger in my throat and kissed each of his fingers, trying to convey my silent apology. I felt like an ass. *What the hell was wrong with me? Why didn't I take care of him the way Grayson took care of Jayden? Why did I always assume he was okay?* I peered into

Alex's eyes and saw the exhaustion there. Those swirling brown orbs were slightly sunken, and I wondered how stressful it must have been for him to take the bus for several hours and then be told he couldn't even come into the venue. Cupping his chin, I pressed a fleeting kiss to his cold lips and sighed. "I'm so sorry."

"Don't be. I'm fine," Alex laughed, and his hands gripped my waist. "I was just happy you saw me. Just once. I didn't abandon you, Evans."

22

REBOUND AND REDEMPTION

EVANS MULRONEY

I deepened the kiss, licking the seam of his mouth, tasting the icy winds on his tongue. His natural scent filled my nostrils, and I threaded my fingers through his hair. I wanted to show him how fucking sorry I was for making him miss this moment. Our moment. Yes, I was the one drafted, but Alex had been there with me every step of the way. He should have been there with me tonight. The way Grayson and Jayden held each other in public, it made me realize I didn't give a fuck what people had to say. *I love Alex.* I wanted him by my side. I kissed down his neck, gripping his jeans as I lost myself to the smell of his clean scent. "I missed you."

He chuckled, but didn't push me away. A shiver rolled through him when I licked down his neck and collarbone before dropping to my knees in front of him. Alex's jeans were threadbare, and I didn't know why the fuck I never noticed it before. Tears stung my eyes as the realization of his predicament sank deep into my chest. I unbuckled his jeans, nuzzling against his thick cock that was straining at his white Calvin Kline underwear. "These are my boxers," I laughed, pressing a kiss to the tip of his dick.

"Yeah, I was in a rush," Alex replied, breathless. "Fuck, seeing you in that suit today ... it was so fucking hot. I hope I get a chance to enjoy it."

"You will," I said, hooking my thumbs in the waistband of his underwear. "Later." I pulled them down enough for his cock to spring free, hard and aching. The mushroom tip glistened with beady pearls, and my mouth watered. Mouthing at the base, I lapped at the wrinkly skin, inhaling his musk and rubbing my nose against his dark pubic hair. Alex shuddered. His hand came up to grip my blond hair, trying not to thrust into my mouth. "Fuck baby, you taste so good." I latched onto the side of his dick, running my tongue along the thick, pulsing vein before taking him down my throat.

Alex cried out. I hummed around his length, hollowing my cheeks and staring up into his brown eyes. His irises were like polished mahogany, drawing me in with a mysterious allure, auburn pools reflecting hidden depths. "I'm close—fuck—" Alex grunted as I worked up a rhythm, just getting into the flow when I felt the first spurts of his precum flood my mouth. Bobbing my head, I worked hard, sucking him off and taking him deep until my chin almost touched his balls. Alex groaned, biting his bottom lip as a flush spread across his cheeks.

I stroked his balls, rolling them between my thumb and forefinger before I felt his body jerk and then come flooding my mouth in searing waves. Swallowing what I could, I let the rest dribble down my chin. Alex's chest heaved; he exhaled a harsh breath before he staggered back to sit on the bed.

"I think my legs are numb," he said, panting.

I laughed, crawling over to him, and then laying down on the bed beside him. "Good, because that was round one."

Alex bit back a smile. "So, how was it?"

Turning onto my side, I stared up at him with a dreamy expression. "Amazing. I met with the CEO of Nike, Sports Check fucking Tim Hortons, but their coffee isn't that good so I don't know what the fuck all that hype is about in Canada."

"I think Tim Hortons is like the only major coffee shop in Canada. Well, aside from Starbucks. Who wants their overpriced crap?"

I chucked at that. "Yeah, fuck man, I meet Coach Daryl from the Pittsburgh Penguins, dude is built like a four by four."

"Really?" Alex's brows rose. "No, shit?"

"Yeah, it was crazy. Grayson had his tongue down Jayden's throat as usual and I wished..." My heart tightened. "I wish you were with me. I'm going to tell Keith tomorrow before we have the last game of the season and then graduation."

Alex went eerily silent.

"What is it?" I asked.

"Maybe we shouldn't say anything."

Not this shit again. "Alex..." I said, my brow knitted. I thought back to all the events that happened today and I wondered if Alex had planned not to come at all. It was an ugly thought, but he could have just come with my parents. Why put himself out by taking the bus and wasting time? "What really happened today? Why didn't you come with Mom and Dad?"

Alex's mouth thinned into a hardline. "I was trying to do the right thing."

My eyes narrowed into pinpricks. "What the hell is that supposed to mean? What are you talking about?"

He sighed, shaking his head. "It doesn't matter. We come from different worlds. Of course, I'll support you and I'm happy for you, Evans. I am, but maybe we should cool it for now. I still ... I mean, let's just focus on one thing at a time."

I had no idea what that was supposed to mean. I was drafted to the Pittsburgh Penguins, meaning that once graduation happened, I'd be moving there. *Did Alex not want to move with me?* My heart jammed in my throat and I couldn't bear the thought of leaving here without him. It was the same shit he brought up at my parent's house and fear wrapped around my throat in a vise grip.

"Are you breaking up with me?"

Shock skittered over Alex's face. "What? No—"

"Then why are you acting like things between us won't last? Like you don't want to invest too much into our relationship before it goes south," I fumed.

"You're so stupid sometimes," Alex whispered darkly. "Do you have anything to lose if shit goes south between us? I have nowhere to live Evans. I rely on you for almost everything. Fuck, I knew this was a bad idea."

"So, what the hell do you want? You won't accept my help and you don't want to be with me. What else do you want?" I barked at him, tired of this back and forth. All I wanted was to be with my boyfriend. I didn't care about any of that other stuff. Alex was it for me.

"Evans ... I need time," Alex said quietly. "Since we got together, there's been a power imbalance between us, and as much as I love you for rescuing me, I want to be able to hold my own. To stand next to you and be someone you would be proud to be with."

"I *am* proud to be with you," I shot back. Blood roared in my ears when I took in everything he was saying. It sounded like Alex wanted me to go to Pittsburgh without him.

"Well, I'm not," Alex muttered. "Do you know how humiliating it was to stand outside waiting for you in my shitty sneakers? Or to be told I couldn't come in because of how I was dressed? My life is a mess right now and I can't rely on you to fix it."

"Alex—" I begged. I hated where this conversation was going. "Don't leave me. Please. I love you, so much. Whatever you want, we can do it."

"I'm not leaving you, Evans," Alex said. He placed a palm on my chest. "I want to become better for you. For myself. All my life I looked after my mom and now things are different. Just give me some time to get my life together. Please. I need that."

Staring deep into his eyes, I understood what he was saying. Alex didn't want to bring me down. Since I would be in the spotlight, he knew how important our public image would be. Still, it didn't stop the hurt from flaring in my chest. Alex leaned over and kissed me hard on the lips. "I love you. I promise Evans. I won't leave you, but I need some time to be your rock. I want to finish school. I want to quit this stupid job and I want us to spend the rest of our lives together."

I nodded, then pulled him into my arms. Alex wouldn't let this go, and I knew I had to let him figure out his own way, even if it meant being apart for a while. "Will you still come to my last game?"

"I'm working, so of course I'll be there."

I leaned back, gazing into his eyes, which were like a tapestry of earthy browns and fiery reds, the auburn depths revealing a passionate soul beneath the surface. *Fuck, I love him.* But I knew part of loving Alex was letting him go.

***

I RACED DOWN THE ICE, the adrenaline coursing through my veins. It was the final game of the season, and graduation was just around the corner. Grayson glided past me, with a mischievous grin as he intercepted a pass from the opposing team and sent it over to Chris, who shot forward like a bullet down the rink. I chuckled at the camaraderie of the guys. It was all fun and games.

The deafening roar of the crowd filled the arena as Jayden slammed the puck into the net. We exchanged nods, and the game continued. My heart pounded in my chest as the intermission was called. We were leading 5-3, but the match was far from over. I spotted Keith and Derek in the stands, and they waved at me. I waved back, appreciating their down-to-earth nature. These PR reps were nothing like I had expected - friendly, approachable, and always willing to answer my questions about the job.

During the break, I headed into the locker room, grabbing a bottle of water and downing it to soothe my parched throat. "Hey, man, have you seen this?" Chris held up the local newspaper, and I nearly choked on my drink. The headline featured a picture of me and Zara from a recent party. "Love on the Ice?" it read. I snatched the paper from his hand, my face burning with embarrassment. *What the hell? Did that nosy photographer publish this picture?*

"I hope Alex likes some friendly competition," Chris snickered.

"Shut up, Chris!" several guys shouted.

Fuck. I ran my hand through my hair, trying not to panic. It wasn't a big deal, right? Everybody had their pictures taken. Alex wouldn't be upset about it. He knew Zara and I had broken up, but with how rocky things were between us, I didn't want him to think I would just pretend to be straight. Alex wanted to get on his own feet, and I had to let him do that. But I needed to find him to explain that. I was just about to take out my phone and text him when I saw an ad in the paper for the University of Pittsburgh accepting admissions. Then it dawned on me. Why didn't Alex just finish up his schooling there? That way, we could be together. Granted, it would be easier if he just went back to school here, but he couldn't afford the tuition, but with my income, he didn't have to. I knew Alex fiercely valued his independence, but this way we could still be together and he could get a job in his field. Alex could pay me back if it bothered him and it would be a win-win for both of us.

Tearing off my skates, I threw on a pair of sneakers and began taking off my gear.

"What the hell are you doing, Evans? We have ten minutes before we have to be back on the rink," Coach Cornell barked at me.

"And I'll be back in three!" I said, sprinting out of the locker room. A frenzy of paparazzi was waiting outside the dual doors, so I went through the employees-only corridors until I got into the main foyer and spotted Alex there in his uniform, mopping up the ice people had tracked in from outside. *Fuck, he looked delicious.* Gray overalls hugged his body tight, making his shoulders broad and his waist narrow. He had the sleeves rolled up, exposing his muscular arms which bulged whenever he moved. I'd lavish him with kisses later. I sprinted over to where he was, ignoring the shocked looks of everyone around me as they got their food for the next half of the game.

"Evans—what—"

"The University of Pittsburgh," I gasped out, my lungs cinching from running so damn fast. "You could go there. That way, we can be together."

Alex bit back a smile. "Man, you really are stupid."

"What?"

"Do you want me to take out my crayons to explain it to you?"

I rolled my eyes at his lame joke. "I'm serious. What are you talking about?"

Alex laughed at my expression and took out his phone, showing me his application to the school already. "I wanted it to be a surprise that's why I said to wait until I can get my life together. Jeez, you just got drafted I need some time too."

My heart skipped a beat, and I felt a rush of astonishment flood my senses.

"I didn't want to make any promises in case I didn't get in, but I applied this morning," Alex continued, trying to hold in his laughter.

"You—so last night you said all that shit—"

"I wanted to be realistic, Evans and I meant every word of it. I want us to be together, but I want to stand on my own two feet too. We can do all of that together. I told you before, I wasn't leaving. It's been almost twenty years. You can't get rid of me that easily."

I surged forward, capturing his lips in a heated kiss. Alex laughed and then moaned as I deepened it, fisting the lapels of my jacket. Lights flashed all around us as the room spun. My lungs screamed for air, but I couldn't stop kissing him. Alex was coming to Pittsburgh with me.

And the bastard knew it the whole time.

Alex yanked away breathlessly, while several paparazzi crowded around us screaming at the top of their lungs. But I couldn't care less. "Alex..." I felt my throat constrict with emotions.

"I told you before, I'm not leaving you."

I laughed and kissed him again.

***

"DUMPSTER DIVING FOR LOVE: Hockey Pro Evans Mulroney's Unconventional Romance."

"Hockey Star Evans Mulroney Takes a Shot at Love – with a Janitor's Mop!"

"Stick Handling on and off the Ice: Evans Mulroney's New Romance with the Janitor's Broom."

"These guys are fucking assholes," I muttered, and Alex laughed when I tossed the newspapers into the trash can. The frat guys were sending them to my room by the bulk, laughing their asses off as the headlines got more and more ridiculous as time went on. Whatever. Alex was busy packing up our stuff. Graduation was in a few months, and then we'd be off to look at apartments in Pittsburgh. Spring seemed to be right around the corner, then I'd officially be joining the members of my team there. It was fucking surreal when I looked back on everything that had happened. Alex and I came out to a frenzy of reporters. I got to declare to the world that he was the man I love, regardless of his background.

Alex was a sexy ass janitor; I didn't care what anyone else thought.

We checked the admission office regularly, but there still weren't any updates. I tried not to be impatient. Alex was smart, so I knew he'd have no trouble getting into the Mechanical Engineering program there. My parents were also helping us with house hunting. While Derek and Keith were doing some damage control from having some backlash for kissing Alex in public, but I didn't care. None of my sponsors did either. In fact, all it did was make them want me even more.

I'd have to beat them off with a broom.

Alex's back was to me, and I took a moment to admire his muscular shoulder blades. "Come, look at this," he said, holding up a picture of us in Boston Bruins jerseys.

I walked over, grinning as I peered at the photo. "Man, look at those baby faces. We were such die-hard Bruins fans back then."

Alex chuckled, his deep voice resonating in the room. "We practically lived and breathed Bruins hockey. Remember how we'd paint our faces in their colors for every game?"

"Yeah, and we'd drive for hours to catch their games, chanting their names like fanatics." I nodded, feeling a wave of nostalgia wash over me.

He pointed at the picture, his finger resting on my face. "Look at you, the ultimate Bergeron supporter."

I rolled my eyes. "Hey, Patrice Bergeron is a legend, and I stand by my choice."

"Remember that time we met some of the players after a game?" Alex said, a mischievous twinkle in his auburn eyes.

"How could I forget?" I replied, shaking my head. "We were so starstruck, stumbling over our words."

"And then, we got their autographs on everything we could find," he added, laughing. "Does your dad still have those jerseys?"

"Mhm, probably," I said, pondering that question, encircling my arms around his narrow waist. "But we'd have to dig deep for it. Sometimes I think my dad is more of a hockey fan than I am, with all the memorabilia shit he keeps in the den. I can ask if you want."

"No. Um ... last time we visited, your dad said some things to me..." Alex said.

My brows knitted. "What things?"

Alex chewed on his lower lip. "To be fair, he isn't against us being together he just ... I thought back on what he was trying to say and I realized it wasn't as sinister as I thought."

That got me really confused. My dad knew how I felt about Alex. Was he trying to deliberately break us up? The thought sent a spark of heat to my core. "What did he say?"

"He said he wanted me to help you make the right choice," Alex explained. "I thought he was saying he wanted us to break up, but when I thought about it, I think he meant he wanted me to be there for you when you made your choices. To be your partner. I think he knew you'd give it all up for me and he wanted me to prevent you from doing that."

I pressed my lips together in a frown. "Honestly, if you didn't come to Pittsburgh with me ... I don't know if I would have gone either. I like to think that I would, but I don't want to imagine my life without you, Alex. I can't."

"You don't have to. Ever." Alex turned in my arms and I kissed him gently on the lips.

"Besides, we're tied together for life, especially with cringey headlines like 'Romance Strikes with a Broom-Wielding Janitor!'"

We burst into fits of laughter. Alex's reddish bronze hair was a blaze of warmth, and his eyes, with their foxlike charm, held me rooted to the spot. *Regeneration*. I realized now that I was wrong. Alex wasn't a brazen fire meant to burn the world to ash, but something smooth and steady. Just as fire can purify and cleanse, Alex's influence was a transformative force, burning away the old and fostering the new, not wreaking havoc like an uncontrolled blaze.

His love burned steady and true.

An eternal flame that illuminated the darkest corners of my heart.

23

HAT TRICK OF EMOTIONS

ALEX MAY

Six months later...

Striding into the sterile halls of the rehab center, I looked around for what would be the last time. My mom had a few more months before they released her, and Doctor Reeds wanted to set up more supervised visits between us to help her transition back into the real world, but I couldn't stomach it. Everything Shirley said last time I knew she meant it. All my life, I did what was best. I wanted to be a good son for her. Mostly because I wanted her to love me.

As other mothers did, but deep down I knew she didn't. I approached her room and knocked, my fingers echoing on the heavy wooden door. There was no response, but I opened the door, anyway.

Shirley stood with her back to me, facing the open bay window in a dab gray sweater and track pants. Her hair was pulled into a tight knot and her expression was much calmer than I had ever seen it before. We didn't speak.

My throat constricted with emotions as I tried not to blurt out all the amazing things that happened to me. *Mom, did you know Evans got drafted by the Pittsburgh Penguins? Mom, did you know I got into university again with a full ride and I'd be able to finish up my degree? Evans and I plan to spend the rest of our lives together. Mom! Can't you see how happy he makes me?* I said nothing.

Just basking in the warmth of the sun. '*Fear is the path to the dark side. Fear leads to anger; anger leads to hate. Hate leads to suffering.*' Yoda once said. All my life I felt hate roil through me, thick like black tar as it spread like vines through every inch of my body. At her indifference.

At her selfishness. At her addiction.

Hate the sin, not the sinner, but it was so hard to separate the two. '*Take your weapon, strike me down with all of your hatred and your journey towards the dark side will be complete.*' The emperor sneered at Luke. And God, did I want to. Lash her like a whip with my cruel words. Give her a fraction of the agony she caused me over the years of abandonment. *Did you ever love me?* The words were at the tip of my tongue, burning like acid, but I swallowed them down. I already knew the answer to that question. Maybe she did. *In her own way.*

There weren't always bad times and yet, I felt like now I could let her go. I waited with bated breath for several moments before I sighed long and deep, ready to turn and leave when my mom spoke.

"Pittsburgh Penguins? Their defense is shit," she muttered, keeping her eyes trained outside. My brows knitted, not sure what she was getting at, so I didn't respond. "Make sure Evans whips them into shape." She turned to look at me then, tears in her eyes as her face was backlit by the sun, turning her brown hair into reddish gold.

The world fell from my feet.

She watched the draft. She knew. My heart thudded in my chest, and tears stung my eyes. I couldn't speak. My feet rooted to the floor. *She did care.* My lip trembled, and I forced myself to look away, to ignore the emotions threatening to fall to my knees and weep at her feet. *It was hello, and it was also goodbye.* If she knew Evans had been assigned to the Pittsburgh Penguins, then she knew I was most likely leaving with him. I gave a curt nod and then walked out the door, closing it shut behind me.

Everything fractured. Bursting into fissions of glass as tears spilled down my cheeks.

Large spikes of barbwire tore at my chest, shredding me alive with agony, but I forced my legs to move. I shoved the dual doors open and saw Evans in the parking lot, standing beside his large Ford F-150 beast of a truck, his hands shoved deep into his pockets and a frown marring his handsome face. His Aviator sunglasses reflected the sunlight like mirrors as I stumbled into his awaiting arms.

"Fuck baby," Evans whispered against my ear. "Why didn't you let me go with you?"

I buried my face in his neck and didn't respond. Saying goodbye to my mom was something I needed to do on my own, and I knew Evans being there would just make things worse. Evans pressed a kiss to my temple and held me as my body wracked with sobs.

She watched the draft.

She knew, but it still wasn't enough. I knew my mom was on the road to recovery and hopefully, someday soon, we'd be able to have a good relationship. *I prayed for that day.*

***

The warm breeze tousled our hair as Evans and I hurriedly packed up his truck, eager to hit the road. With the semester just ended and a few weeks of freedom before training camp, we decided on an epic road trip from Michigan to Pittsburgh.

I tossed the last bag into the spacious truck bed, our suitcases snugly tucked in alongside the Ukrainian snacks his mom had lovingly prepared for us. Pirozhki, those delicious stuffed buns, and homemade pierogi were neatly packed in a cooler, their scent tempting our taste buds.

Beside me, Evans checked the tire pressure and adjusted the mirrors. Nearby, Kateryna stood with her arms crossed and a pout on her face, upset about not joining us on the road trip. She was stuck in summer school to catch up on a few classes.

"Sorry, pumpkinhead," Evans said, patting his sister's head. "I promise we'll bring you some pierogies from Pittsburgh."

Kateryna sighed dramatically but finally broke into a small smile. "You better, or else."

With everything set, we bid farewell to the house we had shared during our college years and loaded ourselves into the truck. Evans' mom made her way over to us, holding a basket of fresh, still-warm pirozhki. "For the road," she said, her eyes glistening with maternal warmth.

"Thanks, Mrs. Mulroney," I replied, accepting the basket with gratitude.

"Make sure you boys stay safe on your adventure," she added, giving her son an affectionate hug.

"We will, Mom," Evans assured her. "We'll be in touch. Love you."

Mr. Mulroney approached me and held out his hand, and I shook it. "Look, about what I said last time..." He rubbed the back of his neck. "I never meant to imply you were less than Alex ... I just want what's best for Evans and it should have occurred to me that you are what's best. So, I apologize."

"It's fine."

Mr. Mulroney nodded. "Okay, then, good luck. We'll be in touch..." he paused then. "And don't worry about Shirley. We'll keep an eye on her."

Words of gratitude clogged my throat. It was more than I could ask. I knew what he meant when he spoke that day. He wanted to make sure that I wasn't going to leave Evans. That I would be there no matter what happened. With goodbyes said, we set off, embarking on a journey of exploration and adventure, all the while savoring the delightful snacks his mom had prepared for us. The road stretched out before us, a promise of exciting experiences and new memories to be made. Evans' hand intertwined with mine as we drove, the highway speeding past us. The engine purring beneath us, Evans turned on the radio, and I waited for some classic road trip tunes, but what filled the truck was not what I expected. It was the unmistakable epic sound of the "Star Wars" soundtrack.

I stared at Evans, utterly perplexed. "Is this... the entire 'Star Wars' soundtrack?"

Evans, sporting a mischievous grin, nodded with delight. "Yup, all five hours of pure Death Star symphony. You're welcome."

I couldn't help but burst into laughter. "Nerd."

Evans kissed the back of my hand, his oceanic eyes shining with so much light that it made my heart soar. Like two swords clashing, our love will cross blades with life's challenges, forging a bond strong enough to weather any storm.

THE END

— · —

OTHER WORKS

Melting the Ice Between Us (Book #1.5)

High school reunions? Yeah, they're about as enjoyable as a root canal. This one's no exception. Flashbacks of those bullies, those epic wedgies, they all flood back as I step into this vortex of nostalgia-gone-wrong. Look at them now, the once-mighty jocks and cheerleaders turned into potato sacks with legs. Schadenfreude much? Don't mind me, I'm just here for the booze.

Speaking of booze, I spin around and kaboom! There's Blake Byrne, looking as sinful as ever. Those blue eyes, the tattoos that make you wanna commit a crime just to get a closer look, and don't even get me started on that lip piercing. I mean, come on! But no, hold up. Not falling into that trap again. Blake and I? Yeah, that's a rollercoaster I've no intention of riding.

He humiliated me in a field full of his friends because he was too deep in the closet to come out. Blake, Mr. Popular, decided to make me his personal punching bag just to keep his closet door locked tight.

Nope. Not this time. This time things will be different.

I'm not sticking around for long, just a few days. And those days? Oh, they're dedicated to one thing and one thing only: Blake's sweet taste of payback. Revenge is a dish best served cold.

Good thing my heart's already turned into a freezer.

Blades of Desire (Book #1)

Hockey became my battleground, my escape from a troubled existence overshadowed by my brother's devastating injury. Blinded by a burning desire for revenge, I yearned for the moment I could face Grayson Hayes, the hockey player responsible for my brother's crippling fate. Finally, my chance arrives, and I relish the opportunity to break him.

Driven by a thirst for retribution, I relentlessly pursue Grayson, determined to force him to his knees for the pain he inflicted. But as the lines between predator and prey blur, a chilling realization dawns upon me—I am the one being played.

The fiery passion I once held for revenge transforms into an insatiable craving for Grayson himself. Desperate to resist, I grapple with conflicting emotions and the unraveling of a sinister plot that goes deeper than our bitter rivalry. Can I emerge triumphant, not only on the ice but also in the arms of my sworn enemy?

Crossed Blades (Book #2)

Once inseparable, my best friend and I were torn apart after a night of fiery passion—a memory forever etched in my mind, its details lost in a hazy fog. Now, Alex May is my bitter rival, his indifference cutting deeper than any blade. The looming national state championships intensify the stakes, fueling the fire of that unforgettable night.

In the arena's dim light, tension crackles. Each stride, each thud of the puck, echoes unspoken words. The remnants of our once unbreakable bond intertwine with a burning desire for vindication.

I yearn to reach out to Alex, hoping he'll give me a second chance. But his walls are high, his heart guarded. Will he ever forgive me for the mistakes of our past and allow love to mend our broken connection?

Heated Rivalry (Book #3)

With graduation looming, I'm forced to take an extra credit athletic course in hockey—a sport I despise. The ice, the cold, and the game itself are everything I detest. But when a bone-shattering shove on the ice threatens to fracture my knee, I must confront my fears and learn to play.

In a shocking revelation, I discovered it was Devon who had shoved me hard on the ice.

Devon Black.

A demon. A force to be reckoned with, notorious for his bullying tactics on and off the ice. I hate Devon with every fiber of my being, yet beneath the surface of my hatred lies an undeniable and confusing attraction. It's as if the very essence of him is both repulsive and magnetic, drawing me in against my will. Graduation approaches and the choices we make will determine our fate—whether bitter separation or a love that transcends the icy battleground we call home. Can Devon and I bridge the divide, or will life's forces tear us apart?

Eternal Ice (Book #4)

Coach Casey. A real piece of work. Rude, uptight—a complete jerk. It felt like nothing I did could ever please him. I was there to play hockey, not jump through hoops like a circus monkey in a suit. The way his mouth curled over his lips when he smiled? Hated it. The way he pushed me harder than ever before? Hated that too.

Then there was that one night we spent together, and suddenly my whole world was upside down. Hated it. Hated him. Yup, Coach Casey was a jerk, but weirdly, I think I might have just liked it. But let's be real, there was no way we could be anything more than enemies. He was my coach, after all, and I was so deep in the closet that I didn't even know where the door was.

Things took a turn for the worse when I found out Coach Casey wasn't exactly who he said he was. Our relationship was forbidden, and Casey's past threatened to unravel all of it. Would we survive? Or would we remain enemies, stuck between love and hatred on the eternal ice?

—∘—

AUTHOR'S NOTE

J.M. Jackie is a writer who specializes in crafting dark and twisted novels, exploring complex human relationships and the darker side of love and desire. She enjoys drinking black coffee and taking long walks with her two large dogs for inspiration. While her writing can be intense, she aims to create stories that challenge readers to confront their own assumptions and beliefs while providing an escape into a richly imagined world of adventure, magic, and occasionally martial arts!

www.ingramcontent.com/pod-product-compliance
Lightning Source LLC
Chambersburg PA
CBHW022013010726
47494CB00003B/1020